LEVIATHAN

LEVIATHAN

BORIS AKUNIN

Translated by
Andrew Bromfield

Weidenfeld & Nicolson
LONDON

First published in Great Britain in 2004
by Weidenfeld & Nicolson

First published in Russia as *Leviafan* in 1998
by I. Zakharov

A CIP catalogue record for this book
is available from the British Library.

ISBN 0 297 64552 8

Typeset at The Spartan Press Ltd,
Lymington, Hants

Printed in Great Britain by
Clays Ltd, St Ives plc

Weidenfeld & Nicolson

The Orion Publishing Group Ltd
Orion House
5 Upper Saint Martin's Lane
London, WC2H 9EA

From Commissioner
Gauche's black file

Record of an examination of the scene of the crime carried out on the
evening of 15 March 1878 in the mansion of Lord Littleby on the rue de
Grenelle (7th arrondissement of the city of Paris) [A brief extract]

. . . For reasons unknown all the household staff were gathered
in the pantry, which is located on the ground floor of the mansion to the left of the entrance hall (room 3 on diagram 1). The
precise locations of the bodies are indicated on diagram 4, in
which:

No. 1 is the body of the butler, Étienne Delarue, age 48 years
No. 2 is the body of the housekeeper, Laura Bernard, age 54
  years
No. 3 is the body of the master's manservant, Marcel Prout, age
  28 years
No. 4 is the body of the butler's son, Luc Delarue, age 11 years
No. 5 is the body of the maid, Arlette Foche, age 19 years
No. 6 is the body of the housekeeper's granddaughter, Anne-
  Marie Bernard, age 6 years
No. 7 is the position of the security guard Jean Lesage, age 42
  years, who died in the St-Lazare hospital on the morning of
  16 March without regaining consciousness
No. 8 is the body of the security guard Patrick Trois-Bras, age 29
  years
No. 9 is the body of the porter, Jean Carpentier, age 40 years.

The bodies shown as Nos. 1–6 are in sitting positions around the
large kitchen table. Nos. 1–3 are frozen with their heads lowered

onto their crossed arms, No. 4 is resting his cheek on his hands, No. 5 is reclining against the back of the chair and No. 6 is in a kneeling position beside No. 2. The faces of Nos. 1–6 are calm, without any indication whatever of fear or suffering. On the other hand, Nos. 7–9, as the diagram shows, are lying at a distance from the table and No. 7 is holding a whistle in his hand. However, none of the neighbours heard the sound of a whistle yesterday evening. The faces of No. 8 and No. 9 are set in expressions of horror, or at the very least of extreme consternation (photographs will be provided tomorrow morning). There are no signs of a struggle. A rapid examination also failed to reveal any sign of injury to the bodies. The cause of death cannot be determined without a post-mortem. From the degree of rigor mortis the forensic medical specialist Maître Bernhem determined that death occurred at various times between ten o'clock in the evening (No. 6) and six o'clock in the morning, while No. 7, as stated above, died later in hospital. Anticipating the results of the medical examination, I venture to surmise that all of the victims were exposed to a potent and fast-acting poison inducing a narcotic effect, and the time at which their hearts stopped beating depended either on the dose of poison received or the physical strength of each of the victims.

The front door of the mansion was closed but not locked. However, the window of the conservatory (item 8 on diagram 1) bears clear indications of a forced entry: the glass is broken and on the narrow strip of loose cultivated soil below it there is the indistinct imprint of a man's shoe with a sole 26 centimetres in length, a pointed toe and a steel-shod heel (photographs will be provided). The felon probably gained entry to the house via the garden only after the servants had been poisoned and sank into slumber, otherwise they would certainly have heard the sound of breaking glass. It remains unclear, however, why, after the servants had been rendered harmless, the perpetrator found it necessary to enter the house through the garden, when he could quite easily have walked through into the house from the pantry. In any event, the perpetrator made his way from the conservatory up to the second floor, where Lord Littleby's personal apartments are located (see diagram 2). As the diagram shows, the left-hand section of the second floor consists of only two rooms: a hall, which houses a collection of Indian curios, and the master's bedroom, which communicates directly with the hall. Lord Littleby's body is indicated on diagram 2 as No. 10 (see also the outline drawing). His Lordship was dressed in a smoking jacket and woollen pantaloons and his right foot was heavily bandaged. An initial examination of the body indicates that death occurred as a result of an extraordinarily powerful blow to the parietal region of the skull with a heavy, oblong-shaped object. The blow was inflicted from the front. The carpet is spattered with blood and brain tissue to a distance of several metres from the body. Likewise spattered with blood is a broken glass display case which, according to its nameplate, previously contained a statuette of the Indian god Shiva (the inscription on the nameplate reads: 'Bangalore, 2nd half XVIII century, gold'). The missing sculpture was displayed against a background of painted Indian shawls, one of which is also missing.

From the report by Dr Bernhem on the results of pathological and anatomical examination of the bodies removed from the rue de Grenelle

. . . however, whereas the cause of Lord Littleby's death (body No. 10) is clear and the only aspect which may be regarded as unusual is the force of the blow, which shattered the cranium into seven fragments, in the case of Nos. 1–9 the picture was less obvious, requiring not only a post-mortem but in addition chemical analyses and laboratory investigation. The task was simplified to some extent by the fact that J. Lesage (No. 7) was still alive when he was initially examined and certain typical indications (pinhole pupils, suppressed breathing, cold clammy skin, rubefaction of the lips and the ear lobes) indicated a presumptive diagnosis of morphine poisoning. Unfortunately, during the initial examination at the scene of the crime we had proceeded on the apparently obvious assumption that the poison had been ingested orally, and therefore only the victims' oral cavities and glottises were subjected to detailed scrutiny. Since no pathological indications were discovered, the forensic examination was unable to provide any conclusive answers. It was only during examination in the morgue that each of the nine deceased was discovered to possess a barely visible injection puncture on the inner flexion of the left elbow. Although it lies outside my sphere of competence, I can venture with reasonable certainty the hypothesis that the injections were administered by a person with considerable experience in such procedures: 1) the injections were administered with great skill and precision, not one of the subjects bore any visible signs of haematoma; 2) since the normal interval before narcotic coma ensues is three minutes, all nine injections must have been administered within that period of time. Either there were several operatives involved (which is unlikely), or a single operative possessing truly remarkable skill – even if we are to assume that he had prepared a loaded syringe for each victim in advance. Indeed, it is hard to imagine that a person in full possession of

4

his faculties would offer his arm for an injection if he had just witnessed someone else lose consciousness as a result of the procedure. Admittedly, my assistant Maître Jolie believes that all of these people could have been in a state of hypnotic trance, but in all my years in this line of work I have never encountered anything of the sort. Let me also draw the commissioner's attention to the fact that Nos. 7–9 were lying on the floor in poses clearly expressive of panic. I assume that these three were the last to receive the injection (or that they offered greater resistance to the narcotic) and that before they lost consciousness they realized that something suspicious was happening to their companions. Laboratory analysis has demonstrated that each of the victims received a dose of morphine approximately three times in excess of the lethal threshold. Judging from the condition of the body of the little girl (No. 6), who must have been the first to die, the injections were administered between nine and ten o'clock on the evening of 15 March.

TEN LIVES FOR A GOLDEN IDOL!

Nightmare crime in fashionable district

Today, 16 March, all of Paris is talking of nothing but the spine-chilling crime which has shattered the decorous tranquillity of the aristocratic rue de Grenelle. The Revue parisienne's correspondent was quick to arrive at the scene of the crime and is prepared to satisfy the legitimate curiosity of our readers.

And so, this morning as usual, shortly after seven o'clock, postman Jacques Le Chien rang the doorbell of the elegant two-storey mansion belonging to the well-known British collector Lord Littleby. M. Le Chien was surprised when the porter Carpentier, who always took in the post for his Lordship in person, failed to open up, and noticing that the entrance door was slightly ajar, he stepped into the hallway. A few moments later the 70-year-old veteran of the postal service ran back out onto the street, howling wildly. Upon being summoned to the house, the police discovered a scene from the kingdom of Hades – seven servants and two children (the 11-year-old son of the butler and the six-year-old granddaughter of the housekeeper) lay in the embrace of eternal slumber. The police ascended the stairs to the second floor and there they discovered the master of the house, Lord Littleby, lying in a pool of blood, murdered in the very repository which housed his celebrated collection of oriental rarities. The 55-year-old Englishman was well known in the highest social circles of our capital. Despite his reputation as an eccentric and unsociable individual, archaeological scholars and orientalists respected Lord Littleby as a genuine connoisseur of Indian history and culture. Repeated attempts by the directors of the Louvre to purchase items from the lord's diverse collection had been disdainfully rejected. The deceased prized especially highly a golden statuette of Shiva, the value of which is estimated by competent experts to be at least half a million francs. A deeply mistrustful man, Lord Littleby was very much afraid of thieves, and two armed guards were on duty in the repository by day and night.

It is not clear why the guards left their post and went down to the ground floor. Nor is it clear what mysterious power the malefactor was able to employ in order to subjugate all of the inhabitants of the house to his will without the slightest resistance (the police suspect that use was made of some quick-acting poison). It is clear, however, that he did not expect to find the master of the house himself at home, and his fiendish calculations were evidently thwarted. No doubt we should see in this the explanation for the bestial ferocity with which the venerable collector was slain. The murderer apparently fled the scene of the crime in panic, taking only the statuette and one of the painted shawls displayed in the same case. The shawl was evidently required to wrap the golden Shiva – otherwise the bright lustre of the sculpture might have attracted the attention of some late-night passer-by. Other valuables (of which the collection contains a goodly number) remained untouched. Your correspondent has ascertained that Lord Littleby was at home yesterday by chance, through a fatal confluence of circumstances. He had been due to depart that evening in order to take the waters, but a sudden attack of gout resulted in his trip being postponed – and condemned him to death.

The immense blasphemy and cynicism of the murders on the rue de Grenelle defy the imagination. What contempt for human life! What monstrous cruelty! And for what? For a golden idol which it is now impossible to sell! If melted down the Shiva will be transformed into an ordinary two kilogram ingot of gold. A mere 200 grams of yellow metal, such is the value placed by the criminal on each of the ten souls who have perished. Well may we exclaim after Cicero: *O tempora! O mores!*

There is, however, reason to believe that this supremely heinous crime will not go unpunished. That most experienced of detectives at the Paris préfecture, M. Gustave Gauche, to whom the investigation has been entrusted, has confidentially informed your correspondent that the police are in possession of a certain important piece of evidence. The commissioner is absolutely certain that retribution will be swift. When asked whether the crime was committed by a member of the professional fraternity of thieves, M. Gauche smiled slyly into his grey moustaches and enigmatically replied: 'Oh no, young man, the thread here leads into good society.' Your humble servant was unable to extract so much as another word from him.

J. du Roi

WHAT A CATCH!

The golden Shiva is found! Was the 'Crime of the Century' on the rue de Grenelle the work of a madman?

Yesterday, 17 March, between five o'clock and six o'clock in the afternoon, 13-year-old Pierre B. was fishing by the Pont des Invalides when his hook became snagged so firmly at the bottom of the river that he was obliged to wade into the cold water. ('I'm not so stupid as to just throw away a genuine English hook!' the young fisherman told our reporter.) Pierre's valour was richly rewarded: the hook had not caught on some common tree root but on a weighty object half buried in the silt. Once extracted from the water the object shone with an unearthly splendour, blinding the eyes of the astonished fisherman. Pierre's father, a retired sergeant and veteran of the Battle of Sedan, guessed that it must be the famous golden Shiva for which ten people had been killed only two days earlier, and he handed in the find at the préfecture.

What are we to make of this? For some reason a criminal who did not baulk at the cold-blooded and deliberate murder of so many people has chosen not to profit from the spoils of his monstrous initiative! Police investigators and public alike have been left guessing in the dark. The public appears inclined to believe that belated pangs of conscience must have led the murderer, aghast at the horror of his awful deed, to cast the golden idol into the river. Many go so far as to surmise that the miserable wretch also drowned himself somewhere close at hand. The police, however, are less romantically inclined and they discern clear indications of insanity in the inconsistency of the criminal's actions.

Shall we ever learn the true background to this nightmarish and unfathomable case?

A bevy of Parisian beauties

A series of 20 photocards forwarded cash on delivery for a price of 3 fr. 99 cent., including the cost of postage. A unique offer! Hurry – this is a limited edition! Paris, rue Cuypel, 'Patoux et fils' printing house.

PART ONE
Port Said to Aden

Commissioner Gauche

At Port Said a new passenger had boarded the *Leviathan*, occupying stateroom No. 18, the last first-class cabin still vacant, and Gustave Gauche's humour had immediately improved. This newcomer looked highly promising: that self-assured and unhurried way of carrying himself, that inscrutable expression on the handsome face which at first glance appeared altogether young, until the subject removed his bowler hat, unexpectedly revealing hair greying at the temples. A curious specimen, the commissioner decided. It was clear straight away that he had character and what they call *a past*. All in all, definitely a potential client for papa Gauche.

The passenger walked up the gangway swinging his holdall while the porters sweated as they struggled under the weight of his ample baggage: expensive squeaky suitcases, high-class pigskin travelling bags, voluminous bundles of books and even a folding tricycle (one large wheel, two small ones and a bundle of gleaming metal tubes). Bringing up the rear came two poor devils lugging an imposing set of gymnastic weights.

Gauche's heart, the heart of an old sleuth (as the commissioner himself was fond of testifying), had thrilled to the lure of the hunt when this newcomer proved to have no golden badge – neither on the silk lapel of his dandified summer coat, nor on his jacket, nor on his watch chain. Warmer now, very warm, thought Gauche as he vigilantly scrutinized the fop from beneath his bushy brows and puffed on his favourite clay pipe. But of course, why had he, old dunderhead that he was, assumed that the murderer would definitely board the steamship at Southampton? The crime was committed on 15 March and today was already 1 April. It would have been perfectly easy to reach Port Said while the *Leviathan* was rounding the western contour of Europe. And there you had it, everything fitted: clearly the right kind of character for a client, plus a first-class ticket, plus the most important thing – no golden whale.

For some time now Gauche's dreams had been haunted by that accursed badge with the acronym for the steamship company of the Jasper–Artaud Partnership, and without exception his dreams had been uncommonly bad ones. Take the most recent case, for instance.

The commissioner was out boating with Mme Gauche in the Bois de Boulogne. The sun was shining high in the sky and the birds were twittering in the trees. Suddenly a gigantic golden face with inanely goggling eyes loomed up over the treetops, opened cavernous jaws that could have accommodated the Arc de Triomphe with ease, and began sucking in the pond. Gauche broke into a sweat and laid into the oars. Meanwhile it transpired that events were not taking place in the park at all, but in the middle of a boundless ocean. The oars buckled like straws, Mme Gauche was jabbing him painfully in the back with her umbrella, and an immense gleaming carcass blotted out the entire horizon. When it spouted a fountain that eclipsed half the sky, the commissioner woke up and began fumbling around on his bedside table with trembling fingers – where were his pipe and those matches?

Gauche had first laid eyes on the golden whale on the rue de Grenelle when he was examining Lord Littleby's mortal remains. The Englishman lay there with his open mouth frozen in a soundless scream – his false teeth had come halfway out and his forehead was crowned by a bloody soufflé. Gauche squatted down on his haunches: he thought he had spotted a glint of gold between the corpse's fingers. Taking a closer look, he chortled in delight. Here was a stroke of uncommonly good luck, the kind that only occurred in crime novels. The helpful corpse had literally handed the investigation an important clue – and not even on a plate, but on the palm of its hand. There you are, Gustave, take that. Now may you die of shame if you dare let the person who smashed my head open get away, you old blockhead!

The golden emblem (at first, of course, Gauche had not known that it was an emblem, he had thought it was a bracelet charm or a monogrammed hairpin) could only have belonged to the murderer. But naturally, just to be sure, the commissioner had shown the whale to the junior manservant (what a lucky lad he was – 15 March was his day off and that had saved his life!), but the manservant had never seen his Lordship with the trinket before.

After that the entire ponderous mechanism of the police system had whirred into action, flywheels twirling and pinions spinning, as the minister and the prefect threw their very finest forces into solving the 'Crime of the Century'. By the evening of the following day Gauche already knew that the three letters on the golden whale were not the initials of some high liver hopelessly mired in debt, but the insignia of a newly established Franco-British shipping consortium. The whale proved to be the emblem of the miracle-ship *Leviathan*, newly launched from the slipway at Bristol and currently being readied for its maiden voyage to India.

The newspapers had been trumpeting the praises of the gigantic steamship for more than a month. Now it transpired that on the eve of the *Leviathan*'s first sailing the London Mint had produced gold and silver commemorative badges: gold for the first-class passengers and senior officers of the ship, silver for second-class passengers and subalterns. Aboard this luxurious vessel, where the achievements of modern science were combined with an unprecedented degree of comfort, no provision at all was made for third class. The company guaranteed travellers a comprehensive service, making it unnecessary to take any servants along on the voyage. 'The shipping line's attentive valets and tactful maids are on hand to ensure that you feel entirely at home on the *Leviathan*,' promised the advertisement printed in newspapers right across Europe. Those fortunate individuals who had booked a cabin for the first cruise from Southampton to Calcutta received a gold or silver whale with their ticket, according to their class – and a ticket could be booked in any major European port from London to Constantinople.

Very well then, the emblem of the *Leviathan* was not as good as the initials of its owner, but this only complicated the problem slightly, the commissioner had reasoned. There was a strictly limited number of gold badges. All he had to do was to wait until 19 March (that was the day appointed for the triumphant first sailing), go to Southampton, board the steamer and look to see which of the first-class passengers had no golden whale. Or else (which was more likely), which of the passengers who had laid out the money to buy a ticket failed to turn up for boarding. He would be papa Gauche's client. Simple as potato soup.

Gauche thoroughly disliked travelling, but this time he couldn't resist. He badly wanted to solve the 'Crime of the Century' himself. Who could tell, they might just give him a division at long last. He only had three years left to retirement. A third-class pension was one thing, but a second-class pension was a different matter altogether. The difference was 1500 francs a year, and that kind of money didn't exactly grow on trees.

In any case, he had put himself forward. He thought he would just nip across to Southampton and then, at worst, sail as far as Le Havre (the first stop) where there would be gendarmes and reporters lined up on the quayside. A tall headline in the *Revue parisienne*: ' "Crime of the Century" solved: our police rise to the occasion.' Or better still: 'Old sleuth Gauche pulls it off!'

Ha! The first unpleasant surprise had been waiting for the commissioner at the shipping line office in Southampton, where he discovered that the infernally huge steamship had 100 first-class cabins and ten senior officers. The tickets had all been sold. All 132 of them. And a gold badge had been issued with each and every one. A total of 142 suspects, if you please! But then only one of them would have no badge, Gauche had reassured himself.

On the morning of 19 March the commissioner, wrapped up against the damp wind in a warm woolly muffler, had been standing close to the gangway beside the captain, Mr Josiah Cliff, and the first lieutenant, M. Charles Renier. They were greeting the passengers. The brass band played English and French marching tunes by turns, the crowd on the pier generated an excited hubbub and Gauche puffed away in a rising fury, biting down hard on his entirely blameless pipe. For alas, due to the cold weather all of the passengers were wearing raincoats, overcoats, greatcoats or capotes. Now just try figuring out who has a badge and who doesn't! That was unpleasant surprise number two.

Everyone who was due to board the steamship in Southampton had arrived, indicating that the criminal must have shown up for the sailing despite having lost the badge. Evidently he must think that policemen were total idiots. Or was he hoping to lose himself in such an immense crowd? Or perhaps he simply had no option?

In any case, one thing was clear: Gauche would have to go along as far as Le Havre. He had been allocated the cabin reserved for honoured guests of the shipping line.

Immediately after the ship had sailed a banquet was held in the first-class grand saloon, an event of which the commissioner had especially high hopes since the invitations bore the instruction: 'Admission on presentation of a gold badge or first-class ticket'. Why on earth would anyone bother to carry around a ticket, when it was so much simpler to pin on your little gold leviathan?

At the banquet Gauche let his imagination run wild as he mentally frisked everyone present. He was even obliged to stick his nose into some ladies' décolletés to check whether they had anything dangling in there on a gold chain, perhaps a whale, perhaps simply a pendant. He had to check, surely?

Everyone was drinking champagne, nibbling on various savoury delicacies from silver trays and dancing, but Gauche was hard at work, eliminating from his list those who had their badge in place. It was the men who caused him the greatest problems. Many of the swines had attached the whale to their watch chains or even stuck it in their waistcoat pockets, and the commissioner was obliged to inquire after the exact time on eleven occasions.

Surprise number three: all of the officers had their badges in place, but there were actually four passengers wearing no emblem, including two of the female sex! The blow that had cracked open Lord Littleby's skull like a nutshell was so powerful it could surely only have been struck by a man, and a man of exceptional strength at that. On the other hand, as a highly experienced specialist in criminal matters, the commissioner was well aware that in a fit of passion or hysterical excitement even the weakest of little ladies was capable of performing genuine miracles. He had no need to look far for examples. Why, only last year a milliner from Neuilly, a frail little chit of a thing, had taken her unfaithful lover, a well-nourished *rentier* twice as fat and half as tall again as herself and thrown him out of a fourth-floor window. So it would not do at all to eliminate women who happened to have no badge from the list of suspects. Although who had ever heard of a woman, especially from good society, mastering the knack of giving injections like that?

What with one thing and another, the investigation on board the *Leviathan* threatened to drag on, and so the commissioner had set about dealing with things in his customary thorough fashion. Captain Josiah Cliff was the only officer of the steamship who had been made privy to the secret investigation, and he had instructions from the management of the shipping company to afford the French guardian of the law every possible assistance. Gauche exploited this privilege quite unceremoniously by demanding that all the individuals of interest to him be assigned to the same saloon.

It should be explained at this point that out of considerations of privacy and comfort (after all, the ship's advertisement had boasted: 'On board you will discover the atmosphere of a fine old English country estate') those individuals travelling first class were not expected to take their meals in the vast dining hall together with the 600 bearers of democratic silver whales, but were assigned to their own comfortable 'saloons', each of which bore its own aristocratic title and in appearance resembled a high-society hotel, with crystal candelabra, fumed oak and mahogany, velvet-upholstered chairs, gleaming table silver, prim waiters and officious stewards. For his own purposes Commissioner Gauche had singled out the Windsor saloon. Located on the upper deck in the bow section, it had three walls of continuous windows affording a magnificent view, so that even when the day was overcast there was no need to switch on the lights. The velvet upholstery here was a fine shade of golden brown and the linen table napkins were adorned with the Windsor coat of arms.

Standing around the oval table with its legs bolted to the floor (a precaution against any likelihood of severe pitching and rolling) there were ten chairs, with their tall backs carved in designs incorporating a motley assortment of gothic knick-knacks. The commissioner liked the idea of everyone sitting around the same table and he had ordered the steward not to set out the name plates at random but with strategic intent: he had seated the four passengers without badges directly opposite himself so that he could keep a close eye on those particular pigeons. It had not proved possible to seat the captain himself at the head of the table, as Gauche had planned. Mr Josiah Cliff did not wish (as he himself had expressed it) 'to have any part in this charade', and had chosen to base himself in the York saloon where the new Viceroy of India was taking his meals with his wife and two generals of the Indian army. York was located in the prestigious stern, as far removed as possible from plague-stricken Windsor, where the head of the table was taken by first mate Charles Renier. The commissioner had taken an instant dislike to Renier, with that face bronzed by the sun and the wind, that honeyed way of speaking, that head of dark hair gleaming with brilliantine, that dyed moustache with its two spruce little curls. A buffoon, not a sailor.

In the course of the twelve days that had elapsed since they sailed, the commissioner had subjected his saloon-mates to close scrutiny, absorbed the rudiments of society manners (that is, he had learned not to smoke during a meal and not to mop up his gravy with a crust of bread), more or less mastered the complex geography of this floating city and grown accustomed to the ship's pitching, but he had still made no progress towards his goal.

The situation was now as follows:

Initially his list of suspects had been headed by Sir Reginald Milford-Stokes, an emaciated, ginger-haired gentleman with tousled sideburns. He looked about twenty-eight or thirty years old and behaved oddly, either gazing vaguely into the distance with those wide green eyes of his and not responding to questions, or suddenly becoming animated and prattling on about the island of Tahiti, coral reefs, emerald lagoons and huts with roofs made of palm leaves. Clearly some kind of mental case. Why else would a baronet, the scion of a wealthy family, go travelling to some God-forsaken Oceania at the other end of the world? What did he think he would find there? And note, too, that this blasted aristocrat had twice ignored a question about his missing badge. He stared straight through the commissioner, and when he did happen to glance at him he seemed to be scrutinizing some insignificant insect. A rotten snob. Back in Le Havre (where they had stood for four hours) Gauche had made a dash to the telegraph and sent off an inquiry about Milford-Stokes to Scotland Yard: who was he, did he have any record of violent behaviour, had he ever dabbled in the study of medicine? The reply that had arrived just before they sailed contained nothing of great interest, but it had explained away the strange mannerisms. Even so, he did not have a golden whale, which meant it was still too early for Gauche to remove the ginger gentleman from his list of potential clients.

The second suspect was M. Gintaro Aono, a 'Japanese noble-man' (or so it said in the register of passengers). He was a typical Oriental, short and skinny. He could be almost any age, with that thin moustache and those narrow, piercing eyes. He remained silent most of the time at table. When asked what he did, he mumbled in embarrassment: 'An officer of the Imperial Army.' When asked about his badge he became even more embarrassed, cast a glance of searing hatred at the commissioner, excused himself and left the room, without even finishing his soup. Decidedly suspicious! An absolute savage. He fanned himself in the saloon with a bright-coloured paper contraption, like some pederast from one of those dens of dubious delight behind the rue de Rivoli, and he strolled about the deck in his wooden slippers and cotton robe without any trousers at all. Of course, Gustave Gauche was all in favour of liberty, equality and fraternity, but a popinjay like that really ought not to have been allowed into first class.

And then there were the women.

Mme Renate Kleber. Young, barely twenty perhaps. The wife of an employee of a Swiss bank, travelling to join her husband in Calcutta. She could hardly be described as a beauty, with that pointy nose, but she was lively and talkative. She had informed him she was pregnant the very moment they were introduced. All her thoughts and feelings were governed by this single circumstance. A sweet and ingenuous woman, but absolutely insupportable. In twelve days she had succeeded in boring the commissioner to death by chattering about her precious health, embroidering nightcaps and other such nonsense. Nothing but a belly on legs, although she was not very far along yet and the belly was only just beginning to show. Gauche, naturally, had chosen his moment and asked where her emblem was. The Swiss lady had blinked her bright little eyes and complained that she was always losing things. Which seemed very likely to be true. For Renate Kleber the commissioner felt a mixture of irritation and protectiveness, but he did not take her seriously as a client.

When it came to the second lady, Miss Clarissa Stamp, the worldly-wise detective felt a far keener interest. There was something about her that seemed not quite right. She appeared to be a typical Englishwoman, nothing out of the ordinary. No longer young, with dull, colourless hair and rather sedate manners, but just occasionally those watery eyes would give a flash of devilment. He'd seen her type before. What was it the English said about still waters? There were a few other little details worthy of note. Mere trifles really, no one else would have paid any attention to that kind of thing, but nothing escaped Gauche, the sly old dog. Miss Stamp's dresses and her wardrobe in general were expensive and brand new, everything in the latest Parisian style. Her handbag was genuine tortoiseshell (he'd seen one like it in a shop window on the Champs-Elysées – three hundred and fifty francs), but the notebook she took out of it was old and made of cheap writing paper. On one occasion she had sat on the deck wearing a shawl (it was windy at the time), and it was exactly like one that Mme Gauche had, made of dog's hair. Warm, but not at all the thing for an English lady. And it was curious that absolutely all of Clarissa Stamp's new things were expensive but her old things were shoddy and of the very poorest quality. This was a clear discrepancy. One day just before five o'clock tea Gauche had asked her: 'Why is it, my dear lady, that you never put on your golden whale? Do you not like it? It seems to me a very stylish trinket.' And what was her response? She had blushed an even deeper colour than the 'Japanese nobleman' and said that she had worn it already but he simply hadn't noticed. It was a lie. Gauche would have noticed all right. The commissioner had a certain subtle ploy in mind, but he would have to choose exactly the right psychological moment. Then he would see how she would react, this Clarissa.

Since there were ten places at the table and he only had four passengers without their emblems, Gauche had decided to make up the numbers with other specimens who were also noteworthy in their own way, even though they had badges. It would widen his field of inquiry: the places were there in any case.

First of all he had demanded that the captain assign the ship's chief physician, M. Truffo, to Windsor. Josiah Cliff had muttered a little but eventually he had given way. The reason for Gauche's interest in the physician was clear enough – skilled in the art of giving injections, he was the only medic on board the *Leviathan* whose status entitled him to a golden whale. The doctor turned out to be a rather short, plump Italian with an olive complexion, a tall forehead and a bald patch with a few sparse strands of hair combed backwards across it. It was simply impossible to imagine this comical specimen in the role of a ruthless killer. In addition to the doctor, another place had to be allocated to his wife. Having married only two weeks previously, the physician had decided to combine duty and pleasure by making this voyage his honeymoon. The chair occupied by the new Mme Truffo was completely wasted. The dreary, unsmiling Englishwoman who had found favour with the shipboard Aesculapius appeared twice as old as her twenty years and inspired in Gauche a deadly ennui – as, indeed, did the majority of her female compatriots. He immediately dubbed her 'the sheep' for her white eyelashes and bleating voice. As it happened, she rarely opened her mouth, since she did not know French and for the most part conversations in the saloon were, thank God, conducted in that most noble of tongues. Mme Truffo had no badge of any kind, but that was only natural, since she was neither an officer nor a paying passenger.

The commissioner had also spotted in the register of passengers a certain specialist in Indian archaeology, Anthony F. Sweetchild by name, and decided that an Indologist might just come in handy. After all, the deceased Lord Littleby had also been something of the kind. Mr Sweetchild, a lanky beanpole with round-rimmed spectacles and a goatee, had himself struck up a conversation about India at the very first dinner. After the meal Gauche had taken the professor aside and cautiously steered the conversation round to the subject of Lord Littleby's collection. The Indian specialist had contemptuously dismissed his late lordship as a dilettante and his collection as a 'cabinet of curiosities' assembled without any scholarly framework. He claimed that the only item of genuine value in it was the golden Shiva and said it was a good thing the Shiva had turned up on its own, because everybody knew the French police were good for nothing but taking bribes. This grossly unjust remark set Gauche coughing furiously, but Sweetchild merely advised him to smoke less. The scholar went on to remark con-descendingly that Littleby had, admittedly, acquired a fairly decent collection of decorative fabrics and shawls, which happened to include some extremely curious items, but that really had more to do with the native applied arts and crafts of India. The sixteenth-century sandalwood chest from Lahore with carvings on a theme from the *Mahabharata* was not too bad either – and then he had launched into a rigmarole that soon had the commissioner nodding off.

Gauche had selected his final saloon-mate by eye, as they say. Quite literally so. The commissioner had only recently finished reading a most diverting volume translated from the Italian. Cesare Lombroso, a professor of forensic medicine from the Italian city of Turin, had developed an entire theory of criminal-istics according to which congenital criminals were not re-sponsible for their antisocial behaviour. In accordance with Dr Darwin's theory of evolution, mankind passed through a series of distinct stages in its development, gradually approaching perfection. But a criminal was an evolutionary reject, a random throwback to a previous stage. It was therefore a very simple matter to identify the potential robber or murderer: he re-sembled the monkey from which we were all descended. The commissioner had pondered long and hard about what he had read. On the one hand, by no means every one of the motley crew of robbers and murderers with whom he had dealt in the course of thirty years of police work had resembled gorillas, some of them had been such sweet little angels that a single glance at them brought a tender tear to the eye. On the other hand, there had been plenty of anthropoid types too. And as a convinced anticlerical, old Gauche did not believe in Adam and Eve. Darwin's theory appeared rather more sound to him. And then he had come across a certain individual among the first-class passengers, a type who might have sat for a picture entitled 'The Typical Killer': low forehead, prominent ridges above little eyes, flat nose and crooked chin. And so the commissioner had requested that this Étienne Boileau, a tea trader, be assigned to the Windsor saloon. He had turned out to be an absolutely charming fellow – a ready wit, father of eleven children and confirmed philanthropist.

It had looked as though papa Gauche's voyage was unlikely to terminate even in Port Said, the next port of call after Le Havre. The investigation was dragging on. And, moreover, the keen intuition developed by the commissioner over the years was already hinting to him that he had drawn a blank and there was no serious candidate among the company he had assembled. He was beginning to glimpse the sickening prospect of cruising the entire confounded length of the route to Port Said and Aden and Bombay and Calcutta – and then hanging himself in Calcutta on the first palm tree. He couldn't go running back to Paris with his tail between his legs! His colleagues would make him a laughing stock, his bosses would start carping about the small matter of a first-class voyage at the treasury's expense. They might even kick him out on an early pension . . .

At Port Said, since the voyage was turning out to be a long one, with an aching heart Gauche bankrupted himself by buying some more shirts, stocked up on Egyptian tobacco and, for lack of anything else to fill his time, spent two francs on a cab ride along the famous waterfront. In fact, there was nothing exceptional about it. An enormous lighthouse, a couple of piers as long as your arm. The town itself produced a strange impression, neither Asia nor Europe. Take a look at the residence of the governor-general of the Suez Canal and it seemed like Europe. The streets in the centre were crowded with European faces, there were ladies strolling about with white parasols and wealthy gentlemen in panama hats and straw boaters plodding along, paunches to the fore. But once the carriage turned into the native quarter a fetid stench filled the air and everywhere there were flies, rotting refuse and grubby little Arab urchins pestering people for small change. Why did these rich idlers bother to go travelling? It was the same everywhere: some grew fat from gorging on delicacies while others had their bellies swollen by hunger.

Exhausted by these pessimistic observations and the heat, the commissioner had returned to the ship feeling dejected. But then he had a stroke of luck – a new client, and he looked like a promising one.

The commissioner paid the captain a visit and made inquiries. So, his name was Erast P. Fandorin and he was a Russian subject. For some reason this Russian subject had not given his age. A diplomat by profession, he had arrived from Constantinople, was travelling to Calcutta and going on from there to Japan to take up his post. From Constantinople? Aha! He must have been involved in the peace negotiations that had concluded the recent Russo-Turkish War. Gauche punctiliously copied all the details onto a sheet of paper and stowed it away in the special calico-bound file where he kept all the materials on the case. He was never parted from his file. He leafed through it and reread the reports and newspaper clippings, and in pensive moments he drew little fishes and houses in the margins of the papers. It was the secret dream of his heart breaking through to the surface. The dream of how he would become a divisional commissioner, earn a decent pension, buy a nice little house somewhere in Normandy and live out his days there with Mme Gauche. The retired Paris *flic* would go fishing and press his own cider. What was wrong with that? Ah, if only he had a little bit of capital to add to his pension – he needed twenty thousand at least . . .

He was obliged to make another visit to the port – luckily the ship was delayed as it waited for its turn to enter the Suez Canal – and dash off a brief telegram to the préfecture, asking whether the Russian diplomat Erast P. Fandorin was known in Paris and whether he had entered the territory of the Republic of France at any time in the recent past.

The reply arrived quickly, after only two and a half hours. It turned out that the chap had crossed French territory not once, but twice. The first time in the summer of 1876 (well, we can let that go) and the second time in December 1877, just three months earlier. His arrival from London had been recorded at the passport and customs control point in Pas-de-Calais. It was not known how much time he had spent in France. He could quite possibly still have been in Paris on 15 March. He could even have dropped round to the rue de Grenelle with a syringe in his hand – stranger things had happened.

It now seemed he would have to free one of the places at the table. The best thing, of course, would be to get rid of the doctor's wife, but he could hardly encroach on the sacred institution of marriage. After some thought, Gauche decided to pack the tea trader off to a different saloon, since the theoretical hopes he had inspired had proved to be unfounded and he was the least promising of all the candidates. The steward could reassign him, tell him there was a place with more important gentlemen or prettier ladies. After all, that was what stewards were for, to arrange such things.

The appearance of a new personality in the saloon caused a minor sensation. In the course of the journey they had all become thoroughly bored with each other, and now here was a fresh gentleman, and such a superior individual at that. Nobody bothered to inquire after poor M. Boileau, that representative of a previous stage of evolution. The commissioner noted that the person who evinced the liveliest reaction was Miss Clarissa Stamp, the old maid, who started babbling about artists, the theatre and literature. Gauche himself was fond of passing his leisure hours in an armchair with a good book, preferring Victor Hugo to all other authors. Hugo was at once so true to life and high-minded, he could always bring a tear to the eye. Besides, he was marvellous for dozing over. But, of course, Gauche had never even heard of these Russian writers with those hissing sibilants in their names, so he was unable to join in the conversation. Anyway, the old English trout was wasting her time, *M. Fandorine* was far too young for her.

Renate Kleber was not slow off the mark either. She made an attempt to press the new arrival into service as one of her minions, whom she bullied mercilessly into bringing her shawl or her parasol or a glass of water. Five minutes after dinner began Mme Kleber had already initiated the Russian into the detailed history of her delicate condition, complained of a migraine and asked him to fetch Dr Truffo, who for some reason was late that day. However, the diplomat seemed to have realized immediately whom he was dealing with and politely objected that he did not know the doctor by sight. The ever-obliging Lieutenant Renier, the pregnant banker's wife's most devoted nursemaid, had volunteered and gone racing off to perform the errand.

The initial impression made by Erast Fandorin was that he was taciturn, reserved and polite. But he was a bit too spruce and trim for Gauche's taste: that starched collar sticking up like alabaster, that jewelled pin in the necktie, that red carnation (oh, very suave!) in the buttonhole, that perfectly smooth parting with not a single hair out of place, those carefully manicured nails, that narrow black moustache that seemed to be drawn on with charcoal.

It was possible to tell a great deal about a man from his moustache. If it was like Gauche's, a walrus moustache drooping at the corners of his mouth, it meant the man was a down-to-earth fellow who knew his own worth, not some featherbrain who was easily taken in. If it was curled up at the ends, especially into points, he was a lady's man and bon vivant. If it merged into his sideburns, he was a man of ambition with dreams of becoming a general, senator or banker. And when it was like *M. Fandorine*'s, it meant he entertained romantic notions about himself.

What else could he say about the Russian? He spoke decent enough French, even though he stammered. There was still no sign of his badge. The diplomat showed most interest in the Japanese, asking him all sorts of tiresome questions about Japan, but the samurai answered guardedly, as if anticipating some kind of trick. The point was that the new passenger had not explained to the company where he was going and why, he had simply given his name and said that he was Russian. The commissioner, though, could understand the Russian's inquisitiveness, since he knew he was going to live in Japan. Gauche pictured to himself a country in which every single person was the same as M. Aono, everybody lived in dolls' houses with bowed roofs and disembowelled themselves at the slightest provocation. No indeed, the Russian was not to be envied.

After dinner, when Fandorin took a seat to one side in order to smoke a cigar, the commissioner settled into the next armchair and began puffing away at his pipe. Gauche had previously introduced himself to his new acquaintance as a Parisian *rentier* who was making the journey to the East out of curiosity (that was the cover he was using). But now he turned the conversation to the matter at hand, approaching it obliquely and with due caution. Fiddling with the golden whale on his lapel (the very same one retrieved from the rue de Grenelle) he said with a casual air, as though he were simply striking up a conversation:

'A beautiful little bauble. Don't you agree?'

The Russian glanced sideways at his lapel but said nothing.

'Pure gold. So stylish!' said Gauche admiringly.

Another pregnant silence followed, but a perfectly civil one. The man was simply waiting to see what would come next. His blue eyes were alert. The diplomat had clear skin, as smooth as a peach, with a bloom on the cheeks like a young girl's. But he was no mama's boy, that much was obvious straight away.

The commissioner decided to try a different tack.

'Do you travel much?'

A non-committal shrug.

'I believe you're in the diplomatic line?'

Fandorin inclined his head politely in assent, extracted a long cigar from his pocket and cut off the tip with a little silver knife.

'And have you ever been in France?'

Again an affirmative nod of the head. *Monsieur le russe is no great shakes as a conversationalist*, thought Gauche, but he had no intention of backing down.

'More than anything I love Paris in the early spring, in March,' the detective mused out loud. 'The very best time of the year!'

He cast a keen glance at the other man, wondering what he would say.

Fandorin nodded twice, though it wasn't clear whether he was simply acknowledging the remark or agreeing with it. Beginning to feel irritated, Gauche knitted his brows in an antagonistic scowl.

'So you don't like your badge then?'

His pipe sputtered and went out.

The Russian gave a short sigh, put his hand into his waistcoat pocket, extracted a golden whale between his finger and thumb and finally condescended to open his mouth.

'I observe, monsieur, that you are interested in my b-badge? Here it is, if you please. I do not wear it because I do not wish to resemble a caretaker with a name tag, not even a golden one. That is one. You yourself do not much resemble a *rentier*, M. Gauche – your eyes are too probing. And why would a Parisian *rentier* lug a civil service file around with him? That is two. Since you are aware of my professional orientation, you would appear to have access to the ship's documents. I assume therefore that you are a detective. That is three. Which brings us to number four. If there is something you need to find out from me, please do not beat about the bush, ask directly.'

Just try having a nice little chat with someone like that!

Gauche had to wriggle out of it somehow. He whispered confidentially to the excessively perspicacious diplomat that he was the ship's house detective, whose job it was to see to the passengers' safety, but secretly and with the greatest possible delicacy in order to avoid offending the refined sensibilities of his public. It was not clear whether Fandorin believed him, but at least he did not ask any questions.

Every cloud has a silver lining. The commissioner now had, if not an intellectual ally, then at least an interlocutor, and one who possessed remarkable powers of observation as well as quite exceptional knowledge on matters of criminology.

They often sat together on the deck, glancing now and then at the gently sloping bank of the canal as they smoked (Gauche his pipe, the Russian his cigar) and discussed various intriguing subjects, such as the very latest methods for the identification and conviction of criminals.

'The Paris police conducts its work in accordance with the very latest advances in scientific method,' Gauche once boasted. 'The préfecture there has a special identification unit headed by a young genius, Alphonse Bertillon. He has developed a complete system for classifying and recording criminal elements.'

'I met with Dr Bertillon during my last visit to Paris,' Fandorin said unexpectedly. 'He told me about his anthropometric method. Bertillonage is a clever theory, very clever. Have you already begun to apply it in practice? What have the results been like?'

'There haven't been any yet,' the commissioner said with a shrug. 'First one has to apply bertillonage to all the recidivists, and that will take years. It's bedlam in Alphonse's department: they bring in the prisoners in shackles, measure them up from every angle like horses at a fair, and jot down the data on little cards. But then pretty soon it will make police work as easy as falling off a log. Let's say you find the print of a left hand at the scene of a burglary. You measure it and go to the card index. Aha, middle finger eighty-nine millimetres long, look in section No. 3. And there you find records of seventeen burglars with a finger of the right length. After that, the whole thing is as easy as pie: check where each of them was on the day of the robbery and nab the one who has no alibi.'

'You mean criminals are divided up into categories according to the length of the middle finger?' the Russian asked with lively interest.

Gauche chuckled condescendingly into his moustache.

'There is a whole system involved, my young friend. Bertillon divides all people into three groups, according to the length of the skull. Each of *these* three groups is divided into three sub-groups, according to the width of the skull. That makes nine sub-groups in all. Each sub-group is in turn divided into three sections, according to the size of the middle finger of the left hand. Twenty-seven sections. But that's not all. There are three divisions in each section, according to the size of the right ear. So how many divisions does that make? That's right, eighty-one. Subsequent classification takes into account the height, the length of the arms, the height when seated, the size of the foot and the length of the elbow joint. A total of eighteen thousand six hundred and eighty-three categories! A criminal who has undergone full bertillonage and been included in our card index will never be able to escape justice again. They used to have it so easy – just give a false name when you're arrested and you could avoid any responsibility for anything you did before.'

'That is remarkable,' the diplomat mused. 'However, bertillonage does not offer much help with the solution of a particular crime if an individual has not been arrested before.'

Gauche spread his arms helplessly.

'Well, that is a problem that science cannot solve. As long as there are criminals, people will not be able to manage without us professional sleuths.'

'Have you ever heard of fingerprints?' Fandorin asked, presenting to the commissioner a narrow but extremely firm hand with polished nails and a diamond ring.

Glancing enviously at the ring (a commissioner's annual salary at the very least), Gauche laughed.

'Is that some kind of gypsy palm reading?'

'Not at all. It has been known since ancient times that the raised pattern of papillary lines on the tips of the fingers is unique to every individual. In China coolies seal their contracts of hire with the imprint of their thumb dipped in ink.'

'Well now, if only every murderer were so obliging as to dip his thumb into ink and leave an imprint at the scene of the crime . . .' The commissioner laughed good-naturedly.

The diplomat, however, was not in the mood for joking.

'Monsieur ship's detective, allow me to inform you that modern science has established with certainty that an imprint is left when a finger comes into contact with any dry, firm surface. If a criminal has so much as touched a door in passing, or the murder weapon, or a window pane, he has left a trace which allows the p-perpetrator to be identified and unmasked.'

Gauche was about to retort ironically that there were twenty thousand criminals in France, that between them they had two hundred thousand fingers and thumbs and you would go blind staring at all of them through your magnifying glass, but he hesitated, recalling the shattered display case in the mansion on the rue de Grenelle. There had been fingerprints left all over the broken glass. But it had never entered anyone's head to copy them and the shards had been thrown out with the garbage.

My, what an amazing thing progress was! Just think what it meant. All crimes were committed with hands, were they not? And now it seemed that hands could snitch every bit as well as paid informants. Just imagine, if you were to copy the fingers of every bandit and petty thief, they wouldn't dare turn those filthy hands of theirs to any more dirty work. It would be the end of crime itself.

The very prospect was enough to set a man's head spinning.

Reginald Milford-Stokes

2 April 1878
18 hours, 34½ minutes, Greenwich time

My precious Emily,
Today we entered the Suez Canal. In yesterday's letter I described the history and topography of Port Said to you in detail, and now I simply cannot resist the temptation of relating to you certain curious and instructive facts concerning the Great Canal, this truly colossal monument to human endeavour, which next year celebrates its tenth anniversary. Are you aware, my adorable little wife, that the present canal is actually the fourth to have existed and that the first was excavated as long ago as the fourteenth century Before Christ, during the reign of the great Pharaoh Rameses? When Egypt fell into decline the desert winds choked up the channel with sand, but under the Persian king Darius, five hundred years Before Christ, slaves dug out another canal at the cost of 120,000 human lives. Herodotus tells us that the voyage along it took four days and that two triremes travelling in opposite directions could easily pass each other without their oars touching. Several ships from Cleopatra's shattered fleet fled to the Red Sea by this route and so escaped the fearful wrath of the vengeful Octavian Caesar.

Following the fall of the Roman Empire, time again separated the Atlantic and Indian Oceans with a barrier of shifting sand one hundred miles wide, but no sooner was a powerful state established in these barren lands by the followers of the Prophet Mohammed than people took up their mattocks and pickaxes once again. As I sail through these dead salt-meadows and endless sand-dunes, I marvel unceasingly at the stubborn courage and ant-like diligence of humankind in waging its never-ending struggle, doomed to inevitable defeat, *against all-powerful Chronos. Vessels laden with grain plied the Arabian canal for two hundred years, and then the earth erased this pitiful wrinkle from its forehead and the desert was plunged into sleep for a thousand years.*

Regrettably the father of the new Suez was not a Briton, but the Frenchman Lesseps, a representative of a nation which, my darling Emily, I quite justifiably hold in the most profound contempt. This crafty diplomat persuaded the Egyptian governor to issue a firman for the establishment of The Universal Company of the Suez Maritime Canal. The Company was granted a 99-year lease on the future waterway, and the Egyptian government was allotted only 15 per cent of the net revenue. And these villainous French dare to label us British pillagers of the backward peoples! At least we win our privileges with the sword, not by striking grubby bargains with greedy local bureaucrats.

Every day 1600 camels delivered drinking water to the workers digging the Great Canal, but still the poor devils died in their thousands from thirst, intense heat and infectious diseases. Our Leviathan is sailing over corpses, and I seem to see the yellow teeth of fleshless, eyeless skulls grinning out at me from beneath the sand. It took ten years and 15 million pounds sterling to complete this gargantuan work of construction. But now a ship can sail from England to India in almost half the time it used to take. A mere 25 days or so and you arrive in Bombay. It is quite incredible! And the scale of it! The canal is more than 100 feet deep, so that even our gigantic ark can sail fearlessly here, with no risk of running aground.

Today at lunch I was overcome by a quite irresistible fit of laughter. I choked on a crust of bread, began coughing and simply could not calm myself. The pathetic coxcomb Renier (I wrote to you about him, he is the Leviathan's first lieutenant) inquired with feigned interest what was the cause of my merriment and I was seized by an even stronger paroxysm, for I certainly could not tell him about the thought that had set me laughing: that the French had built the canal, but the fruits had fallen to us, the English. Three years ago Her Majesty's government bought a controlling block of shares from the Egyptian khedive, and now we British are the masters of Suez. And incidentally, a single share in the canal, which was once sold for fifteen pounds, is now worth three thousand! How's that! How could I help but laugh?

But I fear I must have wearied you with these boring details. Do not blame me, my dear Emily, for I have no other recreation apart from writing long letters. While I am scraping my pen across the vellum paper, it is as though you are here beside me and I am making leisurely conversation with you. You know, thanks to the hot climate here I am feeling very much better. I no longer remember the terrible dreams that haunt me in the night. But they have not gone away. In the morning when I wake up, the pillowcase is still soaked with tears and sometimes gnawed to shreds.

But that is all nonsense. Every new day and every mile of the journey bring me closer to a new life. There, under the soothing sun of the Equator, this dreadful separation that is tearing my very soul apart will finally come to an end. How I wish it could be soon! How impatient I am to see your tender, radiant glance once again, my dear friend.

What else can I entertain you with? Perhaps at least with a description of our Leviathan, *a more than worthy theme. In my earlier letters I have written too much about my own feelings and dreams and I have still not presented you with a full picture of this great triumph of British engineering.*

The Leviathan *is the largest passenger ship in the history of the world, with the single exception of the colossal* Great Eastern, *which has been furrowing the waters of the Atlantic Ocean for the last 20 years. When Jules Verne described the* Great Eastern *in his book* The Floating City, *he had not seen our* Leviathan – *otherwise he would have renamed the old G.E. 'the floating village'. That vessel now does nothing but lay telegraph cables on the ocean floor, but* Leviathan *can transport 1000 people and in addition 10,000 tons of cargo. This fire-breathing monster is more than 600 hundred feet long and 80 feet across at its widest. Do you know, my dear Emily, how a ship is built? First they lay it out in the moulding loft, that is to say, they make a full-scale drawing of the vessel directly onto the smoothly planed floor of a special building. The drawing of the* Leviathan *was so huge that they had to build a shed the size of Buckingham Palace!*

This miracle of a ship has two steam engines, two powerful paddle-wheels on its sides and in addition a gigantic propeller on its stern. Its six masts, fitted with a full set of rigging, tower up to the very sky and with a fair wind and engines running full speed ahead the ship can make 16 knots! All the very latest advances in shipbuilding have been used in the vessel. These include a double metal hull, which ensures its safety even if it should strike a rock; special side keels which reduce pitching and rolling; electric lighting throughout; waterproof compartments; immense coolers for the spent steam – it is impossible to list everything. The entire experience of centuries of effort by the indefatigably inventive human mind has been concentrated in this proud vessel cleaving fearlessly through the ocean waves. Yesterday, following my old habit, I opened the Holy Scriptures at the first page that came to hand and I was astonished when my eyes fell upon the lines about Leviathan, the fearsome monster of the deep from the Book of Job. I began trembling at the sudden realization that this was no description of a sea serpent, as the ancients believed it to be, nor of a sperm whale, as our modern-day rationalists claim – no, the biblical text clearly refers to the very same Leviathan *that has undertaken to deliver me out of darkness and terror into happiness and light. Judge for yourself: 'He maketh the deep to boil like a pot: he maketh the sea like a pot of ointment. He maketh a path to shine after him: one would think the deep to be hoary. Upon earth there is not his like, who is made without fear. He beholdeth all high things: he is a king over all the children of pride.'*

The pot – that is the steam boiler; the pot of ointment – that is the fuel oil; the shining path – that is the wake at the stern. It is all so obvious!

And I felt afraid, my darling Emily. For these lines contain a terrible warning, either to me personally or to the passengers on the Leviathan, *or to the whole of mankind. From the biblical point of view pride is surely a bad thing? And if man with his technological playthings 'beholdeth all high things', is this not fraught with some catastrophic consequences? Have we not become too proud of the keenness of our intellect and the skill of our hands? Where is this king of pride taking us? What lies in store for us?*

And so I opened my prayer book to pray – the first time for a long, long time. And there I read: 'It is in their thoughts that their houses are eternal and their dwellings are from generation to generation, and they call their lands after their own names. But man shall not abide in honour; he shall be likened unto the beasts who die. This path of theirs is their folly, though those that come after them do commend their opinion.'

But when, in a paroxysm of mystical feeling, I opened the Book once again with a trembling hand, my feverish gaze fell on the boring passage in Numbers where the sacrifices made by the tribes of the Israelites are itemized with a bookkeeper's tedious precision. And I calmed down, rang my silver bell and told the steward to bring me some hot chocolate.

The level of comfort prevailing in the section of the ship assigned to the respectable public is absolutely staggering. In this respect the Leviathan is truly without equal. The times are gone when people travelling to India or China were cooped up in dark, cramped little cubbyholes and piled one on top of another. You know, my dearest wife, how keenly I suffer from claustrophobia, but on board the Leviathan I feel as though I were in the wide open spaces of the Thames Embankment. Here there is everything required to combat boredom: a dance hall, a musical salon for concerts of classical music, even a rather decent library. The decor in a first-class cabin is in no way inferior to a room in the finest London hotel, and the ship has 100 hundred such cabins. In addition there are 250 second-class cabins with 600 berths (I have not looked into them – I cannot endure the sight of squalor) and they say there are also capacious cargo holds. The Leviathan's service personnel alone, not counting sailors and officers, numbers more than 200 stewards, chefs, valets, musicians, chambermaids. Just imagine, I do not regret in the least not bringing Jeremy with me. The idle loafer was always sticking his nose into matters that did not concern him, and here at precisely 11 o'clock the maid comes and cleans the room and carries out any other errands I may have for her. This is both rational and convenient. If I wish I can ring for a valet and have him help me dress, but I regard that as excessive – I dress and undress myself. It is most strictly forbidden for any servant to enter the cabin in my absence, and on leaving it I set a hair across the crack of the door. I am afraid of spies. Believe me, my sweet Emily, this is not a ship, but a veritable city, and it has its share of low riff-raff.

For the most part my information concerning the ship has been garnered from the explanations of Lieutenant Renier, who is a great patriot of his own vessel. He is, however, not a very likeable individual and the object of serious suspicion on my part. He tries his hardest to play the gentleman, but I am not so easily duped. I have a keen nose for bad breeding. Wishing to produce a good impression, this fellow invited me to visit his cabin. I did call in, but less out of curiosity than from a desire to assess the seriousness of the threat that might be posed by this swarthy gentleman (concerning his appearance, see my letter of 20 March). The meagreness of the decor was rendered even more glaringly obvious by his tasteless attempts at bon ton (Chinese vases, Indian incense burners, a dreadful seascape on the wall, and so forth). Standing on the table among the maps and navigational instruments was a large photographic portrait of a woman dressed in black, with an inscription in French: 'Seven feet under the keel, my darling! Françoise B.' I enquired whether it was his wife. It turned out to be his mother. Touching, but it does not allay my suspicions. I am as determined as ever to take independent readings of our course every three hours, even though it means that I have to get up twice during the night. Of course, while we are sailing through the Suez Canal this might seem a little excessive, but I do not wish to lose my proficiency in handling the sextant.

I have more than enough time at my disposal and apart from the writing of letters my leisure hours are filled by observing the Vanity Fair which surrounds me on all sides. Among this gallery of human types there are some who are most amusing. I have already written to you about the others, but yesterday a new face appeared in our salon. He is Russian – can you imagine that? His name is Erast Fandorin. You are aware, Emily, of my feelings regarding Russia, that misshapen excrescence that has extended over half of Europe and a third of Asia. Russia seeks to disseminate its own parody of the Christian religion and its own barbarous customs throughout the entire world, and Albion stands as the only barrier in the path of these new Huns. If *not for the resolute position adopted by Her Majesty's government in the current eastern crisis, Tsar Alexander would have raked in the Balkans with his bear's claws, and . . .*

But I have already written to you about that and I do not wish to repeat myself. And in any case, thinking about politics has rather a bad effect on my nerves. It is now four minutes to eight. As I have already informed you, life on the Leviathan *is conducted according to British time as far as Aden, so that it is already dark here at eight o'clock. I shall go and take readings of the longitude and latitude, then take dinner and continue with my letter.*

16 minutes after ten

I see that I did not finish writing about Mr Fandorin. I do believe that I like him, despite his nationality. Good manners, reticent, knows how to listen. He must be a member of that estate referred to in Russia by the Italian word intelligenzia, *which I believe denotes the educated European class. You must admit, dear Emily, that a society in which the European class is separated off into a distinct stratum of the population and also referred to by a foreign word can hardly be ranked among the civilized nations. I can imagine what a gulf separates a civilized human being like Mr Fandorin from some bearded Kossack or muzhik, who make up 90 per cent of the population of that Tartarian–Byzantine empire. On the other hand, a distance of such magnitude must elevate and ennoble an educated and thinking man to an exceptional degree, a point that I shall have to ponder at greater length.*

I liked the elegant way in which Mr Fandorin (by the way, it seems he is a diplomat, which explains a great deal) put down that intolerable yokel Gauche, who claims to be a rentier, *although it is clear from a mile away that the fellow is involved in some grubby little business or other. I should not be surprised if he is on his way to the East to purchase opium and exotic dancers for Parisian dens of vice.* [The last phrase has been scratched out.] *I know, my darling Emily, that you are a real lady and will not attempt to read what has* been crossed out here. I got a little carried away and wrote something unworthy for your chaste eyes to read.

And so, back to today's dinner. The French bourgeois, who just recently has grown bold and become quite terribly talkative, began discoursing with a self-satisfied air on the advantages of age over youth. 'I am older than anyone else here,' he said condescendingly, à la Socrates. 'Grey-haired, bloated and decidedly not good-looking, but you needn't go thinking, ladies and gentlemen, that papa Gauche would agree to change places with you. When I see the arrogance of youth, flaunting its beauty and strength, its health, in the face of age, I do not feel envious in the least. Why, I think, that's no great trick, I was like that myself once. But you, my fine fellow, still do not know if you will live to my 62 years. I am twice as happy as you are at 30, because I have been fortunate enough to live in this world for twice as long.' And he sipped at his wine, very proud of the originality of his thought and his seemingly unimpeachable logic. Then Mr Fandorin, who had so far not said a word, suddenly remarked with a very serious air: 'That is undoubtedly the case, M. Gauche, if one takes the oriental viewpoint on life, as existence at a single point of reality in an eternal present. But there is also another way of reasoning which regards a man's life as a unified work which can only be judged when the final page has been read. Moreover, this work may be as long as a tetralogy or as short as a novella. And yet who would undertake to assert that a fat, vulgar novel is necessarily of greater value than a short, beautiful poem?' The funniest thing of all was that our rentier, who is indeed both fat and vulgar, did not even understand the reference to himself. Even when Miss Stamp (by no means stupid, but a strange creature) giggled and I gave a rather loud snort, the Frenchie failed to catch on and stuck with his own opinion, for which all credit to him.

It is true, however, that in the conversation that followed over dessert, M. Gauche demonstrated a degree of common sense that quite amazed me. There are, after all, certain advantages in not having a regular education: a mind unfettered by authorities is sometimes capable of making interesting and accurate observations.

Judge for yourself. The amoeba-like Mrs Truffo, the wife of our *muttonhead of a doctor, started up again with her mindless prattle about the joy and delight Mme Kleber will bring to her banker with her 'tiny tot' and 'little angel'. Since Mrs Truffo does not speak French, the task of translating her sickly sentiments on the subject of family happiness being inconceivable without 'baby babble', fell to her unfortunate husband. Gauche huffed and puffed and then suddenly declared: 'I cannot agree with you, madam. A genuinely happy married couple have no need whatsoever of children, for husband and wife are perfectly sufficient for each other. Man and woman are like two uneven surfaces, each with bumps and indentations. If the surfaces do not fit tightly against each other, then glue is required, otherwise the structure – in other words the family – cannot be preserved. Children are that selfsame glue. If, however, the surfaces form a perfect fit, bump to indentation, then no glue is required. Take me and my Blanche, if you like. Thirty-three years we've lived in perfect harmony. Why would we want children? Life is splendid without them.' I am sure you can imagine, dear Emily, the tidal wave of righteous indignation that came crashing down on the head of this subverter of eternal values. The most zealous accuser of all was Mme Kleber, who is carrying the little Swiss in her womb. The sight of her neat little belly so carefully exhibited at every opportunity sets me writhing. I can just see the miniature banker nestled inside with his curly moustache and puffy little cheeks. In time the Klebers will no doubt produce an entire battalion of Swiss Guards.*

I must confess to you, my tenderly adored Emily, that the sight of pregnant women makes me feel sick. They are repulsive! That inane bovine smile, that disgusting manner of constantly listening to their own entrails. I try to keep as far away from Mme Kleber as possible. Swear to me, my darling, that we shall never have children. The fat bourgeois is right a thousand times over! Why do we need children when we are already boundlessly happy without them? All we need to do is survive this forced separation.

But it is already two minutes to 11. Time to take a reading.

Damnation! I have turned the whole cabin upside down. My sextant has disappeared. This is no delusion! It was lying in the trunk together with the chronometer and the compass, and now it is

*not there! I am afraid, Emily! O, I had a premonition of this. My worst
suspicions have been confirmed!*

*Why? What have I done? They are prepared to commit any vileness
in order to prevent our reunion! How can I check now that the ship
is following the right course? It is that Renier, I know! I caught the
expression in his eyes when he saw me handling the sextant on deck
last night! The scoundrel!*

*I shall go to the captain and demand retribution. But what if they
are in it together? My God, my God, have pity on me!*

*I had to pause for a while. I was so agitated that I was obliged to take
the drops prescribed for me by Dr Jenkinson. And I did as he told me,
and started thinking of pleasant things. Of how you and I will sit on a
white veranda and gaze into the distance, trying to guess where the sea
ends and the sky begins. You will smile and say: 'Darling Reggie, here
we are together at last.' Then we will get into a cabriolet and go for a
drive along the seashore.*

Lord, what nonsense is this! What cabriolet?

I am a monster, and there can be no forgiveness for me.

Renate Kleber

She woke up in an excellent mood, smiled affably at the spot of sunlight that crept onto her round cheek where it was creased by the pillow, and listened to her belly. The baby was quiet, but she felt terribly hungry. There were still 50 minutes left until breakfast, but Renate had no lack of patience and she simply did not know the meaning of boredom. In the morning sleep released her as swiftly as it embraced her in the evening, when she simply sandwiched her hands together and laid her head on them, and a second later she was immersed in sweet dreams.

As Renate performed her morning toilet she purred a frivolous little song about poor Georgette who fell in love with a chimney sweep. She wiped her fresh little face with an infusion of lavender and then styled her hair quickly and deftly, fluffing up the fringe over her forehead, drawing her thick chestnut tresses into a smooth bun and arranging two long ringlets over her temples. The effect was precisely what was required – demure and sweet. She glanced out of the porthole. Still the same view: the regular border of the canal, the yellow sand, the white mud-daub houses of a wretched little hamlet. It was going to be hot. That meant the white lace dress, the straw hat with the red ribbon, and she mustn't forget her parasol – a stroll after breakfast was de rigueur. Only she couldn't be bothered to drag her parasol around with her. Never mind, someone would fetch it.

Renate twirled in front of the mirror with evident satisfaction, stood sideways and pulled her dress tight over her belly. Although to tell the truth, there was not much to look at as yet.

Asserting her rights as a pregnant woman, Renate arrived ahead of time for breakfast – the waiters were still laying the table. She immediately ordered them to bring her orange juice, tea, croissants with butter and everything else. By the time the first of her table-mates arrived – it was the fat M. Gauche, another early bird – the mother-to-be had already dealt with three croissants and was preparing to set about a mushroom omelette. The breakfast served on the *Leviathan* was not some trifling Continental affair, but the genuine full English variety: with roast beef, exquisite egg dishes, blood pudding and porridge. The French part of the consortium provided nothing but the croissants. At lunch and dinner, however, the menu was dominated by French cuisine. Well, one could hardly serve kidneys and beans in the Windsor saloon!

The first mate appeared, as always, at precisely nine o'clock. He enquired solicitously as to how Mme Kleber was feeling. Renate lied and said she had slept badly and felt absolutely shattered, and it was all because the porthole didn't open properly and it was too stuffy in the cabin. Alarmed, Lieutenant Renier promised that he would make inquiries in person and have the fault rectified. He did not eat eggs or roast beef – he was a devotee of some peculiar diet, sustaining himself largely on fresh greens. Renate pitied him for that.

Gradually the others also put in an appearance. The conversation over breakfast was usually listless. Those who were a bit older had not yet recovered from a wretched night, while the young people were still not fully awake. It was rather amusing to observe the bitchy Clarissa Stamp attempting to coax a response out of the stammering Russian diplomat. Renate shook her head in disbelief: how could she make such a fool of herself? After all, my dear, he could be your son, despite those impressive streaks of grey. Surely this handsome boy was too tough a morsel for this ageing, simpering creature?

The very last to arrive was the Ginger Lunatic (Renate's private name for the English baronet). Tousled hair sticking out in all directions, red eyes, a twitch at the corner of his mouth – he was a quite appalling mess. But Mme Kleber was not in the least bit afraid of him, and given the chance she never missed the opportunity to have a bit of fun at his expense. This time she passed the milk jug to the Lunatic with a warm, guileless smile. As she had anticipated, Milford-Stokes (what a silly name!) squeamishly moved his cup aside. Renate knew from experience that now he would not even touch the milk jug, and he would drink his coffee black.

'Why do you start back like that, sir?' she babbled in a quavering voice. 'Don't be afraid, pregnancy is not infectious.' Then she concluded, no longer quavering: 'At least not for men.'

The Lunatic cast her a glance of withering scorn that shattered against the serenely radiant glance opposed to it. Lieutenant Renier concealed a smile behind his hand, the *rentier* chuckled. Even the Japanese raised a smile at Renate's prank. Of course, this M. Aono was always smiling, even when there was absolutely no reason for it. Perhaps for the Japanese a smile was not an expression of merriment at all, but indicated something quite different. Boredom, perhaps, or repugnance.

When he had finished smiling, M. Aono disgusted his neighbours at table by playing his usual trick: he took a paper napkin out of his pocket, blew his nose into it loudly, crumpled it up and deposited it neatly on the edge of his dirty plate. A fine ikebana arrangement for them to contemplate. Renate had read about ikebana in one of Pierre Loti's novels and the aura of the word had stuck in her memory. It was an interesting idea – composing bouquets of flowers not simply to look nice, but with a philosophical meaning. She would have to try it some time.

'What flowers do you like?' she asked Dr Truffo.

He translated the question to his English jade, then replied: 'Pansies.'

Then he translated his reply into English as well.

'I just adore flowers!' exclaimed Miss Stamp (what an impossible ingénue!). 'But only live ones. I love to walk across a flowering meadow! My heart simply breaks when I see poor cut flowers wither and drop their petals! That's why I never allow anyone to give me bouquets.' And she cast a languid glance at the handsome young Russian.

What a shame, otherwise absolutely everyone would be tossing bouquets at you, thought Renate, but aloud she said:

'I believe that flowers are the crowning glories of God's creation and I think trampling a flowering meadow is a crime.'

'In the parks of Paris it is indeed considered a crime,' M. Gauche pronounced solemnly. 'The penalty is ten francs. And if the ladies will permit an old boor to light up his pipe, I will tell you an amusing little story on the subject.'

'O, ladies, pray do indulge us!' cried the owlish Indologist Sweetchild, wagging his beard à la Disraeli. 'M. Gauche is such a wonderful raconteur!'

Everyone turned to look at the pregnant Renate, on whom the decision depended, and she rubbed her temple as a hint. Of course, she did not have the slightest trace of a headache – she was simply savouring the sweetness of the moment. However, she too was curious to hear this 'little story', and so she nodded her head with a pained expression and said:

'Very well, smoke. But then someone must fan me.'

Since bitchy Clarissa, the owner of a luxurious ostrich-feather fan, pretended this remark did not apply to her, the Japanese had to fill the breach. Gintaro Aono seated himself beside Renate and set to work, flapping his bright fan with the butterfly design in front of the long-suffering woman's nose so zealously that the bright kaleidoscope rapidly make her feel genuinely giddy. The Japanese received a reprimand for his excessive fervour.

Meanwhile the *rentier* drew on his pipe with relish, puffed out a cloud of aromatic smoke and embarked on his story:

'Believe it or not as you wish, but this is a true story. There was once a gardener who worked in the Luxembourg Gardens, little papa Picard. For forty years he had watered the flowers and pruned the shrubs, and now he had only three years to go until he retired and drew his pension. Then one morning, when little papa Picard went out with his watering can, he saw a swell dolled up in a white shirt and tails sprawling in the tulip bed. He was stretched out full length, basking in the morning sunshine, obviously straight from his nocturnal revels – after carousing until dawn, he had dozed off on the way home.' Gauche screwed up his eyes and surveyed his audience with a sly glance. 'Picard, of course, was furious – his tulips were crushed – and he said: "Get up, monsieur, in our park lying in the flower beds is not allowed! We fine people for it, ten francs." The reveller opened one eye and took a gold coin out of his pocket. "There you are, old man," he said, "now leave me in peace. I haven't had such a wonderful rest in ages." Well, the gardener took the coin, but he did not go away. "You have paid the fine, but I have no right to leave you here, monsieur. Be so good as to get up." At this the gentleman in the tails opened both eyes, but he seemed in no haste to rise. "How much do I have to pay you to get out of my sun? I'll pay any amount you like if you'll just stop pestering me and let me doze for an hour." Old papa Picard scratched his head and moved his lips while he figured something out. "Well then, sir," he said eventually, "if you wish to purchase an hour's rest lying in a flower bed in the Luxembourg Gardens, it will cost you eighty-four thousand francs and not a single sou less." ' Gauche chuckled merrily into his grey moustache and shook his head, as if in admiration of the gardener's impudence. ' "And not a single sou less," he said, so there! And let me tell you that this tipsy gentleman was no ordinary man, but the banker Laffitte himself, the richest man in the whole of Paris. Laffitte was not in the habit of making idle promises: he had said "any amount" and now he was stuck with it. As a banker it would have been shameful for him to back down and break his word. Of course, he didn't want to give away that kind of money to the first impudent rogue he met for a mere how-d'ye-do. But what could he do about it?' Gauche shrugged, mimicking a state of total perplexity. 'Then suddenly Laffitte ups and says: "Right, you old scoundrel, you'll get your eighty-four thousand, but only on one condition. You prove to me that lying for an hour in your rotten flower bed is really worth the money. And if you can't prove it, I'll get up this very moment and give your sides a good drubbing with my cane, and that act of petty hooliganism will cost me a forty franc administrative fine." ' Crazy Milford-Stokes laughed loudly and ruffled up his ginger mane in approval, but Gauche raised a yellow-stained finger, as if to say: don't be so hasty with your laughter, it's not the end yet. 'And what do you think happened, ladies and gentlemen? Old papa Picard, not put out in the slightest, began drawing up the balance: "In half an hour, at precisely eight o'clock, monsieur le directeur of the park will arrive, see you in the flower bed and start yelling at me to get you out of there. I shall not be able to do that, because you will have paid for a full hour, not half an hour. I shall get into an argument with monsieur le directeur, and he will kick me out of my job with no pension and no severance pay. I still have three years to go before I retire and take the pension due to me, which is set at one thousand two hundred francs a year. I intend to live at my ease for twenty years, so altogether that makes twenty-four thousand francs already. Now for the matter of accommodation. They will throw me and my lady wife out of our municipal apartment. And then the question is – where are we going to live? We shall have to buy a house. Any modest little house somewhere in the Loire region will run to twenty thousand at least. Now, sir, consider my reputation. Forty years I've slaved away loyally in this park and anyone will tell you that old papa Picard is an honest man. Then suddenly an incident like this brings shame on my old grey head. This is bribery, this is graft! I think a thousand francs for each year of irreproachable service would hardly be too much by way of moral compensation. So altogether it comes out at exactly eighty-four thousand." Laffitte laughed, stretched himself out a bit more comfortably in the flower bed and closed his eyes again. "Come back in an hour, you old monkey," he said, "and you'll be paid." And that is my wonderful little story, ladies and gentlemen.'

'So a year of faultless conduct went for a thousand f-francs?' the Russian diplomat said with a laugh. 'Not so very expensive. Evidently with a discount for wholesale.'

The company began a lively discussion of the story, expressing the most contradictory opinions, but Renate Kleber gazed curiously at M. Gauche as he opened his black file with a self-satisfied air and began rustling his papers. He was an intriguing specimen, this old grandpa, no doubt about it. And what secrets was he keeping in there? Why was he shielding the file with his elbow?

That question had been nagging at Renate for a long time. Once or twice she had tried to exploit her position as a mother-to-be by glancing over Gauche's shoulder as he conjured with that precious file of his, but the mustachioed boor had rather impudently slammed the file shut in the lady's face and even wagged his finger at her, as much as to say: now that's not allowed.

Today, however, something rather remarkable happened. When M. Gauche, as usual, rose from the table ahead of the others, a sheet of paper slid silently out of his mysterious file and glided gently to the floor. Engrossed in some gloomy thoughts of his own, the *rentier* failed to notice anything and left the saloon. The door had scarcely closed behind him before Renate adroitly raised her body, with its slightly thickened waist, out of her chair. But she was not the only one to have been so observant. The well-brought-up Miss Stamp (such a nimble creature!) was the first to reach the scrap of paper.

'Ah, I think Mr Gauche has dropped something!' she exclaimed, deftly grabbing up the scrap and fastening her beady eyes on it. 'I'll catch up with him and return it.'

But Mme Kleber was already clutching the edge of the paper in tenacious fingers and had no intention of letting go.

'What is it?' she asked. 'A newspaper clipping? How interesting!'

The next moment everyone in the room had gathered around the two ladies, except for the Japanese blockhead, who was still pumping the air with his fan, and Mrs Truffo, who observed this flagrant invasion of privacy with a reproachful expression on her face.

The clipping read as follows:

'THE CRIME OF THE CENTURY': A NEW ANGLE?

The fiendish murder of ten people that took place the day before yesterday on the rue de Grenelle continues to exercise the imagination of Parisians. Of the possible explanations proposed thus far the two most prevalent are a maniacal doctor and a fanatical sect of bloodthirsty Hindu devotees of the god Shiva. However, in the course of conducting our own independent investigation, we at *Le Soir* have uncovered a circumstance which could possibly open up a new angle on the case. It would appear that in recent weeks the late Lord Littleby was seen at least twice in the company of the international adventuress Marie Sanfon, well known to the police forces of many countries. The Baron de M., a close friend of the murdered man, has informed us that his Lordship was infatuated with a certain lady, and on the evening of the fifteenth of March he had intended to set out for Spa for some kind of romantic rendezvous. Could this rendezvous, which was prevented by the most untimely attack of gout suffered by the unfortunate collector, possibly have been arranged with Mlle Sanfon? The editors would not make so bold as to propose our own version of events, but we regard it as our duty to draw the attention of Commissioner Gauche to this noteworthy circumstance. You may expect further reports from us on this subject.

Cholera epidemic on the wane

The municipal health authorities inform us that the foci of the cholera infection which they have been combating energetically since the summer have finally been isolated. The vigorous prophylactic measures taken by the physicians of Paris have yielded positive results and we may now hope that the epidemic of this dangerous disease, which began in July, is beg-

'What could that be about?' Renate asked, wrinkling up her brow in puzzlement. 'Something about a murder, and cholera or something of the kind.'

'Well the cholera obviously has nothing to do with the matter,' said Professor Sweetchild. 'It's simply the way the page has been cut. The important thing, of course, is the murder on the rue de Grenelle. Surely you must have heard about it? A sensational case, the newspapers were all full of it.'

'I do not read the newspapers,' Mme Kleber replied with dignity. 'In my condition it places too much strain on the nerves. And in any case I have no desire to learn about all sorts of unpleasant goings-on.'

'Commissioner Gauche?' said Lieutenant Renier, peering at the clipping and running his eyes over the article once again. 'Could that be our own M. Gauche?'

Miss Stamp gasped:

'Oh, it couldn't be!'

At this point even the doctor's wife joined them. This was a genuine sensation and everyone started talking at once:

'The police, the French police are involved in this!' Sir Reginald exclaimed excitedly.

Renier muttered:

'So that's why the captain keeps interrogating me about the Windsor saloon . . .'

M. Truffo translated as usual for his spouse, while the Russian took possession of the clipping and scrutinized it closely.

'That bit about the Indian fanatics is absolute nonsense,' declared Sweetchild. 'I made my opinion on that clear from the very beginning. In the first place, there is no bloodthirsty sect of followers of Shiva. And in the second place, everyone knows that the statuette was recovered. Would a religious fanatic be likely to throw it into the Seine?'

'Yes, the business of the golden Shiva is a genuine riddle,' said Miss Stamp with a nod. 'They wrote that it was the jewel of Lord Littleby's collection. Is that correct, professor?'

The Indologist shrugged condescendingly.

'What can I say, madam? Lord Littleby only started collecting relatively recently, about twenty years ago. In such a short period it is difficult to assemble a truly outstanding collection. They do say that the deceased did rather well out of the suppression of the Sepoy Rebellion of 1857. The notorious Shiva, for instance, was "presented" to the lord by a certain maharajah who was threatened with court martial for intriguing with the insurgents. Littleby served for many years in the Indian military prosecutor's office, you know. Undoubtedly his collection includes quite a few valuable items, but the selection is rather haphazard.'

'But do tell me, at last, why this lord of yours was killed!' Renate demanded. 'Look, M. Aono doesn't know anything about it either, do you?' she asked, appealing for support to the Japanese, who was standing slightly apart from the others.

The Japanese smiled with just his lips and bowed, and the Russian mimed applause:

'Bravo, Mme Kleber. You have quite c-correctly identified the most important question here. I have been following this case in the press. And in my opinion the reason for the c-crime is more important than anything else. That is where the key to the riddle lies. Precisely in the question "why?". What was the purpose for which ten people were killed?'

'Ah, but that is very simple!' said Miss Stamp with a shrug. 'The plan was to steal everything that was most valuable from the collection. But the thief lost his head when he came face to face with the owner. After all, it had been assumed that his Lordship was not at home. It must be one thing to inject someone with a syringe and quite another to smash a man's head open. But then, I wouldn't know, I have never tried it.' She twitched her shoulders. 'The villain's nerves gave out and he left the job half finished. But as for the abandoned Shiva . . .' Miss Stamp pondered. 'Perhaps *that* is the heavy object with which poor Littleby's brains were beaten out. It is quite possible that a criminal also has normal human feelings and he found it repugnant or even simply frightening to hold the bloody murder weapon in his hand. So he walked as far as the embankment and threw it in the Seine.'

'Concerning the murder weapon that seems very probable,' the diplomat agreed. 'I th-think the same.'

The old maid flushed brightly with pleasure and was clearly embarrassed when she caught Renate's mocking glance.

'You are saying quite outrageous things,' the doctor's wife rebuked Clarissa Stamp. 'Shouldn't we find a more suitable subject for table talk?'

But the colourless creature's appeal fell on deaf ears.

'In my opinion the greatest mystery here is the death of the servants!' said the lanky Indologist, keen to contribute to the analysis of the crime. 'How did they come to allow themselves to be injected with such abominable muck? Not at pistol-point, surely! After all, two of them were guards, and they were both carrying revolvers in holsters on their belts. That's where the mystery lies.'

'I have a hypothesis of my own,' Renier announced with a solemn expression. 'And I am prepared to defend it against any objections. The crime on the rue de Grenelle was committed by a person who possesses exceptional mesmeric powers. The servants were in a state of mesmeric trance, that is the only possible explanation! Animal magnetism is a terrifying force. An experienced manipulator can do whatever he chooses with you. Yes, yes, madam,' the lieutenant said, turning towards Mrs Truffo, who had twisted her face into a doubtful grimace, 'absolutely anything at all.'

'Not if he is dealing with a lady,' she replied austerely.

Tired of playing the role of interpreter, Dr Truffo wiped the sweat from his gleaming forehead with his handkerchief and rushed to the defence of the scientific worldview.

'I am afraid I must disagree with you,' he started jabbering in French, with a rather strong accent. 'Mr Mesmer's teaching has been exposed as having no scientific basis. The power of mesmerism or, as it is now known, hypnotism, has been greatly exaggerated. The Honourable Mr James Braid has proved conclusively that only psychologically suggestible individuals are subject to hypnotic influence, and then only if they have complete trust in the hypnotist and have agreed to allow themselves to be hypnotized.'

'It is quite obvious, my dear doctor, that you have not travelled in the East!' said Renier, flashing his white teeth in a smile. 'At any Indian bazaar the fakir will show you miracles of mesmeric art that would make the most hardened sceptic gape in wonder. But those are merely tricks they use to show off! Once in Kandahar I observed the public punishment of a thief. Under Muslim law theft is punished by the amputation of the right hand, a procedure so intensely painful that those subjected to it frequently die from the shock. On this occasion the accused was a mere child, but since he had been caught for the second time, there was nothing else the judge could do, he had to sentence the thief to the penalty prescribed under shariah law. The judge, however, was a merciful man and he sent for a dervish who was well known for his miraculous powers. The dervish took the convicted prisoner's head in his hands, looked into his eyes and whispered something – and the boy became calm and stopped trembling. A strange smile appeared on his face, and did not leave it even when the executioner's axe severed his arm up to the very elbow! And I saw all this with my own eyes, I swear to you.'

Renate grew angry:

'Ugh, how horrible! You and your Orient, Charles. I am beginning to feel faint!'

'Forgive me, Mme Kleber,' said the lieutenant, taking fright. 'I only wished to demonstrate that in comparison with this a few injections are mere child's play.'

'Once again, I am afraid that I cannot agree with you . . .' The stubborn doctor was preparing to defend his point of view, but just at that moment the door of the saloon swung open and in came either a *rentier* or a policeman – in short, M. Gauche.

Everybody turned towards him in consternation, as if they had been caught out in some action that was not entirely decent.

Gauche ran a keen gaze over their faces and spotted the ill-starred clipping in the hands of the diplomat. His face darkened.

'So that's where it is . . . I was afraid of that.'

Renate went over to this grandpa with a grey moustache, looked his massive figure over mistrustfully from head to toe and blurted out:

'M. Gauche, are you really a policeman?'

'The same C-Commissioner Gauche who was leading the investigation into the "Crime of the Century"?' asked Fandorin (yes, that was the Russian diplomat's name, Renate recalled). 'In that case how are we to account for your masquerade and in general for your p-presence here on board?'

Gauche breathed hard for a few moments, raised his eyebrows, lowered them again and reached for his pipe. He was obviously racking his brains in an effort to decide what he should do.

'Please sit down, ladies and gentlemen,' said Gauche in an unfamiliar, imposing bass and turned the key to lock the door behind him. 'Since this is the way things have turned out, I shall have to be frank with you. Be seated, be seated or else somebody's legs might just give way under them.'

'What kind of joke is this, M. Gauche?' the lieutenant asked in annoyance. 'By what right do you presume to command here, and in the presence of the captain's first mate?'

'That, my young man, is something the captain himself will explain to you,' Gauche replied with a hostile sideways glance at Renier. 'He knows what is going on here.'

Renier dropped the matter and took his place at the table, following the others' example.

The verbose, good-humoured grumbler for whom Renate had taken the Parisian *rentier* was behaving rather differently now. A certain dignity had appeared in the broad set of his shoulders, his gestures had become imperious, his eyes had acquired a new, harder gleam. The mere fact that he could maintain a prolonged pause with such calm confidence said a great deal. The strange *rentier*'s piercing gaze paused in turn on each person present in the room and Renate saw some of them flinch under its weight. To be honest, even she was a little disturbed by it, but then she immediately felt ashamed of herself and tossed her head nonchalantly: he may be a police commissioner, but what of that? He was still an obese, short-winded old duffer and nothing more.

'Please do not keep us guessing any longer, M. Gauche,' she said sarcastically. 'Excitement is dangerous for me.'

'There is probably only one person here who has cause for excitement,' Gauche replied mysteriously. 'But I shall come back to that. First, allow me to introduce myself to the honourable company once again. Yes, my name is Gustave Gauche, but I am not a *rentier*, alas I have no investments from which to draw income. I am, ladies and gentlemen, a commissioner in the criminal police of the city of Paris and I work in the department which deals with particularly serious and complicated crimes. The post I hold is entitled Investigator for Especially Important Cases.' The commissioner pronounced the title with distinct emphasis.

The deadly silence in the saloon was broken only by the hasty whispering of Dr Truffo.

'What a scandal!' squeaked the doctor's wife.

'I was obliged to embark on this voyage, and to travel incognito because . . .' Gauche began flapping his cheeks in and out energetically in an effort to revive his half-extinguished pipe. '. . . because the Paris police have serious grounds for believing that the person who committed the crime on the rue de Grenelle is on board the *Leviathan*.'

'Ah!' The sigh rustled quietly round the saloon.

'I presume that you have already discussed the case, which is a mysterious one in many respects.' The commissioner jerked his double chin in the direction of the newspaper clipping, which was still in Fandorin's hands. 'And that is not all, mesdames et messieurs. I know for a fact that the murderer is travelling first class . . .' (another collective sigh) '. . . and, moreover, happens to be present in this saloon at this very moment,' Gauche concluded. Then he seated himself in a satin-upholstered armchair by the window and folded his arms expectantly just below his silver watch chain.

'Impossible!' cried Renate, clutching involuntarily at her belly.

Lieutenant Renier leapt to his feet.

The ginger baronet began chortling and applauding demonstratively.

Professor Sweetchild gulped convulsively and removed his glasses.

Clarissa Stamp froze with her fingers pressed against the agate brooch on her soft collar.

Not a single muscle twitched in the face of the Japanese, but the polite smile instantly disappeared.

The doctor grabbed his wife by the elbow, forgetting to translate the most important thing of all, but to judge from the frightened expression in her staring eyes, Mrs Truffo had guessed for herself.

The Russian diplomat asked quietly:

'What reasons do you have for this assertion?'

'My presence here,' the commissioner replied imperturbably, 'is explanation enough. There are other considerations, but there is no need for you to know about them . . . Well then' – there was a clear note of disappointment in the policeman's voice – 'I see that no one is about to swoon and cry out: "Arrest me, I killed them!" But of course, I was not really counting on that. So listen to me.' He raised a stubby finger in warning. 'None of the other passengers must be told about this. And it is not in your interests to tell them – the rumour would spread instantly and people would start treating you like lepers. Do not attempt to transfer to a different saloon – that will merely increase my suspicion. And you will not be able to do it; I have an arrangement with the captain.'

Renate began babbling in a trembling voice.

'Darling M. Gauche, can you not at least spare me this nightmare? I am afraid to sit at the same table as a murderer. What if he sprinkles poison in my food? I shan't be able to swallow a single morsel now. You know it's dangerous for me to be worried. I won't tell anyone, anyone at all, honestly!'

'My regrets, Mme Kleber,' the sleuth replied coolly, 'but there can be no exceptions. I have grounds to suspect every person here, and not least of all you.'

Renate threw herself against the back of her chair with a weak moan and Lieutenant Renier stamped his foot angrily.

'You take too many liberties, monsieur . . . Investigator for Especially Important Cases! I shall report everything to Captain Cliff immediately.'

'Go right ahead,' said Gauche indifferently. 'But not just at this moment, a bit later. I haven't quite finished my little speech. So, as yet I do not know for certain which of you is my client, but I am close, very close, to my goal.'

Renate expected these words to be followed by an eloquent glance and she strained her entire body forward in anticipation, but no, the policeman was looking at his stupid pipe. He was probably lying and didn't have his eye on anyone in particular.

'You suspect a woman, it's obvious!' exclaimed Miss Stamp with a nervous flutter of her hands. 'Otherwise why would you be carrying around a newspaper article about some Marie Sanfon? Who is this Marie Sanfon? And anyway, it doesn't matter who she is. It's plain stupid to suspect a woman! How could a woman ever be capable of such brutality!'

Mrs Truffo rose abruptly to her feet, ready to rally to the banner of female solidarity.

'We shall speak of Mlle Sanfon on some other occasion,' the detective replied, looking Clarissa Stamp up and down. 'I have plenty of these little articles and each of them contains its own version of events.' He opened his file and rustled the newspaper clippings. There must have been several dozen of them. 'Very well, mesdames et messieurs, I ask you please not to interrupt me any more!' The policeman's voice had turned to iron. 'Yes, there is a dangerous criminal among us. Possibly a psychopath.' (Renate noticed the professor quietly shift his chair away from Sir Reginald.) 'Therefore I ask you all to be careful. If you notice something out of the ordinary, even the very slightest thing, come to me immediately. And it would be best, of course, if the murderer were to make a full and frank confession. There is no escape from here in any case. That is all I have to say.'

Mrs Truffo put her hand up like a pupil in school.

'In fact I *have* seen something extraordinary only yesterday! A charcoal-black face, it was definitely not human, looked in at me from outside while I was in our cabin! I was so scared!' She turned to her other half and jabbed him with her elbow: 'I told you, but you paid no attention!'

'Oh,' said Renate with a start, 'and yesterday a mirror in a genuine tortoiseshell frame disappeared from my toiletry set.'

Monsieur the Lunatic apparently also had something to report, but before he had a chance the commissioner slammed his file shut.

'Do not try to make a fool of me! I am an old bloodhound. You won't throw Gustave Gauche off the scent. If necessary I shall have every one of you put ashore and we will deal with each of you separately. Ten people have been killed, this is not a joke. Think, mesdames et messieurs, think!'

He left the saloon, slamming the door loudly behind him.

'Gentlemen, I am not feeling well,' Renate declared in a weak voice. 'I shall go to my cabin.'

'I shall accompany you, Mme Kleber,' said Charles Renier, immediately leaping to her side. 'This is simply intolerable! Such incredible insolence!'

Renate pushed him away.

'No thank you. I shall manage quite well on my own.'

She walked unsteadily across the room and leaned against the wall by the door for a moment. In the corridor, which was empty, her stride quickened. Renate opened her cabin and went inside, took a travelling bag out from under the bed and thrust a trembling hand in under its silk lining. Her face was pale but determined. In an instant her fingers had located a small metal box.

Inside the box, glittering with cold glass and steel, lay a syringe.

Clarissa Stamp

Things had begun to go wrong first thing in the morning, when Clarissa quite distinctly spotted two new wrinkles in the mirror – two fine, barely visible lines running from the corners of her eyes to her temples. It was all the sun's fault. It was so bright here that no parasol or hat could save you. Clarissa spent a long time inspecting herself in that pitiless polished surface and stretching her skin with her fingers, hoping it might be the way she'd slept and it would smooth out. Just as she finished her inspection, she turned her neck and spotted a grey hair behind her ear. That really made her feel glum. Might that perhaps be the sun's fault too? Did hairs fade? Oh no, Miss Stamp, no point in deceiving yourself. As the poet said:

November's chill breath trimmed her braids with silver,
Whispering that youth and love were lost forever.

She took greater pains than usual with her appearance. That grey hair was mercilessly plucked out. It was stupid, of course. Wasn't it John Donne who said the secret of female happiness was knowing when to make the transition from one age to the next, and there were three ages of woman: daughter, wife and mother? But how could she progress from the second state to the third, when she had never been married?

The best cure for thoughts like that was a walk in the fresh air, and Clarissa set out to take a turn round the deck. Huge as *Leviathan* was, it had long since been measured out in her leisurely, even paces – at least the upper deck, which was intended for the first-class passengers. The distance round the perimeter was 355 paces. Seven and a half minutes, if she didn't pause to admire the sea or chat with casual acquaintances.

At this early hour there were none of her acquaintances on deck, and Clarissa completed her promenade along the starboard side of the ship unhindered, all the way to the stern. The ship was ploughing a smooth path through the brownish surface of the Red Sea and a lazy grey furrow extended from its powerful propeller right out to the horizon. Oh, but it was hot!

Clarissa looked enviously at the sailors polishing up the copper fittings one level below. Lucky beasts, in nothing but their linen trousers – no bodice, no bloomers, no stockings with tight garters, no long dress. You couldn't help envying that outrageous Mr Aono, swanning about the ship in his Japanese dressing gown, and no one in the least bit surprised because he was an Oriental.

She imagined herself lying in a canvas deckchair with absolutely nothing on. No, she could be in a light tunic, like a woman in Ancient Greece. And it was perfectly normal. In a hundred years or so, when the human race finally rid itself of prejudice, it would be absolutely natural.

There was Mr Fandorin riding towards her with a squeak of rubber tyres on his American tricycle. They did say that kind of exercise was excellent for developing the elasticity of the muscles and strengthening the heart. The diplomat was dressed in a light sports outfit: check pantaloons, gutta-percha shoes with gaiters, a short jacket and a white shirt with the collar unbuttoned. His bronze-tanned face lit up in a friendly smile of greeting. Mr Fandorin politely raised his cork helmet and went rustling by. He did not stop.

Clarissa sighed. The idea of a stroll had been a failure, all she had succeeded in doing was to soak her underwear with perspiration. She had to go back to her cabin and change.

Breakfast had been spoiled for Clarissa by that poseuse Mme Kleber. What an incredible ability to transform her own weakness into a means of exploiting others! At the precise moment when the coffee in Clarissa's cup had cooled to the required temperature, that unbearable Swiss woman had complained that she felt stifled and asked for someone to loosen the bodice of her dress. Clarissa usually pretended not to hear Renate Kleber's whinges and some male volunteer was always found, but a man was clearly not suitable for such a delicate task, and as luck would have it Mrs Truffo was not there – she was helping her husband attend to some lady who had fallen ill. Apparently the tedious creature had previously worked as a nurse. What remarkable social climbing, straight up to the wife of the senior doctor and dining in first class! And she tried to act like a real British lady, but overdid it rather.

Anyway, Clarissa had been forced to fiddle with Mme Kleber's lacing, and in the meantime her coffee had gone completely cold. It was a trivial matter, of course, but it was that Kleber woman to an absolute T.

After breakfast she went out for a walk, did ten circuits and began feeling tired. Taking advantage of the fact that there was no one nearby she peeped cautiously in at the window of cabin No. 18. Mr Fandorin was sitting at the secretaire, wearing a white shirt with red, white and blue braces, a cigar clenched in the corner of his mouth. He was tapping terribly loudly with his fingers on a bizarre black apparatus made of iron, with a round roller and a large number of keys. Clarissa was so intrigued that she let her guard down and was caught red-handed. The diplomat jumped to his feet, bowed, threw on his jacket and came across to the open window.

'It's a Remington t-typewriter,' he explained. 'The very latest model, only just on sale. A most c-convenient device, Miss Stamp, and quite light. Two porters can carry it with no difficulty. Quite indispensable on a journey. You see, I am p-practising my stenography by copying out a piece of Hobbes.'

Still red with embarrassment, Clarissa nodded slightly and walked away, then sat down under a striped awning close by. There was a fresh breeze blowing. She opened *La Chartreuse de Parme* and began reading about the selfless love of the beautiful but ageing duchess Sanseverina for the youthful Fabrice del

Dongo. Moved to shed a sentimental tear, she wiped it away with her handkerchief, and as if by design, at that very moment, Mr Fandorin emerged onto the deck, wearing a white suit with a broad-brimmed panama hat and carrying a cane. He looked exceptionally handsome.

Clarissa called to him. He approached, bowed and sat down beside her. Glancing at the cover of her book, he said:

'I am willing to b-bet that you skipped the description of the Battle of Waterloo. A pity – it is the finest passage in the whole of Stendhal. I have never read a more accurate description of war.'

Strangely enough, Clarissa was indeed reading *La Chartreuse de Parme* for the second time and both times she had simply leafed through the battle scene.

'How could you tell?' she asked curiously. 'Are you a clairvoyant?'

'Women always miss out the battle episodes,' said Fandorin with a shrug. 'At least women of your temperament.'

'And just what is my temperament?' Clarissa asked in a wheedling voice, feeling that she cut a poor figure as a coquette.

'An inclination to view yourself sceptically and the world around you romantically.' He looked at her, his head inclined slightly to one side. 'And specifically concerning yourself I can say that recently there has been some kind of sudden change for the b-better in your life and that you have suffered some k-kind of shock.'

Clarissa started and glanced at her companion in frank alarm.

'Don't be frightened,' the astonishing diplomat reassured her. 'I know absolutely nothing about you. It is simply that I have developed my powers of observation and analysis with the help of special exercises. Usually a single insignificant detail is enough for me to recreate the entire p-picture. Show me a charming button like that (he pointed delicately to a large, ornamental pink button on her jacket) and I will tell you immediately who lost it – a very big pig or a very small elephant.'

Clarissa smiled and asked:

'And can you see right through absolutely everybody?'

'Not right through, but I do see a lot. For instance, what can you tell me about that gentleman over there?'

Fandorin pointed to a thickset man with a large moustache observing the shoreline through a pair of binoculars.

'That's Mr Babble, he's . . .'

'Stop there!' said Fandorin, interrupting her. 'I'll try to guess myself.'

He looked at Mr Babble for about 30 seconds, then said:

'He is travelling to the East for the first time. He married recently. A factory owner. Business is not going well, there is a whiff of imminent bankruptcy about this gentleman. He spends almost all his time in the billiard room, but he plays badly.'

Clarissa had always prided herself on being observant and she began inspecting Mr Babble, the Manchester industrialist, more closely.

A factory owner? Well, that was possible to guess. If he was travelling first class, he must be rich. It was clear from his face that he was no aristocrat. And he didn't look like a businessman either, in that baggy frock coat, and his features lacked animation. All right then.

Recently married? Well, that was simple enough – the ring on his third finger gleamed so brightly it was obvious straightaway that it was brand new.

Plays billiards a lot? Why was that? Aha, his jacket was smeared all over with chalk.

'What makes you think that Mr Babble is travelling to the East for the first time?' she asked. 'Why is there a whiff of bankruptcy about him? And what is the basis for your assertion that he is a poor billiards player? Perhaps you have been there and seen him play?'

'No, I have not been in the b-billiard room, because I cannot stand pastimes that involve gambling, and I have never laid eyes on this gentleman before,' Fandorin replied. 'It is evident that he is travelling this way for the first time from the stubborn persistence with which he is studying the empty shoreline. Otherwise

Mr Babble would be aware that he will not see anything of interest on that side until we reach the Strait of Mandeb. That is one. This gentleman's business affairs must be going very badly, otherwise he would never have embarked on such a long journey, especially so soon after his wedding. A badger like that might leave his set if the end of the world is nigh, but certainly not before. That is two.'

'What if he is taking a honeymoon voyage together with his wife?' asked Clarissa, knowing that Mr Babble was travelling alone.

'And lingering forlornly on the deck like that, and loitering in the billiard room? And he plays quite incredibly badly – his jacket is all white at the front. Only absolutely hopeless players scrape their bellies along the edge of the table like that. That is three.'

'Oh, all right, but what will you say about that lady over there?'

Clarissa, now completely engrossed in the game, pointed to Mrs Blackpool, who was proceeding majestically along the deck, arm in arm with her female companion.

Fandorin scanned the estimable lady in question with a disinterested glance.

'With this one everything is written in the face. She is on her way back from England to join her husband. She has been to visit their grown-up children. Her husband is a military man. A colonel.'

Mr Blackpool was indeed a colonel in command of a garrison in some city or other in northern India. This was simply too much.

'Explain!' Clarissa demanded.

'Ladies of that kind do not travel to India on their own b-business, only to their husbands' place of service. She is not of the right age to have embarked on a journey like this for the first time – so she must be going back somewhere. Why could she have travelled to England? Only in order to see her children. I am assuming that her parents have already passed away. It is clear from her determined and domineering expression that she is a woman used to command. That is the look of the first lady of a garrison or a regiment. They are usually regarded as a level of command senior to the commanding officer himself. Perhaps you would like to know why she must be a colonel's wife? Well, because if she were a general's wife she would be travelling first class, and this lady, as you can see, has a silver badge. But let us not waste any more time on trifles.' Fandorin leaned closer and whispered: 'Let me tell you about that orang-utan over there. A curious specimen.'

The monkey-like gentleman who had halted beside Mr Babble was M. Boileau, the former Windsor habitué who had left the ill-fated saloon and so slipped through Commissioner Gauche's net.

Speaking in a low voice directly into Clarissa's ear, the diplomat told her:

'The man you see here is a criminal and a villain. Most probably a dealer in opium. He lives in Hong Kong and is married to a Chinese woman.'

Clarissa burst into laughter.

'Well, you're really wide of the mark this time! That is M. Boileau from Lyon, a philanthropist and the father of eleven completely French children. And he deals in tea, not opium.'

'I rather think not,' Fandorin replied calmly. 'Look closely, his cuff has bent up and you can see the blue circle of a tattoo on his wrist. I have seen one like that before in a book about China. It is the mark of one of the Hong Kong triads, secret criminal societies. Any European who becomes a member of a triad must be a master criminal operating on a truly grand scale. And of course, he has to marry a Chinese woman. A single look at the face of this "philanthropist" should make everything clear to you.'

Clarissa didn't know whether to believe him or not, but Fandorin continued with a serious expression:

'And that is by no means all, Miss Stamp. I can tell a lot about a person even if I am b-blindfolded – from the sounds that he makes and his smell. Why not test me for yourself?'

And so saying he untied his white satin necktie and handed it to Clarissa.

She fingered the fabric – it was dense and non-transparent – and then blindfolded the diplomat with it. As though by accident she touched his cheek – it was smooth and hot.

The ideal candidate soon put in an appearance from the direction of the stern – the well-known suffragette, Lady Campbell, making her way to India in order to collect signatures for her petition for married women to be given the vote. Mannish and massive, with cropped hair, she lumbered along the deck like a carthorse. He would never guess that this was a lady and not a boatswain.

'Right, who is this coming our way?' Clarissa asked, choking in anticipatory laughter.

Alas, her merriment was short-lived.

Fandorin wrinkled up his brow and began tossing out staccato phrases:

'A skirt hem rustling. A woman. A heavy stride. A strong c-character. Elderly. Plain. Smokes tobacco. Short-cropped hair.'

'Why does she have short-cropped hair?' Clarissa squealed, covering her eyes and listening carefully to the suffragette's elephantine footfall. How, how did he do it?

'If a woman smokes, she must have bobbed hair and be progressive in her views,' Fandorin declared in a firm voice. 'And this one also despises fashion and wears a kind of shapeless robe, bright green with a scarlet belt.'

Clarissa was dumbstruck. This was quite incredible! She took her hands away from her eyes in superstitious terror and saw that Fandorin had already removed the necktie and even retied it in an elegant knot. The diplomat's blue eyes were sparkling in merriment.

All this was very pleasant, but the conversation had ended badly. When she stopped laughing, Clarissa very delicately broached the subject of the Crimean War and what a tragedy it had been for both Europe and Russia. She touched cautiously on her own memories of the time, making them somewhat more infantile than they were in reality. She was anticipating reciprocal confidences, and hoping to learn exactly how old Fandorin really was. Her worst fears were confirmed:

'I was still not b-born then,' he confessed, artlessly clipping Clarissa's wings.

After that everything had gone from bad to worse. Clarissa had tried to turn the conversation to painting, but she got everything so mixed up that she couldn't even explain properly why the Pre-Raphaelites had called themselves Pre-Raphaelites. He must have thought her an absolute idiot. Ah, but what difference did it make now?

As she was making her way back to her cabin, feeling sad, something terrifying happened.

She saw a gigantic black shadow quivering in a dark corner of the corridor. Clutching at her heart, Clarissa let out an immodest squeal and made a dash for her own door. Once she was in her cabin it was a long time before she could calm her wildly beating heart. What was that thing? Neither man nor beast. Some concretion of evil, destructive energy. Her guilty conscience. The phantom of her Paris nightmare.

No more, she told herself, she had put all that behind her. It was nothing. It was delirium, a delusion, no more. She had sworn that she would not torment herself with remorse. This was a new life, bright and happy – 'And may your mansion be illumined by the lamp of bliss.'

To soothe her nerves, she put on her most expensive day dress, the one she had not even tried yet (white Chinese silk with a pale-green bow at the back of the waist) and put her emerald necklace round her neck. She admired the gleam of the stones.

Very well, so she wasn't young. Or beautiful either. But she was far from stupid and she had money. And that was far better than being an ugly, ageing fool without a penny to her name.

Clarissa entered the saloon at precisely two o'clock, but the entire company was already assembled. Strangely enough, rather than fragmenting the Windsor contingent, the commissioner's astounding announcement of the previous day had brought them closer together. A common secret that cannot be shared with anyone else binds people to each other more tightly than a common cause or a common interest. Clarissa noticed that her fellow diners now gathered around the table in advance of the times set for breakfast, lunch, five o'clock tea and dinner, and lingered on afterwards, something that had hardly ever happened before. Even the captain's first mate, who was only indirectly involved in this whole affair, spent a lot of time sitting on in the Windsor saloon with the others rather than hurrying off about his official business (but then, of course, the lieutenant might possibly be acting on the captain's orders). It was as though all the Windsorites had joined some elite club that was closed to the uninitiated. Several times Clarissa caught swift, stealthy glances cast in her direction. Glances that could mean one of two things: 'Are you the murderer?' or 'Have you guessed that I am the murderer?' Every time it happened she felt a sweet trembling sensation welling up from somewhere deep inside, a pungent cocktail of fear and excitement. The image of the rue de Grenelle rose up clearly before her eyes, the way it looked in the evening: beguilingly quiet and deserted, with the bare branches of the black chestnut trees swaying against the sky. God forbid that the commissioner should somehow find out about the Ambassador Hotel. The very thought of it terrified Clarissa, and she cast a furtive glance in the policeman's direction.

Gauche presided at the table like the high priest of a secret sect. They were all constantly aware of his presence and followed the expression on his face out of the corners of their eyes, but Gauche appeared not to notice that at all. He assumed the role of a genial philosopher happy to relate his 'little stories', while the others listened tensely.

By unspoken agreement, *that* was only discussed in the saloon and only in the commissioner's presence. If two Windsorites chanced to meet somewhere in neutral territory – in the music salon, on the deck, in the reading hall – they did not discuss *that* under any circumstances. And not even in the saloon did they return to the tantalizing subject on every occasion. It usually happened spontaneously, following some entirely unrelated remark.

Today at breakfast, for instance, a general conversation had completely failed to materialize, but now as Clarissa took her seat the discussion was in full swing. She began studying the menu with a bored expression on her face, as though she had forgotten what she had ordered for lunch, but she could already feel that familiar tingle of excitement.

'The thing that bothers me about the crime,' Dr Truffo was saying, 'is the blatant senselessness of it all. Apparently all those people were killed for absolutely nothing. The golden Shiva ended up in the Seine, and the killer was left empty-handed.'

Fandorin rarely participated in these discussions, preferring to remain silent most of the time, but for once even he felt compelled to express an opinion:

'That is not quite true. The p-perpetrator was left with the shawl.'

'What shawl?' asked the doctor, confused.

'The painted Indian shawl. In which, if we are to believe the newspapers, the killer wrapped the stolen Shiva.'

This joke was greeted with rather nervous laughter.

The doctor spread his hands expressively.

'But a mere shawl . . .'

Sweetchild gave a sudden start and lifted his spectacles off his nose, a gesture of his which indicated intense agitation.

'No, don't laugh! I made inquiries as to exactly which shawl was stolen. And it is, gentlemen, an extremely unusual piece of material, with a story of its own. Have you ever heard of the Emerald Rajah?'

'Wasn't he some kind of legendary Indian nabob?' asked Clarissa.

'Not legendary, but quite real, madam. It was the name given to Bagdassar, the ruler of the principality of Brahmapur. The principality is located in a large, fertile valley, surrounded on all sides by mountains. The rajahs trace their line of descent from the great Babur and are adherents of Islam, but that did not prevent them from reigning in peace for three hundred years over a little country in which the majority of the population are Hindus. Despite the difference in religion between the ruling caste and their subjects, the principality never suffered a single rebellion or feud, the rajahs prospered and grew rich and by Bagdassar's time the house of Brahmapur was regarded as the wealthiest in the whole of India after the Nizams of Hyderabad, whose wealth, as you are no doubt aware, eclipses that of every monarch in the world, including Queen Victoria and the Russian emperor Alexander.'

'The greatness of our queen does not consist in the extent of her personal fortune, but in the prosperity of her subjects,' Clarissa remarked primly, stung by the professor's remark.

'Undoubtedly,' agreed Sweetchild, who was already in full spate and not to be halted. 'However, the wealth of the rajahs of Brahmapur was of a very special kind. They did not hoard gold, they did not stuff trunks to overflowing with silver, they did not build palaces of pink marble. No, for three hundred years these rulers knew only one passion – precious stones. Do you know what the Brahmapur Standard is?'

'Isn't it a style of faceting diamonds?' Dr Truffo asked uncertainly.

'The Brahmapur Standard is a jewellers' term which refers to a diamond, sapphire, ruby or emerald that is faceted in a particular manner and is the size of a walnut, which corresponds to one hundred and sixty tandools, in other words eighty carats in weight.'

'But that is a very large size,' Renier exclaimed in amazement. 'Stones as large as that are very rare. If my memory does not deceive me, even the Regent diamond, the glory of the French state jewels, is not very much larger.'

'No, Lieutenant, the Pitt diamond, also known as the Regent, is almost twice as large,' the professor corrected him with an air of authority, 'but eighty carats is still a considerable size, especially if one is dealing with stones of the first water. But can you believe, ladies and gentlemen, that Bagdasssar had five hundred and twelve such stones, and all of absolutely irreproachable quality!'

'That's impossible!' exclaimed Sir Reginald.

Fandorin asked:

'Why exactly five hundred and t-twelve?'

'Because of the sacred number eight,' Sweetchild gladly explained. 'Five hundred and twelve is eight times eight times eight, that is eight to the power of three, or eight cubed, the so-called "ideal number". There is here, undoubtedly, some influence from Buddhism, in which the number eight is regarded with particular reverence. In the north-eastern part of India, where Brahmapur lies, religions are intertwined in the most bizarre fashion imaginable. But the most interesting thing of all is where this treasure was kept and how.'

'And where was it kept?' Renate Kleber inquired curiously.

'In a simple clay casket without any adornment whatever. In 1852 I visited Brahmapur as a young archaeologist and met the Rajah Bagdassar. An ancient temple had been discovered in the jungle on the territory of the principality, and the rajah invited me to assess the significance of the find. I carried out the necessary research, and what do you think I discovered? The temple turned out to have been built in the time of King Chandragupta, when . . .'

'Stop-stop-stop!' the commissioner interrupted. 'You can tell us about archaeology some other time. Let's get back to the rajah.'

'Ah yes indeed,' said the professor, fluttering his eyelashes. 'That really would be best. Well then, the rajah was pleased with me and as a token of his favour he showed me his legendary casket. Oh, I shall never forget that sight!' Sweetchild narrowed his eyes as he continued: 'Imagine a dark dungeon with only a single torch burning in a bronze bracket beside the door.

The rajah and I were alone, his retainers remained outside the massive door, which was protected by a dozen guards. I got no clear impression of the interior of this treasure house, for my eyes had no time to adjust to the semi-darkness. I only heard the clanging of locks as his Highness opened them. Then Bagdassar turned to me and in his hands I saw a cube that was the colour of earth and appeared to be very heavy. It was the size of . . .' Sweetchild opened his eyes and looked around. Everyone was sitting and listening with bated breath, and Renate Kleber had even parted her lips like a child. 'Oh, I don't know. I suppose about the size of Miss Stamp's hat, if one were to place that piece of headgear in a square box.' As though on command, everyone turned and began staring curiously at the diminutive Tyrolean hat decorated with a pheasant's feather. Clarissa endured this public scrutiny with a dignified smile, in the manner she had been taught as a child. 'This cube resembled most of all one of the ordinary clay bricks that they use for building in those parts. His Highness later explained to me that the coarse, dull uniformity of the clay surface made a far better foil than gold or ivory for the magnificent glimmering light of the stones. Indeed, I was able to see that for myself when Bagdassar slowly raised a hand studded with rings to the lid of the casket, then opened it with a rapid movement and . . . I was blinded, ladies and gentlemen!' The professor's voice quavered. 'It . . . it is impossible to express it in words! Picture to yourselves a mysterious, multicoloured, lambent radiance spilling out of that dark cube and painting the gloomy vaults of that dungeon with shimmering patches of rainbow-coloured light. The round stones were arranged in eight layers, and in each layer there were sixty-four faceted sources of quite unbearable brilliance. And the effect was certainly enhanced by the flickering flame of the solitary torch. I can still see Rajah Bagdassar's face bathed from below in that magical light . . .'

The professor closed his eyes again and fell silent.

'And how much, for instance, are these glass baubles worth?' the commissioner's rasping voice enquired.

'Yes indeed, how much?' Mme Kleber repeated enthusiastically. 'Say, in your English pounds?'

Clarissa heard Mrs Truffo whisper rather loudly to her husband:

'She's so vulgar!' But even so she pushed her mousy curls back off her ear in order not to miss a single word.

'You know,' Sweetchild said with a genial smile, 'I have often wondered about that. It's not an easy question to answer, since the value of precious stones fluctuates according to the market, but as things stand today . . .'

'Yes, please, as things stand today, not in the time of King Chandragupta,' Gauche put in gruffly.

'Hmm . . . I don't know exactly how many diamonds, how many sapphires and how many rubies the rajah had. But I do know that he valued emeralds most of all, which was how he acquired his popular name. In the course of his reign seven emeralds were acquired from Brazil and four from the Urals, and for each of them Bagdassar gave one diamond and some additional payment. You see, each of his ancestors had a favourite stone that he preferred to all others and tried to acquire in greater numbers. The magical number of five hundred and twelve stones had already been reached in the time of Bagdassar's grandfather, and since then the ruler's primary goal had been not to increase the number of stones but to improve their quality. Stones which fell even slightly short of perfection, or which the present ruler did not favour for some reason, were sold – hence the fame of the Brahmapur Standard, which gradually spread around the world. Their place in the casket was taken by other, more valuable stones. Bagdassar's ancestors carried their obsession with the Brahmapur Standard to quite insane lengths! One of them purchased a yellow sapphire weighing three hundred tandools from the Persian Shah Abbas the Great, paying ten caravans of ivory for this marvel, but the stone was larger than the standard size and the rajah had his jewellers cut away all the excess!'

'That is terrible, of course,' said the commissioner, 'but let us get back to the question of the stones' value.'

This time, however, it proved less easy to direct the flow of the Indologist's speech into the required channel.

'The question of value can wait for a moment,' he said, peremptorily dismissing the detective's request. 'Is that really so important? When one considers a noble stone of such size and quality, the first thing that comes to mind is not money but the magical properties that have been attributed to it since ancient times. The diamond, for instance, is considered a symbol of purity. Our ancestors used to test their wives' fidelity by placing a diamond under their sleeping spouse's pillow. If she was faithful, then she would immediately turn to her husband and embrace him without waking. If she was unfaithful, she would toss and turn and attempt to throw the diamond onto the floor. And the diamond is also reputed to guarantee its owner's invincibility. The ancient Arabs used to believe that in battle the general who owned the larger diamond would be victorious.'

'Ancient Arab mistaken,' said Gintaro Aono, interrupting the inspired speaker in full flow.

Everyone stared in astonishment at the Japanese, who very rarely joined in the general conversation and never interrupted anyone. The Oriental continued hastily in that odd accent of his:

'In the Academy of St Cyr we were taught that the Duke of Burgundy, Charles the Bold, specially took the huge Sancy diamond with him into battle against the Swiss, but it did not save him from defeat.'

Clarissa felt sorry for the poor devil for making a rare attempt to show off his knowledge at such an inopportune moment.

The Japanese gentleman's remark was greeted with deadly silence, and Aono blushed in painful embarrassment.

'Yes indeed, Charles the Bold . . .' the professor said with a sharp nod of dissatisfaction and concluded without his former ardour. 'The sapphire symbolizes devotion and constancy, the emerald confers improved sharpness of vision and foresight, the ruby protects against illness and the evil eye . . . But you were asking about the value of Bagdassar's treasures?'

'I realize that it must be an incredibly huge sum, but could you at least give us an approximate idea of how many zeros there are in it?' Mme Kleber enunciated clearly, as if she were addressing a dull-witted pupil, demonstrating yet again that once a banker's wife, always a banker's wife.

Clarissa would have enjoyed listening to more on the subject of the magical properties of precious stones and would have preferred to avoid talk of money. Apart from anything else, it was so vulgar.

'Very well then, let me just tot it up.' Sweetchild took a pencil out of his pocket and poised himself to write on a paper napkin. 'Formerly the diamond was considered the most expensive stone, but since the discovery of the South African mines it has fallen significantly in value. Large sapphires are found more often than other precious stones, and so on average they are only worth a quarter as much as diamonds, but that does not apply to yellow and star sapphires, and they made up the majority of Bagdassar's collection. Pure rubies and emeralds of great size are also rare and have a higher value than diamonds of the same weight . . . Very well, for simplicity's sake, let us assume that all five hundred and twelve stones are diamonds, and all of the same value. Each of them, as I have already said, weighing eighty carats. According to Tavernier's formula, which is used by jewellers all over the world, the value of a single stone is calculated by taking the market value of a one carat diamond and multiplying it by the square of the number of carats in the stone concerned. That would give us . . . A one carat diamond costs about fifteen pounds on the Antwerp exchange. Eighty squared is six thousand four hundred. Multiply by fifteen . . . Mmm . . . Ninety-six thousand pounds sterling – so that is the value of an average stone from the Brahmapur casket . . . Multiply by five hundred and twelve . . . About fifty million pounds sterling. And in actual fact even more, because as I have already explained, coloured stones of such a great size are more valuable than diamonds,' Sweetchild concluded triumphantly.

'Fifty million pounds? As much as that?' Renier asked in a voice suddenly hoarse. 'But that's one and a half billion francs!'

Clarissa caught her breath, all thoughts of the romantic properties of precious stones driven out of her head by astonishment at this astronomical figure.

'Fifty million! But that's half the annual budget of the entire British Empire!' she gasped.

'That's three Suez Canals!' mumbled the red-headed Milford-Stokes. 'Or even more!'

The commissioner also took a napkin and became absorbed in some calculations of his own.

'It is my salary for three hundred thousand years,' he announced in dismay. 'Are you not exaggerating, professor? The idea of some petty native princeling possessing such immense wealth!'

Sweetchild replied as proudly as if all the treasure of India belonged to him personally:

'Why, that's nothing! The jewels of the Nizam of Hyderabad are estimated to be worth three hundred million, but of course you couldn't get them all into one little casket. In terms of compactness, certainly, Bagdassar's treasure had no equal.'

Fandorin touched the Indologist's sleeve discreetly:

'Nonetheless, I p-presume that this sum is rather abstract in nature. Surely no one would be able to sell such a huge number of gigantic p-precious stones all at once? It would bring down the market price.'

'You are mistaken to think so, monsieur diplomat,' the scholar replied with animation. 'The prestige of the Brahmapur Standard is so great that there would be no shortage of buyers. I am certain that at least half of the stones would not even leave India – they would be bought by the local princes, in the first instance by the Nizam whom I have already mentioned. The remaining stones would be fought over by the banking houses of Europe and America, and the monarchs of Europe would not let slip the chance to add the masterpieces of Brahmapur to their treasuries. If he had wished, Bagdassar could have sold the contents of his casket in a matter of weeks.'

'You keep referring to this man in the p-past tense,' remarked Fandorin. 'Is he dead? And if so, what happened to the casket?'

'Alas, that is something that nobody knows. Bagdassar's own end was tragic. During the Sepoy Mutiny the rajah was incautious enough to enter into secret dealings with the rebels, and the viceroy declared Brahmapur enemy territory. There was malicious talk of Britannia simply wishing to lay its hands on Bagdassar's treasure, but of course it was untrue. That is not the way we English go about things.'

'Oh, yes,' nodded Renier with a dark smile, exchanging glances with the commissioner.

Clarissa stole a cautious glance at Fandorin – surely he could not also be infected with the bacillus of Anglophobia? The Russian diplomat, however, was sitting there with an air of perfect equanimity.

'A squadron of dragoons was dispatched to Bagdassar's palace. The rajah attempted to escape by fleeing to Afghanistan, but the cavalry overtook him at the Ganges crossing. Bagdassar considered it beneath his dignity to submit to arrest and he took poison. The casket was not found on him; in fact, there was nothing but a small bundle containing a note in English. In the note, which was addressed to the British authorities, the rajah swore that he was innocent and requested them to forward the bundle to his only son. The boy was studying in a private boarding school somewhere in Europe – it's the done thing among Indian grandees of the new breed. I should mention that Bagdassar was no stranger to the spirit of civilization, he visited London and Paris several times. He even married a French woman.'

'Oh, how unusual!' Clarissa exclaimed. 'To be an Indian rajah's wife! What became of her?'

'Never mind the blasted wife, tell us about the bundle,' the commissioner said impatiently. 'What was in it?'

'Absolutely nothing of any interest,' said the professor with a regretful shrug of his shoulders. 'A volume of the Koran. But the casket disappeared without trace, although they looked for it everywhere.'

'And was it a perfectly ordinary Koran?' asked Fandorin.

'It could hardly have been more ordinary: printed by a press in Bombay, with devout comments in the deceased's own hand in the margins. The squadron commander decided that the Koran could be forwarded as requested, and for himself he took only the shawl in which it was wrapped as a souvenir of the expedition. The shawl was later acquired by Lord Littleby for his collection of Indian paintings on silk.'

To clarify the point the commissioner asked:

'So that is the same shawl in which the murderer wrapped the Shiva?'

'The very same. It is genuinely unusual. Made of the very finest silk, almost weightless. The painting is rather trivial – an image of the bird of paradise, the sweet-voiced Kalavinka, but it possesses two unique features which I have never encountered in any other Indian shawl. Firstly, where Kalavinka's eye should be there is a hole, the edges of which have been sewn up with minute care with brocade thread. Secondly, the shawl itself is an interesting shape – not rectangular, but tapering. A sort of irregular triangle, with two crooked sides and one absolutely straight.'

'Is the shawl of any g-great value?' asked Fandorin.

'All this talk about the shawl is boring,' complained Mme Kleber, sticking out her lower lip capriciously. 'Tell us more about the jewels! They ought to have searched a bit more thoroughly.'

Sweetchild laughed.

'Oh, madam, you cannot even imagine how thoroughly the new rajah searched for them. He was one of the local zamindars who had rendered us invaluable service during the Sepoy War and received the throne of Brahmapur as a reward. But greed unhinged the poor man's mind. Some wit whispered to him that Bagdassar had hidden the casket in the wall of one of the buildings. And since in size and appearance the casket looked exactly like an ordinary clay brick, the new rajah ordered all buildings constructed of that material to be taken apart. The houses were demolished one after another and each brick was smashed under the personal supervision of the new ruler. Bearing in mind that in Brahmapur ninety per cent of all structures are built of clay bricks, in a few months a flourishing city was transformed into a heap of rubble. The insane rajah was poisoned by his own retainers, who feared a popular revolt even more fierce than the Sepoy Mutiny.'

'Serve him right, the Judas,' Renier declared with feeling. 'Nothing is more abominable than treachery.'

Fandorin patiently repeated his question:

'But nonetheless, professor, is the shawl of any g-great value?'

'I think not. It is more of a rarity, a curiosity.'

'But why are things always b-being wrapped in the shawl – first the Koran, and then the Shiva? Could this piece of silk perhaps have some ritual significance?'

'I've never heard of anything of the sort. It is simply a coincidence.'

Commissioner Gauche got to his feet with a grunt and straightened his numbed shoulders.

'Mmm, yes, an entertaining story, but unfortunately it has nothing to contribute to our investigation. The murderer is unlikely to be keeping this piece of cloth as a sentimental souvenir. It would be handy if he was, though,' he mused. 'One of you, my dear suspects, simply takes out a silk shawl with a picture of the bird of paradise – out of sheer absent-mindedness – and blows his, or her, nose into it. Old papa Gauche would know what to do then all right.'

The detective laughed, clearly in the belief that his joke was very witty. Clarissa gave the coarse lout a disapproving look.

Catching her glance, the commissioner narrowed his eyes.

'By the way, Mlle Stamp, about your wonderful hat. A very stylish item, the latest Parisian chic. Is it long since your last visit to Paris?'

Clarissa braced herself and replied in an icy tone:

'The hat was bought in London, Commissioner. And I have never been to Paris.'

What was Mr Fandorin staring at so intensely? Clarissa followed the line of his gaze and turned pale.

The diplomat was studying her ostrich-feather fan, and the words inscribed in gold on its ivory handle: MEILLEURS SOUVENIRS! HÔTEL AMBASSADEUR. RUE DE GRENELLE, PARIS.

What an appalling blunder!

Gintaro Aono

The fifth day of the fourth month
In sight of the Eritrean coast

Below – the green stripe of the sea,
Between – the yellow stripe of sand,
Above – the blue stripe of the sky.
Such are the colours
Of Africa's flag.

This trivial pentastich is the fruit my one-hour-and-a-half-long efforts to attain a state of inner harmony – that confounded harmony that has stubbornly refused to be restored.

I have been sitting alone on the stern, watching the dreary coastline of Africa and feeling my infinite isolation more acutely than ever. I can at least be thankful that the noble habit of keeping a diary was instilled in me from childhood. Seven years ago as I

set out to study in the remote country of Furansu, I dreamed in secret that one day the diary of my travels would be published as a book and bring fame to me and the entire clan of Aono. But alas, my intellect is too imperfect and my feelings are far too ordinary for these pitiful pages ever to rival the great diaristic literature of former times.

And yet if not for these daily entries I should certainly have gone insane long ago.

Even here, on board a ship travelling to east Asia, there are only two representatives of the yellow race – myself and a Chinese eunuch, a court official of the eleventh rank who has travelled to Paris to obtain the latest perfumes and cosmetic products for the Empress Dowager Tz'u Hsi. For the sake of economy he is travelling second class, of which he is greatly ashamed, and our conversation was broken off the moment it emerged that I am travelling first class. What a disgrace for China! In the court official's place I should certainly have died of humiliation, for on this European vessel each of us is the representative of a great Asian power. I understand Courtier Chan's state of mind, but it is nonetheless a pity that he feels too ashamed even to leave his cramped cabin – there are things that we could have talked about. That is, although we could not talk about them, we could communicate with the aid of ink, brush and paper, for while we speak different languages, we use the same hieroglyphs.

Never mind, I tell myself, hold on. The difficulties remaining are mere trifles. In a month or so you will see the lights of Nagasaki, and from there it is a mere stone's throw to your home town of Kagoshima. And what do I care that my return promises me only humiliation and disgrace, that I shall be a laughing stock to all my friends! For I shall be home once again and, after all, no one will dare to express his contempt for me openly, since everyone knows that I was carrying out my father's will, and that orders are not a matter for discussion. I have done what I had to do, what my duty obliged me to do. My life may be ruined, but if that is what the welfare of Japan requires . . . Enough, no more of that!

And yet who could have imagined that the return to my homeland, the final stage of my seven year ordeal, would prove so hard? In France at least I could take my food alone, I could delight in taking solitary walks and communing with nature. But here on the ship I feel like a grain of rice that has fallen by accident into a bowl of noodles. Seven years of life among the red-haired barbarians have failed to inure me to some of their disgusting habits. When I see the fastidious Kleber-san cut a bloody beefsteak with her knife and then lick her red-stained lips with her pink tongue it turns my stomach. And these English washbasins in which you have to plug the drain and wash your face in contaminated water! And those appalling clothes, the invention of some perverted mind! They make you feel like a carp wrapped in greased paper that is being roasted over hot coals. Most of all, I hate the starched collars that leave a red rash on your chin and the leather shoes, a genuine instrument of torture. Exploiting my position as an 'oriental savage' I take the liberty of strolling around the deck in a light yukata, while my unfortunate dining companions stew in their clothes from morning till night. My sensitive nostrils suffer greatly from the smell of European sweat, so harsh, greasy and fleshy. Equally terrible is the round-eyes' habit of blowing their noses into handkerchiefs and then putting them back into their pockets, together with the mucus, then taking them out and blowing their noses into them again. They will simply not believe it at home, they will think I have made it all up. But then seven years is a long time. Perhaps by now our ladies are also wearing those ridiculous bustles on their hindquarters and tottering along on high heels. It would be interesting to see how Kyoko-san looks in a costume like that. After all, she is quite grown up now – 13 years old already. In another year or two they will marry us. Oh to be home soon!

Today I found it especially difficult to attain inner harmony because:

1. I discovered that my finest instrument, capable of easily cutting through the very thickest muscle, has been stolen from my travelling bag. What does this strange theft mean?

2. At lunch I once again found myself in a position of humiliation – far worse than the incident with Charles the Bold (see my entry for yesterday). Fandorin-san, who continues as before to be very curious concerning Japan, began questioning me about bushido and samurai traditions. The conversation moved on to my family and my ancestors. Since I had introduced myself as an officer, the Russian began to question me about the weapons, uniforms and service regulations of the Imperial Army. It was terrible! When it emerged that I had never even heard of the Berdan rifle, Fandorin-san looked at me very strangely. He must have thought the Japanese army is staffed with absolute ignoramuses. In my shame I completely forgot my manners and ran out of the saloon, which of course only rendered the incident even more embarrassing.

It was a long time before I was able to settle my nerves. First I went up onto the boat deck, which is deserted because the sun is at its fiercest there. I stripped to my loincloth and for half an hour practised the kicking technique of *mawashi-geri*. When I had reached the right condition and the sun began to look pink, I seated myself in the zazen pose and attempted to meditate for 40 minutes. And only after that did I dress myself and go to the stern to compose a tanka.

All of these exercises were helpful. Now I know how to save face. At dinner I shall tell Fandorin-san that we are forbidden to talk to strangers about the Imperial Army and that I ran out of the saloon in such haste because I am suffering from terrible diarrhoea. I think that will sound convincing and in the eyes of my neighbours at table I shall not appear to be an ill-mannered savage.

The evening of the same day

So much for harmony! Something quite catastrophic has happened. My hands are trembling in shame, but I must immediately note down all the details. It will help me to concentrate and take the correct decision.

To begin with only the facts, conclusions later.

And so.

Dinner in the Windsor saloon began as usual at eight o'clock. Although during the afternoon I had ordered red beet salad, the waiter brought me bloody, half-raw beef. Apparently he thought I had said 'red beef'. I prodded the slaughtered animal's flesh, still oozing blood, and observed with secret envy the captain's first mate, who was eating a most appetizing vegetable stew with lean chicken.

What else happened?

Nothing out of the ordinary. Kleber-san, as always, was complaining of a migraine but eating with a voracious appetite. She looks the very picture of health, a classic example of an easy pregnancy. I am sure that when her time comes the child will pop out of her like a cork from sparkling French wine.

There was talk of the heat, of tomorrow's arrival in Aden, of precious stones. Fandorin-san and I discussed the relative advantages of Japanese and English gymnastics. I found myself in a position to be condescending, since in this sphere the superiority of the East over the West is self-evident. The difference, of course, is that for them physical exercise is sport, a game, but for us it is the path to spiritual self-improvement. It is spiritual improvement that is important. Physical perfection is of no importance; it is automatically dragged along behind, as the carriages follow a steam locomotive. I should mention that the Russian is very interested in sport and has even heard something of the martial arts schools of Japan and China. This morning I was meditating on the boat deck earlier than usual and I saw Fandorin-san there. We merely bowed to each other and did not enter into conversation, because each of us was occupied with his own business: I was bathing my soul in the light of the new day, while he, dressed in gymnast's tights, was performing squats and press-ups on each arm in turn and lifting weights which appeared to be very heavy.

Our common interest in gymnastics rendered our evening conversation unforced and I felt more relaxed than usual. I told the Russian about ju-jitsu. He listened with unflagging interest.

At about half past eight (I did not notice the precise time) Kleber-san, having drunk her tea and eaten two cakes, complained of feeling dizzy. I told her that this happens to pregnant women when they eat too much. For some reason she evidently took offence at my words and I realized that my comment was out of place. How many times have I sworn not to speak out of turn. After all, I was taught by wise teachers: when you find yourself in strange company, sit, listen, smile pleasantly and from time to time nod your head – you will acquire the reputation of a well-bred individual and at the very least you will not say anything stupid. It is not the place of an 'officer' to be giving medical advice!

Renier-san immediately leapt to his feet and

volunteered to accompany the lady to her cabin. He is in general a most considerate man, and especially with Kleber-san. He is the only one who is not yet sick of her interminable caprices. He stands up for the honour of his uniform, and I applaud him for it.

When they left, the men moved to the armchairs and began smoking. The Italian ship's doctor and his English wife went to visit a patient and I attempted to din it into the waiter's head that they should not put either bacon or ham in my omelette for breakfast. After so many days they should have grown used to the idea by now.

Perhaps about two minutes later we suddenly heard a woman's high-pitched scream.

Firstly, I did not immediately realize that it was Kleber-san screaming. Secondly, I did not understand that her blood-curdling scream of 'Oscure! Oscure!' meant 'Au secours! Au secours!' But that does not excuse my behaviour. I behaved disgracefully, quite disgracefully. I am unworthy of the title of samurai!

But everything is in order.

The first to reach the door was Fandorin-san, fol-lowed by the commissioner of police, then Milford-Stokes-san and Sweetchild-san, and I was still glued to the spot. They have all decided, of course, that the Japanese army is staffed by pitiful cowards. In actual fact, I simply did not understand immediately what was happening.

When I did understand it was too late – I was the last to come running up to the scene of the incident, even behind Stamp-san.

Kleber-san's cabin is very close to the saloon, the fifth door on the right along the corridor. Peering over the shoulders of those who had reached the spot before me I saw a quite incredible sight. The door of the cabin was wide open. Kleber-san was lying on the floor and moaning pitifully, with some immense, heavy, shiny black mass slumped across her. I did not immediately realize that it was a negro of immense stature. He was wearing white canvas trousers. The handle of a sailor's dirk was protruding from the back of his neck. From the position of his body I knew immediately that the negro was dead. A blow like that, struck to the base of the skull, requires great strength and precision, but it kills instantly and surely.

Kleber-san was floundering in a vain effort to wriggle out from under the heavy carcass that had pinned her down. Lieutenant Renier was bustling about beside her. His face was whiter than the collar of his shirt. The dirk scabbard hanging at his side was empty. The lieutenant was completely flustered, torn between dragging this unsavoury dead-weight off the pregnant woman, and turning to us and launching into an incoherent explanation to the commissioner of what had happened.

Fandorin-san was the only one who remained calm and composed. Without any visible effort he lifted up the heavy corpse and dragged it off to one side (I remembered his exercises with the weights), helped Kleber-san into an armchair and gave her some water. Then I came to my senses and checked swiftly to make sure that she had no wounds or bruises. There did not seem to be any. Whether there is any internal damage will become clear later. Everyone was so agitated that they were not surprised when I examined her. White people are convinced that all Orientals are part-shaman and know the art of healing. Kleber-san's pulse was 95, which is perfectly understandable.

Interrupting each other as they spoke, Renier-san and Kleber-san told us the following story.

The lieutenant:

He saw Kleber-san to her cabin, wished her a pleasant evening and took his leave. However, he had scarcely taken two steps away from her door when he heard her desperate scream.

Kleber-san:

She went into her cabin, switched on the electric light and saw a gigantic black man standing by her dressing table with her coral beads in his hands (I actually saw these beads on the floor afterwards). The negro threw himself on her without speaking, tossed her to the floor and grabbed hold of her throat with his massive hands. She screamed.

The lieutenant:

He burst into the cabin, saw the appalling (he said 'fantastic') scene and for a moment was at a loss. He grabbed the negro by the shoulders, but was unable to shift the giant by even an inch. Then he kicked him in the head, but again without the slightest effect. It was only then, fearing for the life of Kleber-san and her child, that he grabbed his dirk out of its sheath and struck a single blow.

It occurred to me that the lieutenant must have spent a turbulent youth in taverns and bordellos, where skill in handling a knife determines who will be sober up the following morning and who will be carried off to the cemetery.

Captain Cliff and Dr Truffo came running up. The cabin became crowded. No one could understand how the African had come to be on board the *Leviathan*. Fandorin-san carefully inspected a tattoo covering the dead man's chest and said that he had come across one like it before. Apparently, during the recent Balkan conflict he was held prisoner by the Turks, and there he saw black slaves with precisely the same zigzag lines surrounding the nipples in concentric circles. They are the ritual markings of the Ndanga tribe, recently discovered by Arab slave traders in the very heart of Equatorial Africa. Ndanga men are in great demand at markets throughout the East.

It seemed to me that Fandorin-san said all of this with a rather strange expression on his face, as though he were perplexed by something. However, I could be mistaken, since the facial expressions of Europeans are freakish and do not correspond at all to ours.

Commissioner Gauche listened to the diplomat carefully. He said that there were two questions that interested him as a representative of the law: how the negro had managed to get on board and why he had attacked Mme Kleber.

Then it emerged that things had begun disappearing in a mysterious fashion from the cabins of several of the people present. I remembered the item that had disappeared from my cabin, but naturally I said nothing. It was also established that people had seen a massive black shadow (Miss Stamp) or a black face peeping in at their windows (Mrs Truffo). It is clear now that these were not hallucinations and not the fruit of morbid imaginings.

Everyone threw themselves on the captain. Apparently, the passengers had been in mortal danger all the time they had been on board and the ship's command had not even been aware of it. Cliff-san was scarlet with shame. And it must be admitted that a terrible blow has been struck at his prestige. I tactfully turned away so that he would suffer less from his loss of face.

Then the captain asked all the witnesses to the incident to move into the Windsor saloon and addressed us with a speech of great power and dignity. Above all he apologized for what had happened. He asked us not to tell anyone about this 'regrettable occurrence', since it might cause mass psychosis on board the ship. He promised that his sailors would immediately comb all the holds, the 'tween-decks space, the wine cellar, the store rooms and even the coal holes. He gave us his guarantee that there would not be any more black burglars on board his ship.

The captain is a good man, a genuine old sea dog. He speaks awkwardly, in short, clipped phrases, but it is clear that he is strong in spirit and he takes his job with serious enthusiasm. I once heard Truffo-sensei telling the commissioner that Captain Cliff is a widower and he dotes on his only daughter, who is being educated in a boarding school somewhere. I find that very touching.

I seem to be recovering my composure gradually. The lines of writing are more even now and my hand is no longer shaking. I can go on to the most unpalatable moment in all of this.

During my superficial examination of Kleber-san I noticed that she had no bruising. There were also several other observations which ought to be shared with the captain and the commissioner. But I wished above all to reassure a pregnant woman who was struggling to recover her wits after a shock, who seemed intent, in fact, on plunging into hysterics.

I said to her in a most soothing tone of voice:

'Perhaps this black man had no intention of killing you, madam. You entered so unexpectedly and switched on the light and he was simply frightened. After all, he . . .'

Kleber-san interrupted before I could finish.

'He was frightened?' she hissed with sudden venom. 'Or perhaps it was you who was frightened, my dear Oriental monsieur? Do you think I didn't notice your nasty little yellow face peeping out from behind other people's backs?'

No one has ever insulted me so outrageously. The worst thing of all was that I could not pretend these were the foolish words of a silly hysterical woman and shield myself from them with a smile of disdain. Kleber-san's thrust had found my most vulnerable spot!

There was nothing I could say in reply, I was badly hurt, and the grimace on her tear-stained face when she looked at me was humiliating. If at that moment I could have fallen through the floor into the famous Christian hell, I would certainly have pressed the lever of the trapdoor myself. Worst of all, my sight was veiled by the red mist of rage, and that is the condition which I fear most. It is in this state of frenzy that a samurai commits those deeds that are disastrous for his karma. Then afterwards he must spend the rest of his life seeking to expiate the guilt of that single moment of lost self-control. He can do things for which even seppuku will not be sufficient atonement.

I left the saloon, afraid that I would not be able to restrain myself and would do something terrible to a pregnant woman. I am not sure that I could have controlled myself if a man had said something like that to me.

I locked myself in my cabin and took out the sack of Egyptian gourds that I had bought at the bazaar in Port Said. They are small, about the size of a human head, and very hard. I bought 50 of them.

In order to disperse the scarlet mist in front of my eyes, I set about improving my straight chop with the edge of the hand. Because of my extreme agitation I delivered the blow poorly: instead of two equal halves, the gourds split into seven or eight pieces.

It is hard.

PART TWO

Aden to Bombay

Gintaro Aono

The seventh day of the fourth month
In Aden

The Russian diplomat is a man of profound, almost Japanese intellect. Fandorin-san possesses the most un-European ability to see a phenomenon in all its fullness, without losing his way in the maze of petty details and technicalities. The Europeans are unsurpassed masters of everything that concerns *doing*, they have superlative understanding of *how*. But true wisdom belongs to us Orientals, since we understand *why*. For the hairy ones the fact of movement is more important than the final goal, but we never lower our gaze from the lodestar twinkling in the distance, and therefore we often neglect to pay due attention to what lies closer at hand. This is why time and again the white peoples are the victors in petty skirmishes, but the yellow race maintains its unshakeable equanimity in the certain knowledge that such trivial matters are unworthy of serious attention. In all that is truly important, in the genuinely essential matters, victory will be ours.

Our emperor has embarked on a great experiment: to combine the wisdom of the East with the intellect of the West. Yet while we Japanese strive meekly to master the European lesson of routine daily conquest, we do not lose sight of the ultimate end of human life – death and the higher form of existence that follows it. The red-hairs are too individualistic, their precious ego obscures their vision, distorting their picture of the world around them and making it impossible for them to see a problem from different points of view. The soul of the European is fastened tight to his body with rivets of steel, it cannot soar aloft.

But if Fandorin-san is capable of illumination, he

owes it to the semi-Asiatic character of his homeland. In many ways Russia is like Japan: the same reaching out of the East for the West. Except that, unlike us, the Russians forget the star by which the ship maintains its heading and spend too much time gazing idly around them. To emphasize one's individual 'I' or to dissolve it in the might of the collective 'we' – therein lies the antithesis between Europe and Asia. I believe the chances are good that Russia will turn off the first road onto the second.

However, I have become carried away by my philosophizing. I must move on to Fandorin-san and the clarity of mind which he has demonstrated. I shall describe events as they happened.

The *Leviathan* arrived in Aden before dawn. Concerning this port my guidebook says the following:

The port of Aden, this Gibraltar of the East, serves England as her link with the East Indies. Here steamships take on coal and replenish their reserves of fresh water. Aden's importance has increased immeasurably since the opening of the Suez Canal. The town itself, however, is not large. It has extensive dockside warehouses and shipyards, a number of trading stations, shipping offices and hotels. The streets are laid out in a distinctively regular pattern. The dryness of the local soil is compensated for by 30 ancient reservoirs which collect the rainwater that runs down from the mountains. Aden has a population of 34,000, consisting primarily of Indian Moslems.

For the time being I must be content with this scanty description, since the gangway has not been lowered and no one is being allowed ashore. The alleged reason is quarantine for medical reasons, but we vassals of the principality of Windsor know the true reason for the turmoil and confusion: sailors and police from ashore are combing the gigantic vessel from stem to stern in search of negroes.

After breakfast we stayed on in the saloon to wait for the results of the manhunt. It was then that an important conversation took place between the commissioner and the Russian diplomat in the presence of our entire company (even for me it has already become 'ours').

At first people spoke about the death of the negro, then as usual the conversation turned to the murders in Paris. Although I took no part in the discussion on that topic, I listened very attentively, and at first it seemed to me that they were trying yet again to catch a green monkey in a thicket of bamboo or a black cat in a dark room.

Stamp-san said: 'So, we have nothing but riddles. We don't know how the black man managed to get on board and we don't know why he wanted to kill Mme Kleber. It's just like the rue de Grenelle. More mystery.'

But then Fandorin-san said: 'There's no mystery there at all. It's true that we still haven't cleared up the business with the negro, but I think we have a fairly clear picture of what happened on the rue de Grenelle.'

Everyone stared at him in bewilderment and the commissioner smiled scornfully: 'Is that so? Well then, out with it, this should be interesting.'

Fandorin-san: 'I think what happened was this. That evening someone arrived at the door of the mansion on the rue de Grenelle . . .'

The commissioner (in mock admiration): 'Oh, bravo! A brilliant deduction!'

Someone laughed, but most of us continued listening attentively, for the diplomat is not a man to indulge in idle talk.

Fandorin-san (continuing imperturbably): ' . . . someone whose appearance completely failed to arouse the servants' suspicion. It was a physician, possibly wearing a white coat and certainly carrying a doctor's bag. This unexpected visitor requested everyone in the house to gather immediately in one room, because the municipal authorities had instructed that all Parisians were to receive a prophylactic vaccination.'

The commissioner (starting to get angry): 'What idiotic fantasy is this? What vaccination? Why should the servants take the word of a total stranger?'

Fandorin (sharply): 'If you do not take care, M. Gauche, you may find yourself demoted from

Investigator for Especially Important Cases to Investigator for Rather Unimportant Cases. You do not take sufficient care in studying your own materials, and that is unforgivable. Take another look at the article from *Le Soir* that mentions Lord Littleby's connection with the international adventuress Marie Sanfon.'

The detective rummaged in his black file, took out the article in question and glanced through it.

The commissioner (with a shrug): 'Well, what of it.'

Fandorin (pointing): 'Down here at the bottom. Do you see the headline of the next article: "Cholera epidemic on the wane"? And what it says about "the vigorous prophylactic measures taken by the physicians of Paris"?'

Truffo-sensei: 'Why, yes indeed, gentlemen, Paris has been plagued by outbreaks of cholera all winter. They even set up a medical checkpoint in the Louvre for the boats arriving from Calais.'

Fandorin-san: 'That is why the sudden appearance of a physician did not make the servants suspicious. No doubt their visitor acted confidently and spoke very convincingly. He could have told them it was getting late and he still had several more houses to visit, or something of the kind. The servants evidently decided not to bother the master of the house, since he was suffering from an attack of gout, but of course they called the security guards from the second floor. And it only takes a moment to give an injection.'

I was delighted by the diplomat's perspicacity and the ease with which he had solved this difficult riddle. His words even set Commissioner Gauche thinking.

'Very well then,' he said reluctantly. 'But how do you explain the fact that after poisoning the servants this medic of yours didn't simply walk up the stairs to the second floor, but went outside, climbed over the fence and broke in through a window in the conservatory?'

Fandorin-san: 'I've been thinking about that. Did it not occur to you that two culprits might have been involved? One dealt with the servants, while the other broke in through the window?'

The commissioner (triumphantly): 'Indeed it did occur to me, my dear monsieur clever clogs, it most certainly did. That is precisely the assumption that the murderer wanted us to make. It's perfectly obvious that he was simply trying to confuse the trail! After he poisoned the servants, he left the pantry and went upstairs, where he ran into the master of the house. Very probably the thief simply smashed in the glass of the display case because he thought there was no one else in the house. When his Lordship came out of his bedroom to see what all the noise was about, he was murdered. Following this unexpected encounter the culprit beat a hasty retreat, not through the door, but through the window of the conservatory. Why? In order to pull the wool over our eyes and make it seem like there were two of them. You fell for his little trick hook, line and sinker. But old papa Gauche is not so easily taken in.'

The commissioner's words were greeted with general approval. Renier-san even said: 'Damn it, Commissioner, but you're a dangerous man!' (This is a common turn of speech in various European languages. It should not be taken literally. The lieutenant meant to say that Gauche-san is a very clever and experienced detective.)

Fandorin-san waited for a while and asked: 'Then you made a thorough study of the footprints and came to the conclusion that this person jumped down from the window and did not climb up on to the window sill?'

The commissioner did not answer that, but he gave the Russian a rather angry look.

At this point Stamp-san made a comment that turned the conversation in a new direction.

'One culprit, two culprits – but I still don't understand the most important thing: what was it all done for?' she said. 'Clearly not for the Shiva. But what then? And not for the sake of the scarf either, no matter how remarkable and legendary it may be!'

Fandorin-san replied to this in a matter-of-fact voice, as if he were saying something perfectly obvious: 'But of course it was precisely for the sake of yesterday I try not to look at her – I have a strong urge to jab my finger into the blue vein pulsating on her white neck. One jab would be quite enough to dispatch the loathsome creature. But of course that is one of those evil thoughts that a man must drive out of his head by an effort of will. By confiding my evil thoughts to this diary I have managed to diminish the violence of my hatred a little.

The commissioner put Mme Kleber in her place. 'Please be quiet, madam,' he said sternly. 'Let us hear what other fantasies our diplomat has concocted.'

Fandorin-san: 'This entire story only makes sense if the stolen shawl is especially valuable in some way. That is one. According to what the professor told us, in itself the shawl is of no great value, so it is not a matter of the piece of silk, but of some other thing connected with it. That is two. As you already know, the shawl is connected with the final will and testament of the Rajah Bagdassar, the last owner of the Brahmapur treasure. That is three. Tell me, professor, was the rajah a zealous servant of the Prophet?'

Sweetchild-sensei (after a moment's thought): 'I

the scarf, mademoiselle. The Shiva was only taken in order to divert attention and then thrown into the Seine from the nearest bridge because it was no longer needed.'

The commissioner observed: 'For Russian boyars (I have forgotten what this word means, I shall have to look it up in the dictionary) half a million francs may perhaps be a mere trifle, but most people think differently. Two kilograms of pure gold was "no longer needed"! You really are getting carried away, monsieur diplomat.'

Fandorin-san: 'Oh come now, Commissioner, what is half a million francs compared with the treasure of Bagdassar?'

'Gentlemen, enough of this quarrelling!' the odious Mme Kleber exclaimed capriciously. 'I was almost killed, and here you are still harping on the same old tune. Commissioner, while you were so busy tinkering with an old crime, you very nearly had a new one on your hands!'

That woman simply cannot bear it when she is not the centre of attention. After what happened can't say exactly . . . He didn't build mosques, and he never mentioned the name of Allah in my company. The rajah liked to dress in European clothes, he smoked Cuban cigars and read French novels . . . Ah yes, he drank cognac after lunch! So he obviously didn't take religious prohibitions too seriously.'

Fandorin-san: 'Then that makes four: although he is not overly devout, Bagdassar makes his son a final gift of a Koran, which for some reason is wrapped in a shawl. I suggest that the shawl was the most important part of this legacy. The Koran was included for the sake of appearances . . . Or possibly the notes made in the margins in Bagdassar's own hand contained instructions on how to find the treasure with the help of the shawl.'

Sweetchild-sensei: 'But why did it have to be with the help of the shawl? The rajah could have conveyed his secret in the marginalia!'

Fandorin-san: 'He could have, but he chose not to. Why? Allow me to refer you to my argument number one: if the shawl were not immensely valuable in some way, it is unlikely that ten people would have been murdered for it. The shawl is the key to five hundred million francs or, if you prefer, fifty million pounds, which is approximately the same. I believe that is the greatest hidden treasure there has ever been in the whole of human history. And by the way, Commissioner, I must warn you that if you are not mistaken and the murderer really is on board the *Leviathan*, more people could be killed. Indeed, the closer you come to your goal, the more likely it becomes. The stakes are too high and too great a price has already been paid for the key to the mystery.'

These words were followed by deadly silence. Fandorin-san's logic seemed irrefutable, and I believe all of us felt shivers run up and down our spines. All of us except one.

The first to recover his composure was the commissioner. He gave a nervous laugh and said: 'My, what a lively imagination you do have, M. Fandorin. But as far as danger is concerned, you are right. Only you, gentlemen, have no need to quake in your boots. This danger threatens no one but old man

Gauche, and he knows it very well. It comes with my profession. But I'm well prepared for it!' And he glanced round us all menacingly, as if he were challenging us to single combat.

The fat old man is ridiculous. Of everyone there the only person whom he might be able to best is the pregnant Mme Kleber. In my mind's eye I glimpsed a tempting picture: the red-faced commissioner had flung the young witch to the floor and was strangling her with his hairy sausage-fingers, and Mme Kleber was expiring with her eyes popping out of her head and her malicious tongue dangling out of her mouth.

'Darling, I'm scared!' I heard the doctor's wife whisper in a thin, squeaky voice as she turned to her husband, who patted her shoulder reassuringly.

The red-headed freak M.-S.-san (his name is too long for me to write it in full) raised an interesting question: 'Professor, can you describe the shawl in more detail? We know the bird has a hole where its eye should be, and it's a triangle. But is there anything else remarkable about it?'

I should note that this strange gentleman takes part in the general conversation almost as rarely as I do. But, like the author of these lines, if he does say something then it is always off the point, and so the unexpected appropriateness of his question was all the more remarkable.

Sweetchild-sensei: 'As far as I recall, apart from the hole and the unique shape there is nothing special about the shawl. It is about the size of a small fan, but it can easily be hidden in a thimble. Such remarkably fine fabric is quite common in Brahmapur.'

'Then the key must lie in the eye of the bird and the triangular shape,' Fandorin-san concluded with exquisite assurance.

He was truly magnificent.

The more I ponder on his triumph and the whole story in general, the more strongly I feel the unworthy temptation to demonstrate to all of them that Gintaro Aono is also no fool. I also could reveal things that would amaze them. For instance, I could tell Commissioner Gauche certain curious details of yesterday's incident involving the black-skinned savage. Even the wise Fandorin-san has admitted that the matter is not entirely clear to him as yet. What if the 'wild Japanese' were suddenly to solve the riddle that is puzzling him? That could be interesting!

Yesterday's insults unsettled me and I lost my composure for a while. Afterwards, when I had calmed down, I began comparing facts and weighing the situation up, and I have constructed an entire logical argument which I intend to put to the police-man. Let him work out the rest for himself. This is what I shall tell the commissioner.

First I shall remind him of how Mme Kleber humiliated him. It was a highly insulting remark, made in public. And it was made at the precise moment when I was about to reveal what I had observed. Did Mme Kleber not perhaps wish to shut me up? This surely appears suspicious, monsieur Commissioner?

To continue. Why does she pretend to be weak, when she is as fit as a sumo wrestler? You will say this is an irrelevant detail. But I shall tell you, monsieur detective, that a person who is constantly pre-

tending must be hiding something. Take me, for instance. (Ha ha. Of course, I shall not say that.)

Then I shall point out to the commissioner that European women have very delicate white skin. Why did the negro's powerful fingers not leave even the slightest mark on it? Is that not strange?

And finally, when the commissioner decides I have nothing to offer him but the vindictive speculations of an oriental mind bent on vengeance, I shall tell him the most important thing, which will immediately make our detective sit up and take notice.

'M. Gauche,' I shall say to him with a polite smile, 'I do not possess your brilliant mind and I am not attempting, hopeless ignoramus that I am, to interfere in your investigation, but I regard it as my duty to draw your attention to a certain circumstance. You yourself say that the murderer from the rue de Grenelle is one of us. M. Fandorin has expounded a convincing account of how Lord Littleby's servants were killed. Vaccinating them against cholera was a brilliant subterfuge. It tells us that the murderer knows how to use a syringe. But what if the person who came to the mansion on the rue de Grenelle were not a male doctor, but a woman, a nurse? She would have aroused even less apprehension than a man, would she not? Surely you agree? Then let me advise you to take a casual glance at Mme Kleber's arms when she is sitting with her viper's head propped on her hand and her wide sleeve slips down to the elbow. You will observe some barely visible points on the inner flexure, as I have observed them. They are needle marks, monsieur Commissioner. Ask Dr Truffo if he is giving Mme Kleber any injections and the venerable physician will tell you what he has already told me today: no, he is not, for he is opposed in principle to the intravenous injection of medication. And then, oh wise Gauche-sensei, you will add two and two, and you will have something for your grey head to puzzle over.' That is what I shall tell the commissioner, and he will take Mme Kleber more seriously.

A European knight would say that I had behaved villainously, but that would merely demonstrate his own limitations. That is precisely why there are no knights left in Europe, but the samurai are still with us. Our lord and emperor may have set the different estates on one level and forbidden us to wear two swords in our belts, but that does not mean the calling of a samurai has been abolished, quite the opposite. The entire Japanese nation has been elevated to the estate of the samurai in order to prevent us from boasting to each other of our noble origins. We all stand together against the rest of the world. Oh, you noble European knight (who has never existed except in novels)! In fighting with men, use the weapons of a man, but in fighting with women, use the weapons of a woman. That is the samurai code of honour, and there is nothing villainous in it, for women know how to fight every bit as well as men. What contradicts the honour of the samurai is to employ the weapons of a man against a woman or the weapons of a woman against a man. I would never sink as low as that.

I am still uncertain whether the manoeuvre I am contemplating is worthwhile, but my state of mind is incomparably better than it was yesterday. So much so that I have even managed to compose a decent haiku without any difficulty:

The moonlight glinting
Bright upon the steely blade,
A cold spark of ice.

Clarissa Stamp

Clarissa glanced around with a bored look on her face to see if anyone was watching and only then peeped cautiously round the corner of the deck-house.

The Japanese was sitting alone on the quarterdeck with his legs folded up underneath him. His head was thrown right back and she could see the whites of his eyes glinting horribly between the half-closed lids. The expression on his face was absolutely impassive, inhumanly dispassionate.

Br-r-r! Clarissa shuddered. What a strange specimen this Mr Aono was. Here on the boat deck, located just one level above the first-class cabins, there was no one taking the air, just a gaggle of young girls skipping with a rope and two nursery maids exhausted by the heat who had taken refuge in the shade of a snow-white launch. Who but children and a crazy Oriental would be out in such scorching heat? The only structures higher than the boat deck were the control room, the captain's bridge and, of course, the funnels, masts and sails. The white canvas sheets were swollen taut by a following wind and *Leviathan* was making straight for the liquid-silver line of the horizon, puffing smoke into the sky as it went, while all around the Indian Ocean lay spread out like a slightly crumpled table-cloth with shimmering patches of bright bottle-green. From up here she could see that the Earth really was round: the rim of the horizon was clearly lower than the *Leviathan*, and the ship seemed to be running downhill towards it.

But Clarissa had not drenched herself in perspiration for the sake of the sea view. She wanted to see what Mr Aono was up to. Where did he disappear to with such unfailing regularity after breakfast?

And she had been right to be curious. Look at him now, the very image of the inscrutable Oriental! A man with such a motionless, pitiless mask for a face was capable of absolutely anything. The members of the yellow races were certainly not like us, and it was not simply a matter of the shape of their eyes. They looked very much like people on the outside, but on the inside they were a different species altogether. After all, wolves looked like dogs, didn't they, but their nature was quite different. Of course, the yellow-skinned races had a moral code of their own, but it was so alien to Christianity that no normal person could possibly understand it. It would be better if they didn't wear European clothes or know how to use cutlery – that created a dangerous illusion of civilization, when there were things that we couldn't possibly imagine going on under that slickly parted black hair and yellow forehead.

The Japanese stirred almost imperceptibly and blinked, and Clarissa hastily ducked back out of sight. Of course, she was behaving like an absolute fool, but she couldn't just do nothing! This nightmare couldn't be allowed to go on and on for ever. The commissioner had to be nudged in the right direction, otherwise there was no way of knowing how everything might end. Despite the heat, she felt a chilly tremor run through her.

There was obviously something mysterious about Mr Aono's character and the way he behaved. Like the mystery of the crime on the rue de Grenelle. It was strange that Gauche had still not realized that all the signs pointed to the Japanese as the main suspect.

What kind of officer was he, and how could he have graduated from St Cyr if he knew nothing about horses? One day, acting purely out of humanitarian motives, Clarissa had decided to involve the Oriental in the general conversation and started talking about a subject that should have been of interest to a military man – training and racing horses, the merits and shortcomings of the Norfolk trotter. He was no officer! When she asked him: 'Have you ever taken part in a steeplechase?' he replied that officers of the imperial army were absolutely forbidden to become involved in politics. He simply had no idea what a steeplechase was! Of course, who could tell what kind of officers they had in Japan – perhaps they rode around on sticks of bamboo – but how could an alumnus of St Cyr possibly be so ignorant? No, it was quite out of the question.

She had to bring this to Gauche's attention. Or perhaps she ought to wait and see if she could discover something else suspicious?

And what about that incident yesterday? Clarissa had taken a stroll along the corridor past Mr Aono's cabin after she heard some extremely strange noises. There was a dry crunching sound coming from inside the cabin, as if someone were smashing furniture with precisely regular blows. Clarissa had screwed up her courage and knocked.

The door had opened with a jerk and the Japanese appeared in the doorway – entirely naked except for a loincloth! His swarthy body was gleaming with sweat, his eyes were swollen with blood.

When he saw Clarissa standing there, he hissed through his teeth:

'Chikusho!'

The question that she had prepared in advance ('Mr Aono, do you by any chance happen to have with you some of those marvellous Japanese prints I've heard so much about?') flew right out of her head, and Clarissa froze in stupefaction. Now he would drag her into the cabin and throw himself on her! And afterwards he would chop her into pieces and throw her into the sea. Nothing could be simpler. And that would be the end of Miss Clarissa Stamp, the well-brought-up English lady, who might not have been very happy but had still expected so much from her life.

Clarissa mumbled that she had got the wrong door. Aono stared at her without speaking. He gave off a sour smell.

Probably she ought to have a word with the commissioner after all.

Before afternoon tea she ambushed the detective outside the

doors of the Windsor saloon and began sharing her ideas with him, but the way the boorish lout listened was very odd: he kept darting sharp, mocking glances at her, as though he were listening to a confession of some dark misdeed that she had committed.

At one point he muttered into his moustache:

'Ah, how eager you all are to tell tales on each other.'

When she had finished, he suddenly asked out of the blue:

'And how are mama and papa keeping?'

'Whose, Mr Aono's?' Clarissa asked in amazement.

'No, mademoiselle, yours.'

'I was orphaned as a child,' she replied, glancing at the policeman in alarm. Good God, this was no ship, it was a floating lunatic asylum.

'That's what I needed to establish,' said Gauche with a nod of satisfaction, then the boor began humming a song that Clarissa didn't know and walked into the saloon ahead of her, which was incredibly rude.

That conversation had left a bad taste in her mouth. For all their much-vaunted gallantry, the French were not gentlemen. Of course, they could dazzle you and turn your head, make some dramatic gesture like sending a hundred red roses to your hotel room (Clarissa winced as she thought of that), but they were not to be trusted. Although the English gentleman might appear somewhat insipid by comparison, he knew the meaning of the words 'duty' and 'decency'. But if a Frenchman wormed his way into your trust, he was certain to betray it.

These generalizations, however, had no direct relevance to Commissioner Gauche. And moreover, the reason for his bizarre behaviour was revealed at the dinner table, and in a most alarming man-ner.

Over dessert the detective, who had so far preserved a most untypical silence that had set everyone's nerves on edge, suddenly stared hard at Clarissa and said:

'Yes, by the way, Mlle Stamp' (although she had not said anything), 'you were asking me recently about Marie Sanfon.

You know, the little lady who was supposedly seen with Lord Littleby shortly before he died.'

Clarissa started in surprise and everyone else fell silent and began staring curiously at the commissioner, recognizing that special tone of voice in which he began his leisurely 'little stories'.

'I promised to tell you something about this individual later. And now the time has come,' Gauche continued, with his eyes still fixed on Clarissa, and the longer he looked the less she liked it. 'It will be a rather long story, but you won't be bored, because it concerns a quite extraordinary woman. And in any case, we are in no hurry. Here we all are sitting comfortably, eating our cheese and drinking our orangeade. But if anyone does have business to attend to, do leave by all means. Papa Gauche won't be offended.'

No one moved.

'Then shall I tell you about Marie Sanfon?' the commissioner asked with feigned bonhomie.

'Oh yes! You must!' they all cried.

Only Clarissa said nothing, aware that this topic had been broached for a reason and it was intended exclusively for her ears. Gauche did not even attempt to disguise the fact.

He smacked his lips in anticipation and took out his pipe without bothering to ask permission from the ladies.

'Then let me start at the beginning. Once upon a time, in the Belgian town of Bruges there lived a little girl by the name of Marie. The little girl's parents were honest, respectable citizens, who went to church, and they doted on their little golden-haired darling. When Marie was five years old, her parents presented her with a little brother, the future heir to the Sanfon and Sanfon brewery, and the happy family began living even more happily, until suddenly disaster struck. The infant boy, who was barely a month old, fell out of a window and was killed. The parents were not at home at the time, they had left the children alone with their nanny. But the nanny had gone out for half an hour to see her sweetheart, a fireman, and during her brief absence a stranger in a black cloak and black hat burst into the house. Little Marie managed to hide under the bed, but the man in black grabbed her little brother out of his cradle and threw him out of the window. Then he simply vanished without trace.'

'Why are you telling us such terrible things?' Mme Kleber exclaimed, clutching at her belly.

'Why, I have hardly even begun,' said Gauche, gesturing with his pipe. 'The best – or the worst – is yet to come. After her miraculous escape, little Marie told mama and papa about the "black man". They turned the entire district upside down searching for him, and in the heat of the moment they even arrested the local rabbi, since he naturally always wore black. But there was one strange detail that kept nagging at M. Sanfon: why had the criminal moved a stool over to the window?'

'Oh, God!' Clarissa gasped, clutching at her heart. 'Surely not!'

'You are quite remarkably perceptive, Mlle Stamp,' the commissioner said with a laugh. 'Yes, it was little Marie who had thrown her own baby brother out of the window.'

'How terrible!' Mrs Truffo felt it necessary to interject. 'But why?'

'The girl did not like the way everyone was paying so much attention to the baby, while they had forgotten all about her. She thought that if she got rid of her brother, then she would be mama and papa's favourite again,' Gauche explained calmly. 'But that was the first and the last time Marie Sanfon ever left a clue and was found out. The sweet child had not yet learned to cover her tracks.'

'And what did they do with the infant criminal?' asked Lieutenant Renier, clearly shaken by what he had heard. 'They couldn't try her for murder, surely?'

'No, they didn't try her.' The commissioner smiled craftily at Clarissa. 'The shock, however, was too much for her mother, who lost her mind and was committed to an asylum. M. Sanfon could no longer bear the sight of the little daughter who was the cause of his family's calamitous misfortune, so he placed her with a convent of the Grey Sisters of St Vincent, and the girl was brought up there. She was best at everything, in her studies and in her charity work. But most of all, they say, she liked to read books. The novice nun was just seventeen years old when a disgraceful scandal occurred at the convent.' Gauche glanced into his file and nodded. 'I have the date here. The seventeenth of July 1866. The Archbishop of Brussels himself was staying with the Grey Sisters when the venerable prelate's ring, with a massive amethyst, disappeared from his bedroom. It had supposedly belonged to St Louis himself. The previous evening the monseigneur had summoned the two best pupils, our Marie and a girl from Arles, to his chambers for a talk. Suspicion naturally fell on the two girls. The mother superior organized a search and the ring's velvet case was discovered under the mattress of the girl from Arles. The thief lapsed into a stupor and would not answer any questions, so she was escorted to the punishment cell. When the police arrived an hour later, they were unable to question the criminal – she had strangled herself with the belt of her habit.'

'I've guessed it, the whole thing was staged by that abominable Marie Sanfon!' Milford-Stokes exclaimed. 'A nasty story, very nasty!'

'Nobody knows for certain, but the ring was never found,' the commissioner said with a shrug. 'Two days later Marie came to the mother superior in tears and said everyone was giving her strange looks and begged to be released from the convent. The mother superior's feelings for her former favourite had also cooled somewhat, and she made no effort to dissuade her.'

'They should have searched the little pigeon at the gates,' said Dr Truffo with a regretful sigh. 'You can be sure they would have found the amethyst somewhere under her skirt.'

When he translated what he had said to his wife, she jabbed him with her elbow, evidently regarding his remark as somehow indecent.

'Either they didn't search her or they searched her and found nothing, I don't know which. In any case, after she left the convent, Marie chose to go to Antwerp, which, as you are aware, is regarded as the world capital of precious stones. The former nun suddenly grew rich and ever since she has lived in the grand style. Sometimes, just occasionally, she has been left without a sou to her name, but not for long. With her sharp mind and brilliant skill as an actress, combined with a total lack of moral scruple' – at this point the commissioner raised his voice and then paused – 'she has always been able to obtain the means required for a life of luxury. The police of Belgium, France, England, the United States, Brazil, Italy and a dozen other countries have detained Marie Sanfon on numerous occasions, on suspicion of all sorts of offences, but no charges have ever been brought against her. Always it turns out that either no crime has actually been committed or there is simply not enough evidence. If you like, I could tell you about a couple of episodes from her distinguished record. Are you not feeling bored yet, Mlle Stamp?'

Clarissa did not reply, she felt it was beneath her dignity. But in her heart she felt alarmed.

'Eighteen seventy,' Gauche declared, after another glance into his file. 'The small but prosperous town of Fettburg in German-speaking Switzerland. The chocolate and ham industries. Eight and a half thousand pigs to four thousand inhabitants. A land of rich, fat idiots – I beg your pardon, Mme Kleber, I did not mean to insult your homeland,' said the policeman, suddenly realizing what he had said.

'Never mind,' said Mme Kleber with a careless shrug. 'I come from French-speaking Switzerland. And anyway, the area around Fettburg really is full of simpletons. I believe I have heard this story, it is very funny. But never mind, carry on.'

'Some might think it funny,' Gauche sighed reproachfully, and suddenly he winked at Clarissa, which was going too far altogether. 'One day the honest burghers of the town were thrown into a state of indescribable excitement when a certain peasant by the name of Möbius, who was known in Fettburg as an idler and a numskull, boasted that he had sold his land, a narrow strip of stony desert, to a certain grand lady who styled herself the Comtesse de Sanfon. This damn fool of a countess had shelled out three thousand francs for thirty acres of barren land on which not even thistles could grow. But there were people smarter than Möbius on the town council, and they thought his story sounded suspicious. What would a countess want with thirty acres of sand and rock? There was something fishy going on. So they dispatched the very smartest of the town's citizens to Zurich to find out what was what, and he discovered that the Comtesse de Sanfon was well known there as woman who knew how to enjoy life on a grand scale. Even more interestingly, she often appeared in public in the company of Mr Goldsilber, the director of the state railway company. The director and the countess were rumoured to be romantically involved. Then, of course, the good burgers guessed what was going on. The little town of Fettburg had been dreaming for a long time of having its own railway line, which would make it cheaper to export its chocolate and ham. The wasteland acquired by the countess just happened to run from the nearest railway station to the forest where the communal land began. Suddenly everything was clear to the city fathers: having learned from her lover about plans to build a railway line, the countess had bought the key plot of land, intending to turn a handsome profit. An outrageously bold plan began to take shape in the good burghers' heads. They dispatched a deputation to the countess, which attempted to persuade her Excellency to sell the land to the noble town of Fettburg. The beautiful lady was obstinate at first, claiming that she knew nothing about any branch railway line, but when the burghomaster hinted subtly that the affair smacked of a conspiracy between her Excellency and his Excellency the Director of State Railways, and that was a matter which fell within the competence of the courts, the woman's nerve finally gave way and she agreed. The wasteland was divided into thirty lots of one acre each and auctioned off to the citizens of the town. The Fettburgers almost came to blows over it and the price for some lots rose as high as fifteen thousand francs. Altogether the countess received . . .' The commissioner ran his finger along a line of print. 'A little less than two hundred and eighty thousand francs.'

Mme Kleber laughed out loud and gestured to Gauche as if to say: I'm saying nothing, go on, go on.

'Weeks went by, then months, and still the construction work had not started. The citizens of the town sent an inquiry to the government and received a reply that no branch line to Fettburg was planned for the next fifteen years . . . They went to the police and explained what had happened and said that it was daylight robbery. The police listened to the victims' story with sympathy, but there was nothing they could do to help: Mlle Sanfon had said that she knew nothing about any railway line and she had not wanted to sell the land. The sales were properly registered, it was all perfectly legal. As for calling herself a countess, that was not a very nice thing to do, but unfortunately it was not a criminal offence.'

'Very clever!' laughed Renier. 'It really was all perfectly legal.'

'But that's nothing,' said the commissioner, leafing further through his papers. 'I have another story here that is absolutely fantastic. The action is set in the Wild West of America, in 1873. Miss Cleopatra Frankenstein, the world-famous necromancer and Grand Dragoness of the Maltese Lodge, whose name in her passport is Marie Sanfon, arrives in the goldfields of California. She informs the prospectors that she has been guided to this savage spot by the voice of Zarathustra, who has ordered his faithful handmaiden to carry out a great experiment in the town of Golden Nugget. Apparently, at that precise longitude and latitude the cosmic energy was focused in such a way that on a starry night, with the help of a few cabbalistic formulas, it was possible to resurrect someone who had already crossed the great divide between the kingdom of the living and the kingdom of the dead. And Cleopatra intended to perform this miracle that very night, in public and entirely without charge, because she was no circus conjurer but the medium of the supreme spheres.

And what do you think?' Gauche asked, pausing for effect. 'Before the eyes of five hundred bearded onlookers, the Dragoness worked her magic over the burial mound of Red Coyote, the legendary Indian chief who had died a hundred years earlier, and suddenly the earth began to stir – it gaped asunder, you might say – and an Indian brave in a feather headdress emerged from the mound, complete with a tomahawk and painted face. The onlookers trembled and Cleopatra, in the grip of her mystical trance, screeched: "I feel the power of the cosmos in me! Where is the town cemetery? I will bring everyone in it back to life." It says in this article,' the policeman explained, 'that the cemetery in Golden Nugget was vast, because in the goldfields someone was dispatched to the next world every day of the week. Apparently, the headstones outnumbered the town's living inhabitants. When the prospectors imagined what would happen if all those troublemakers, drunks and gallows birds suddenly rose from their graves, panic set in. The situation was saved by the Justice of the Peace, who stepped forward and asked politely whether the Dragoness would agree to halt her great experiment if the town's inhabitants gave her a saddlebag full of gold dust as a modest donation towards the requirements of occult science.'

'Well, did she agree?' chuckled the lieutenant.

'Yes, for two bagfuls.'

'And what became of the Indian chief?' asked Fandorin with a smile. He had a quite wonderful smile, except that it was too boyish, thought Clarissa. As they said in Suffolk: a grand pie, but not for your mouth.

'Cleopatra Frankenstein took the Indian chief with her,' Gauche replied with a serious expression. 'For purposes of scientific research. They say he got his throat cut during a drunken brawl in a Denver bordello.'

'This Marie Sanfon really is a very interesting character,' mused Fandorin. 'Tell us more about her. It's a long way from all these clever frauds to cold-blooded mass murder.'

'Oh, please, that's more than enough,' protested Mrs Truffo, turning to her husband. 'My darling, it must be awfully tiresome for you to translate all this nonsense.'

'You are not obliged to stay, madam,' said Commissioner Gauche, offended by the word 'nonsense'.

Mrs Truffo batted her eyelids indignantly, but she had no intention of leaving.

'M. le cosaque is right,' Gauche acknowledged. 'Let me try to dig out a more vicious example.'

Mme Kleber laughed and cast a glance at Fandorin and, nervous as she was, even Clarissa was unable to restrain a smile – the diplomat was so very unlike a wild son of the steppe.

'Here we are, listen to this story about the black baby. It's a recent case, from the year before last, and we have a detailed report of the outcome.' The detective glanced through several sheets of paper clipped together, evidently to refresh his memory of the event. He chuckled. 'This is something of a masterpiece. I have all sorts of things in my little file, ladies and gentlemen.' He stroked the black calico binding lovingly with the stumpy fingers of his plebeian hand. 'Papa Gauche made thorough preparations for his journey, he didn't forget a single piece of paper that might come in useful. The embarrassing events I am about to relate to you never reached the newspapers, and what I have here is the police report. All right. In a certain German principality (I won't say which, because this is a delicate matter), a family of great note was expecting an addition to its number. It was a long and difficult birth. The receiving physician was a certain highly respected Dr Vogel. Eventually the bedroom was filled with the sound of an infant's squalling. The grand duchess lost consciousness for several minutes because she had suffered so much, and then she opened her eyes and said to the doctor: "Ah, Herr Professor, show me my little child." With an expression of extreme embarrassment, Dr Vogel handed her Highness the charming baby that was bawling so loudly. Its skin was a light coffee colour. When the grand duchess fainted again, the doctor glanced out of the door and beckoned with his finger to the grand duke, which, of course, was a gross violation of court etiquette.'

It was obvious that the commissioner was taking great pleasure in telling this story to the prim and proper Windsorites. A police report was unlikely to contain such details – Gauche was clearly allowing himself to fantasise at will. He lisped when he spoke the countess's part and deliberately selected words that sounded pompous: he obviously thought that made the story sound funnier. Clarissa did not consider herself an aristocrat, but even she winced at the bad taste of his scoffing at royalty. Sir Reginald, a baronet and the scion of an ancient line, also knitted his brows in a scowl, but this reaction only seemed to inspire the commissioner to greater efforts.

'His highness, however, did not take offence at his physician in ordinary, because this was a moment of tremendous pathos. Positively overwhelmed by a rising tide of paternal and conjugal feelings, he went dashing into the bedroom . . . You can imagine for yourselves the scene that followed: the crowned monarch swearing like a trooper, the grand duchess sobbing and making excuses and swooning by turns, the little negro child bawling his lungs out and the court physician frozen in reverential horror. Eventually his Highness got a grip on himself and decided to postpone the investigation into her Highness's behaviour until later. In the meantime the business had to be hushed up. But how? Flush the child down the toilet?' Gauche put his hand over his mouth, acting the buffoon. 'I beg your pardon, ladies, it just slipped out. It was impossible to get rid of the child – the entire principality had been eagerly awaiting his birth. In any case, it would have been a sin. If he called his advisers together they might let the cat out of the bag. What was he going to do? And then Dr Vogel coughed deferentially into his hand and suggested a way of saving the situation. He said that he knew a lady by the name of Fräulein von Sanfon who could work miracles and even pluck the phoenix from the sky for the prince if he needed it, let alone find him a newborn white baby. The fräulein knew how to keep her mouth shut, and being a very noble individual she would, of course, not take any money for her services, but she did have a great fondness for old jewels . . . Anyway, within no more than a couple of hours a fine bouncing baby boy, whiter than a little suckling piglet, even with white hair, was reposing on the satin sheets of the cradle and the poor little negro child was taken from the palace. They told her Highness that the innocent child would be transported to southern climes and placed with a good family for upbringing. And so everything was settled as well as could possibly be managed. The grateful duke gave the doctor a monogrammed diamond snuffbox for Fräulein von Sanfon, together with a note of gratitude and an oral request to depart the principality and never return. Which the considerate maiden immediately did.' Gauche chuckled, unable to restrain himself. 'The next morning, after a row that had lasted all night, the grand duke finally decided to take a closer look at his new son and heir. He squeamishly lifted the boy out of the cradle and turned him this way and that, and suddenly on his pink little backside – begging your pardon – he saw a birthmark shaped like a heart. His Highness had one exactly like it on his own hindquarters, and so did his grandfather, and so on to the seventh generation. Totally bemused, the duke sent for his physician in ordinary, but Dr Vogel had set out from the castle for parts unknown the previous night, leaving behind his wife and eight children.' Gauche burst into hoarse laughter, then began coughing and waving his hands in the air. Someone else chuckled uncertainly and Mme Kleber put her hand over her mouth.

'The investigation that followed soon established that the court doctor had been behaving strangely for some time and had even been seen in the gambling houses of neighbouring Baden, in the company, moreover, of a certain jolly young woman whose description closely matched that of Fräulein von Sanfon.' The detective put on a more serious expression. 'The doctor was found two days later in a hospital in Strasbourg. Dead. He'd taken a fatal dose of laudanum and left a note: "I alone am to blame for everything." A clear case of suicide. The identity of the true culprit was obvious, but how could you prove it? As for the snuffbox, it was a gift from the grand duke, and there was a note to go with it. It would not have been worth their Highnesses' while to take the case to court. The greatest mystery, of course, was how they managed to swap the new-born prince for the little negro baby, and where they could have found a chocolate-coloured child in a country of people with blue eyes and blond hair. But then, according to some sources, shortly before the incident described, Marie Sanfon had had a Senegalese maid in her service . . .'

'Tell me, Commissioner,' Fandorin said when the laughter stopped (four people were laughing: Lieutenant Renier, Dr Truffo, Professor Sweetchild and Mme Kleber), 'is Marie Sanfon so remarkably good-looking that she can turn any man's head?'

'No, she is nothing of the kind. It says everywhere that her appearance is perfectly ordinary, with absolutely no distinctive features.' Gauche cast a lingering, impudent glance in Clarissa's direction. 'She changes the colour of her hair, her behaviour, her accent and the way she dresses with the greatest of ease. But evidently there must be something exceptional about this woman. In my line of work I've seen all sorts of things. The most devastating heartbreakers are not usually great beauties. If you saw them in a photograph you would never pick them out, but when you meet them you can feel your skin creep. It's not a straight nose and long eyelashes that a man goes for, it's a certain special smell.'

'Oh, Commissioner,' Clarissa objected at this vulgar comment. 'There are ladies present.'

'There are certainly suspects present,' Gauche parried calmly. 'And you are one of them. How do I know that Mlle Sanfon is not sitting at this very table?'

He fixed his eyes on Clarissa's face. This was getting more and more like a bad dream. She could hardly catch her breath.

'If I have c-calculated correctly, then this person should be twenty-nine now?'

Fandorin's calm, almost indifferent question roused Clarissa to take a grip on herself, and casting female vanity aside, she cried out:

'There is no point in staring at me like that, monsieur detective! You are obviously paying me a compliment that I do not deserve. I am almost ten years older than your adventuress! And the other ladies present are hardly suited to the role of Mlle Sanfon. Mme Kleber is too young and Mrs Truffo, as you know, does not speak French!'

'For a woman of Marie Sanfon's skill it is a very simple trick to add or subtract ten years from her age,' Gauche replied slowly, staring at Clarissa as intently as ever. 'Especially if the prize is so great and failure smacks of the guillotine. So have you really never been to Paris, Mlle Stamp? Somewhere in the region of the rue de Grenelle, perhaps?'

Clarissa turned deathly pale.

'At this point I feel obliged to intervene as a representative of the Jasper–Artaud Partnership,' Renier interrupted irritably. 'Ladies and gentlemen, I can assure you there is absolutely no way that any swindlers and crooks with an international reputation could have joined our cruise. The company guarantees that there are no card-sharps or loose women on board the *Leviathan*, let alone adventuresses known to the police. You can understand why. The maiden voyage is a very great responsibility. A scandal is the very last thing that we need. Captain Cliff and I personally checked and rechecked the passenger lists, and whenever necessary we made inquiries. Including some to the French police, monsieur Commissioner. The captain and I are prepared to vouch for everyone present here. We do not wish to prevent you from carrying out your professional duty, M. Gauche, but you are simply wasting your time. And the French taxpayers' money.'

'Well now,' growled Gauche, 'time will tell.'

Following which, to everyone's relief, Mrs Truffo struck up a conversation about the weather.

Reginald Milford-Stokes

10 April 1878
22 hours 31 minutes
In the Arabian Sea
17°06′ 28″ N 59° 48′ 14″ E

My passionately beloved Emily,
This infernal ark is controlled by the forces of evil, I can sense it in every fibre of my tormented soul. Although I am not sure that a criminal such as I can have a soul. Writing that has set me thinking. I remember that I have committed a crime, a terrible crime which can never ever be forgiven, but the strange thing is, I have completely forgotten what it was that I did. And I very much do not want to remember.

At night, in my dreams, I remember it very well – otherwise how can I explain why I wake up in such an appalling state every morning? How I long for our separation to be over! I feel that if it lasts for even a little longer, I shall lose my mind. I sit in the cabin and stare at the minute hand of the chronometer, but it doesn't move. Outside on the deck I heard someone say, 'It's the tenth of April today,' and I couldn't grasp how it could possibly be April and why it had to be the tenth. I unlocked the trunk and saw that the letter I wrote to you yesterday was dated 9 April and the one from the day before yesterday was dated the eighth. So it's right. It is April. The tenth.

For several days now I have been keeping a close eye on Professor Sweetchild (if he really is a professor). He is a very popular man with our group in Windsor, an inveterate old windbag who loves to flaunt his knowledge of history and oriental matters. Every day he comes up with new, fantastic stories of hidden treasure, each more improbable than the last. And he has nasty, shifty, piggy little eyes. Sometimes there is an insane gleam in them. If only you could hear how voluptu-

ous his voice sounds when he talks about precious stones. He has a positive mania for diamonds and emeralds.

Today at breakfast Dr Truffo suddenly stood up, clapped his hands loudly and announced in a solemn voice that it was Mrs Truffo's birthday. Everybody oohed and aahed and began congratulating her, and the doctor himself publicly presented his plain-faced spouse with a gift for the occasion, a pair of topaz earrings in exceptionally bad taste. What terrible vulgarity, to make a spectacle of giving a present to one's own wife! Mrs Truffo, however, did not seem to think so. She became unusually lively and appeared perfectly happy, and her dismal features turned the colour of grated carrot. The lieutenant said: 'Oh, madam, if we had known about this happy event in advance, we would certainly have prepared some surprise for you. You have only your own modesty to blame.' The empty-headed woman turned an even more luminous shade and muttered bashfully: 'Would you really like to make me happy?' The response was a general lazy mumble of goodwill. 'Well then,' she said, 'let's play my favourite game of lotto. In our family we always used to take out the cards and the bag of counters on Sundays and church holidays. It's such wonderful fun! Gentlemen, it will really make me very happy if you will play!' It was the first time I had heard the doctor's wife speak at such great length. For an instant I thought she was making fun of us, but no, Mrs Truffo was entirely serious. There was nothing to be done. Only Renier managed to slip out, supposedly because it was time for him to go on watch. The churlish commissioner also attempted to cite some urgent business or other as an excuse, but everyone stared at him so reproachfully that he gave in with a bad grace and stayed.

Mr Truffo went to fetch the equipment for this idiotic game and the torment began. Everyone dejectedly set out their cards, glancing long-ingly at the sunlit deck. The windows of the saloon were wide open, but we sat there playing out a scene from the nursery. We set up a prize fund to which everyone contributed a guinea – 'to make things more interesting', as the elated birthday girl said. Our leading lady should have had the best chance of winning, since she was the only one who was watching eagerly as the numbers were drawn. I had the impression that the commissioner would have liked to win the jackpot too, but he had difficulty understanding the childish little jingles that Mrs Truffo kept spouting (for her sake, on this occasion we spoke English).

The pitiful topaz earrings, which are worth ten pounds at the most, prompted Sweetchild to mount his high horse again. 'An excellent present, sir!' he declared to the doctor, who beamed in delight, but then Sweetchild spoiled everything with what he said next. 'Of course, topazes are cheap nowadays, but who knows, perhaps their price will shoot up in a hundred years or so. Precious stones are so unpredictable! They are a genuine miracle of nature, unlike those boring metals gold and silver. Metal has no soul or form, it can be melted down, while each stone has a unique personality. But it is not just anyone who can find them, only those who stop at nothing and are willing to follow their magical radiance to the ends of the earth, or even beyond if necessary.' These bombastic sentiments were accompanied by Mrs Truffo calling out the numbers on the counters in her squeaky voice. While Sweetchild was declaiming: 'I shall tell you the legend of the great and mighty conqueror Mahmud Gaznevi, who was bewitched by the brilliant lustre of diamonds and put half of India to fire and the sword in his search for these magical crystals,' Mrs Truffo said: 'Eleven, gentlemen. Drumsticks!' And so it went on.

But I shall tell you Sweetchild's legend of Mahmud Gaznevi anyway. It will give you a better understanding of this storyteller. I can even attempt to convey his distinctive manner of speech.

'In the year (I don't remember which) of our Lord Jesus Christ, which according to the Moslem chronology was (and of course I don't remember that), the mighty Gaznevi learned that in Sumnat on the peninsula of Guzzarat (I think that was it) there was a holy shrine which contained an immense idol that was worshipped by hundreds of thousands of people. The idol jealously guarded the borders of that land against foreign invasions and anyone who stepped across those borders with a sword in his hand was doomed. This shrine belonged to a powerful Brahmin community, the richest in the whole of India. And these Brahmins of Sumnat also possessed an immense number of precious stones. But unafraid of the power of the idol, the intrepid conqueror gathered his forces together and launched his campaign.

Mahmud hewed off fifty thousand heads, reduced fifty fortresses to ruins and finally burst into the Sumnat shrine. His soldiers defiled the holy site and ransacked it from top to bottom, but they could not find the treasure. Then Gaznevi himself approached the idol, swung his great mace and smote its copper head. The Brahmins fell to the floor before their conqueror and offered him a million pieces of silver if only he would not touch their god. Mahmud laughed and smote the idol again. It cracked. The Brahmins began wailing more loudly than ever and promised this terrible ruler ten million pieces of gold. But the heavy mace was raised once again and it struck for a third time. The idol split in half and the diamonds and precious stones that had been concealed within it spilled out onto the floor in a gleaming torrent. The value of that treasure was beyond all calculation.'

At this point Mr Fandorin announced with a slightly embarrassed expression that he had a full card. Everyone except Mrs Truffo was absolutely delighted and was on the point of leaving when she begged us so insistently to play another round that we had to stay. It started up again: 'Thirty-nine – pig and swine! Twenty-seven – I'm in heaven!' and more drivel of the same kind.

But now Mr Fandorin began speaking and he told us another story in his gentle, rather ironic manner. It was an Arab fairy tale that he had read in an old book, and here is the fable as I remember it.

'Once upon a time three Maghrib merchants set out into the depths of the Great Desert, for they had learned that far, far away among the shifting sands, where the caravans do not go, there was a great treasure, the equal of which mortal eyes had never seen. The merchants walked for forty days, tormented by great heat and weariness, until they had only one camel each left – the others had all collapsed and died. Suddenly they saw a tall mountain ahead of them, and when they grew close to it they could not believe their eyes: the entire mountain consisted of silver ingots. The merchants gave thanks to Allah, and one of them stuffed a sack full of silver and set off back the way they had come. But the others said: "We shall go further." They walked for another forty days, until their faces were blackened by the sun, and their eyes became red and inflamed. Then another mountain appeared ahead of them, this time of gold. The second merchant exclaimed: "Not in vain have we borne so many sufferings! Glory be to the Most High!" He stuffed a sack full of gold and asked his comrade: "Why are you just standing there?" The third merchant replied: "How much gold can you carry away on one camel?" The second said: "Enough to make me the richest man in our city." "That is not enough for me," said the third, "I shall go further and find a mountain of diamonds. And when I return home, I shall be the richest man in the entire world." He walked on, and his journey lasted another forty days. His camel lay down and rose no more, but the merchant did not stop, for he was stubborn and he believed in the mountain of diamonds, and everyone knows that a single handful of diamonds is more valuable than a mountain of silver or a hill of gold. Then the third merchant beheld a wondrous sight ahead of him: a man standing there doubled over in the middle of the desert, bearing a throne made of diamonds on his shoulders, and squatting on the throne was a monster with a black face and burning eyes. "Joyous greetings to you, O worthy traveller," croaked the crooked man. "Allow me to introduce the demon of avarice, Marduf. Now you will bear him on your shoulders until another as avaricious as you and I comes to take your place."'

The story was broken off at that point, because once again Mr Fandorin had a full card, so our hostess failed to win the second jackpot too. Five seconds later Mrs Truffo was the only person left at the table – everyone else had disappeared in a flash.

I keep thinking about Mr Fandorin's story. It is not as simple as it seems.

That third merchant is Sweetchild. Yes, when I heard the end of the story, I suddenly realized that he is a dangerous madman! There is an uncontrollable passion raging in his soul, and if anyone should know what that means, it is me. I have been gliding around after him like an invisible shadow ever since we left Aden.

I have already told you, my precious Emily, that I spent the time we were moored there very profitably. I'm sure you must have thought I meant I had bought a new navigational instrument to replace the one that was stolen. Yes, I do have a new sextant now and I am checking the ship's course regularly once again, but what I meant was something quite different. I was simply afraid to commit my secret to paper. What if someone were to read it? After all, I am surrounded by enemies on every side. But I have a resourceful mind, and I have invented a fine stratagem: starting from today I am writing in milk. To the eye of a stranger it will seem like a clean sheet of paper, quite uninteresting, but my quick-witted Emily will warm the sheets on the lampshade to make the writing appear! What a spiffing wheeze, eh?

Well then, about Aden. While I was still on the steamer, before they let us go ashore, I noticed that Sweetchild was nervous, and more than simply nervous, he was positively jumping up and down in excitement. It began soon after Fandorin announced that the shawl stolen from Lord Littleby was the key to the mythical treasure of the Emerald Rajah. The professor became terribly agitated, started muttering to himself and kept repeating: 'Ah, I must get ashore soon.' But what for, that was the question!

I decided to find out.

Pulling my black hat with the wide brim well down over my eyes, I set off to follow Sweetchild. Everything could not have gone better at first: he didn't glance round once and I had no trouble in trailing him to the square located behind the little custom house. But there I was in for an unpleasant surprise. Sweetchild called one of the local cabbies and drove off with him. His barouche was moving rather slowly, but I could not go running after it, that would have been unseemly. Of course, there were other barouches on the square, I could easily have got into any of them, but you know, my dearest, how heartily I detest open carriages. They are the devil's own invention and only reckless fools ride in them. Some people (I have seen it with my own eyes more than once) even take their wives and innocent children with them. How long can it be before disaster strikes? The two-wheelers which are so popular at home in Britain are especially dangerous. Someone once told me (I can't recall who it was just at the moment) that a certain young man from a very decent family, with a good position in society, was rash enough to take his young wife for a ride in one of those two-wheelers when she was eight months pregnant. It ended badly, of course: the mad fool lost control of the horses, they bolted and the carriage overturned. The young man was all right, but his wife went into premature labour. They were unable to save her or the child. And all because of his thoughtlessness. They could have gone for a walk, or taken a ride in a boat. If it comes to that, one can take a ride on a train, in a separate carriage. In Venice they take rides in gondolas. We were there, do you remember? Do you recall how the water lapped at the steps of the hotel?

I am finding it hard to concentrate, I am constantly digressing. And so, Sweetchild rode off in a carriage, and I was left standing beside the custom house. But do you think I lost my head? Not a bit of it. I thought of something that calmed my nerves almost instantly. While I was waiting for Sweetchild, I went into a sailors' shop and bought a new sextant, even better than the old one, and a splendid navigational almanac with astronomical formulae. Now I can calculate the ship's position much faster and more precisely. See what a cunning customer I am!

I waited for six hours and 38 minutes. I sat on a rock and looked at the sea, thinking about you.

When Sweetchild returned, I pretended to be dozing and he slipped past me, certain that I had not seen him.

The moment he disappeared round the corner of the custom house, I dashed across to his cabby. For sixpence the Bengali told me where our dear professor had been. You must admit, my sweet Emily, that I handled this business most adroitly.

The information I received only served to corroborate my initial suspicions. Sweetchild had asked to be taken from the port directly to the telegraph office. He spent half an hour there, and then went back to the post office building another four times. The cabby said: 'Sahib very-very worried. Run backwards and forwards. Sometimes say: take me to bazaar, then tap me on back: take me back, post office, quick-quick.' It seems quite clear that Sweetchild first sent off an urgent message to someone and then waited impatiently for an answer. The Bengali said that the last time he came out of the post office he was 'not like himself, he wave paper' and told the cabby to drive him back to the ship. The reply must have arrived.

I do not know what was in it, but it is perfectly clear that the professor, or whoever he really is, has accomplices.

That was two days ago. Since then Sweetchild has been a changed man. As I have already told you, he speaks of nothing but precious stones all the time, and sometimes he suddenly sits down on the deck and starts drawing something, either on his cuff or his handkerchief.

This evening there was a ball in the grand saloon. I have already described this majestic hall, which appears to have been transported here from Versailles or Buckingham Palace. There is gilt everywhere and the walls are covered from top to bottom with mirrors. The crystal electric chandeliers tinkle melodically in time to the gentle rolling of the ship. The orchestra (a perfectly decent one, by the way) mostly played Viennese waltzes and, as you know, I regard that dance as indecent, so I stood in the corner, keeping an eye on Sweetchild. He was enjoying himself greatly, inviting one lady after another to dance, skipping about like a goat and trampling on their feet outrageously, but that did not worry him in the least. I was even distracted a little, recalling how we once used to dance and how elegant your arm looked in its white glove as it lay on my shoulder. Suddenly I saw Sweetchild stumble and almost drop his partner, then without even bothering to apologize, he fairly raced across to the tables with the hors d'oeuvres, leaving his partner standing bewildered in the centre of the hall. I must admit that this sudden attack of uncontrollable hunger struck me as rather strange too.

Sweetchild, however, did not even glance at the dishes of pies, cheese and fruit. He grabbed a paper napkin out of a silver napkin holder, hunched over the table and began furiously scribbling something on it. He has become completely obsessed, and obviously no longer feels it necessary to conceal his secret even in a crowded room! Consumed with curiosity, I began strolling casually in his direction. But Sweetchild had already straightened up and folded the napkin into four, evidently intending to put it in his pocket. Unfortunately, I was too late to glance at it over his shoulder. I stamped my foot furiously and was about to turn back when I noticed Mr Fandorin coming over to the table with two glasses of champagne. He handed one to Sweetchild and kept the other for himself. I heard the Russian say: 'Ah, my dear Professor, how terribly absent-minded you are! You have just put a dirty napkin in your pocket.' Sweetchild was embarrassed, he took the napkin out, crumpled it into a ball and threw it under the table. I immediately joined them and deliberately struck up a conversation about fashion, knowing that the Indologist would soon get bored and leave. Which is exactly what happened.

No sooner had he made his apologies and left us alone than Fandorin whispered to me conspiratorially: 'Well, Sir Reginald, which of us is going to crawl under the table?' I realized that the diplomat was as suspicious of the professor's behaviour as I was. We understood each other completely in an instant. 'Yes, it is not exactly convenient,' I agreed. Mr Fandorin glanced around and then suggested: 'Let us do this thing fairly and honestly. If one of us can invent a decent pretext, the other will crawl after the napkin.' I nodded and started thinking, but nothing appropriate came to mind. 'Eureka!' whispered Fandorin, and with a movement so swift that I could barely see it, he unfastened one of my cufflinks. It fell on the floor and the diplomat pushed it under the table with the toe of his shoe. 'Sir Reginald,' he said loudly enough for people standing nearby to hear, 'I believe you have dropped a cufflink.'

An agreement is an agreement. I squatted down and glanced under the table. The napkin was lying quite close, but the dratted cufflink had skidded right across to the wall, and the table was rather broad. Imagine the scene. Your husband crawling under the table on all fours, presenting the crowded hall with a view that was far from edifying. On my way back I ran into a rather embarrassing situation. When I stuck my head out from under the table, I saw two young ladies directly in front of me, engaged in lively conversation with Mr Fandorin. When they spotted my red head at the level of their knees, the ladies squealed in fright, but my perfidious companion merely said calmly: 'Allow me to introduce Baronet Milford-Stokes.' The ladies gave me a distinctly chilly look and left without saying a word. I leapt to my feet, absolutely bursting with fury and exclaimed: 'Sir, you deliberately stopped them so that you could make fun of me!' Fandorin replied with an innocent expression: 'I did stop them deliberately, but not at all in order to make fun of you. It simply occurred to me that their wide skirts would conceal your daring raid from the eyes of the hall. But where is your booty?'

My hands trembled in impatience as I unfolded the napkin, reveal-ing a strange sight. I am drawing it from memory:

What are these geometrical figures? What does the zigzag line mean? And why are there three exclamation marks?

I cast a stealthy glance at Fandorin. He tugged at his ear lobe and muttered something that I didn't catch. I expect it was in Russian.

'What do you make of it?' I asked. 'Let's wait for a while,' the diplomat replied with a mysterious expression. 'He's getting close.'

Who is getting close? Sweetchild? Close to what? And is it a good thing that he is getting close?

I had no chance to ask these questions, because just at that moment there was a commotion in the hall and everyone started applauding. Then M. Driet, the captain's social officer, began shouting deafeningly through a megaphone: 'Ladies and gentlemen, the grand prize in our lottery goes to cabin number eighteen!' I had been so absorbed in the operation with the mysterious napkin that I had paid absolutely no attention to what was going on in the hall. It turned out that they had stopped dancing and set up the draw for the charity raffle 'In Aid of Fallen Women' (I wrote to you about this idiotic undertaking in my letter of 3 April). You are well aware of how I feel about charity and fallen women, so I shall refrain from further comment.

The announcement had a strange effect on my companion – he frowned and ducked, pulling his head down below his shoulders. I was surprised for a moment, until I remembered that No. 18 is Mr Fandorin's cabin. Just imagine that, he was the lucky winner again!

'This is becoming intolerable,' our favourite of fortune mumbled, stammering more than usual. 'I think I shall take a walk,' and he started backing away towards the door, but Mrs Kleber called out in her clear voice: 'That's Mr Fandorin from our saloon! There he is, gentlemen! In the white dinner jacket with the red carnation! Mr Fandorin, where are you going, you've won the grand prize!'

Everyone turned to look at the diplomat and began applauding more loudly than ever as four stewards carried the grand prize into the hall: an exceptionally ugly grandfather clock modelled after Big Ben. It was an absolutely appalling construction of carved oak – one and a half times the height of a man, and it must have weighed at least four stone. I thought I caught a glimpse of something like horror in Mr Fandorin's eyes. I must say I cannot blame him.

After that it was impossible to carry on talking, so I came back here to write this letter.

I have the feeling something terrible is about to happen, the noose is tightening around me. But you pursue me in vain, gentlemen, I am ready for you!

However, the hour is already late and it is time to take a reading of our position.

Goodbye, my dear, sweet, infinitely adored Emily.

Your loving

Reginald Milford-Stokes.

Renate Kleber

Renate lay in wait for Watchdog (that was what she had christened Gauche once she discovered what the old fogy was really like) outside his cabin. It was clear from the commissioner's crumpled features and tousled grey hair that he had only just risen from his slumbers – he must have collapsed into bed immediately after lunch and carried on snoozing until the evening.

Renate deftly grabbed hold of the detective's sleeve, lifted herself up on tiptoe and blurted out:

'Wait till you hear what I have to tell you!'

Watchdog gave her a searching look, crossed his arms and said in an unpleasant voice:

'I shall be very interested to hear it. I've been meaning to have a word with you for some time, madam.'

Renate found his tone of voice slightly alarming, but she decided it didn't really mean anything – Watchdog must be suffering from indigestion, or perhaps he'd been having a bad dream.

'I've done your job for you,' Renate boasted, glancing around to make sure no one was listening. 'Let's go into your cabin, we won't be interrupted in there.'

Watchdog's abode was maintained in perfect order. The familiar black file reposed impressively in the centre of the desk with a neat pile of paper and several precisely pointed pencils lying beside it. Renate surveyed the room curiously, turning her head this way and that, noting the shoe brush and tin of wax polish and the shirt collars hung up to dry on a piece of string. The moustache man was obviously rather stingy, he polished his own shoes and did a bit of laundry to avoid having to give the servants any tips.

'Right then, out with it, what have you got for me?' Watchdog growled irritably, clearly displeased by Renate's inquisitiveness.

'I know who the criminal is,' she announced proudly.

This news failed to produce the anticipated effect on the detective. He sighed and asked:

'Who is it?'

'Need you ask? It's so obvious a blind man could see it,' Renate said with an agitated flutter of her hands as she seated herself in an armchair. 'All the newspapers said that the murder was committed by a loony. No normal person could possibly do anything so insane, could they? And now just think about the people we have sitting round our table. It's a choice bunch of course, perfectly matching blooms, bores and freaks every last one of them, but there's only one loony.'

'Are you hinting at the baronet?' asked Watchdog.

'Now you've got it at last!' said Renate with a pitying nod. 'Why, it's as clear as day. Have you seen his eyes when he looks at me? He's a wild beast, a monster! I'm afraid to walk down the corridors. Yesterday I ran into him on the stairs when there wasn't a soul around. It gave me such a twinge here inside!' She put one hand over her belly. 'I've been watching him for a long time. At night he keeps the light on in his cabin and the curtains are tightly closed. But yesterday they were open just a tiny little crack, so I peeped in. He was standing there in the middle of the cabin waving his arms about and making ghastly faces and wagging his finger at somebody. It was so frightening! Later on, in the middle of the night, my migraine started up again, so I went out for a breath of fresh air, and there I saw the loony standing on the forecastle looking up at the moon through some kind of metal contraption. That was when it dawned on me. He's one of those maniacs whose bloodlust rises at full moon. I've read about them! Why are you looking at me as if I were some kind of idiot? Have you taken a look at the calendar recently?' Renate produced a pocket calendar from her purse with a triumphant air. 'Look at this, I've checked it.

On the fifteenth of March, when ten people were killed on the rue de Grenelle, it was a full moon. See, it's written here in black and white: *pleine lune*.'

Watchdog looked all right, but he didn't seem very interested.

'Why are you goggling at it like a dozy owl?' Renate asked angrily. 'Don't you understand that today is a full moon too? While you're sitting around doing nothing, he'll go crazy again and brain somebody else. And I know who it will be – me. He hates me.' Her voice trembled hysterically. 'Everyone on this loathsome steamer wants to kill me! That African attacked me, and that Oriental of ours keeps glaring and grinding his teeth at me and now it's this crazy baronet!'

Watchdog carried on gazing at her with his dull, unblinking eyes, and Renate waved her hand in front of his nose.

'Coo-ee! M. Gauche! Not fallen asleep have you, by any chance?'

The old grandpa grabbed her wrist in a firm grip. He moved her hand aside and said sternly:

'I'll tell you what, my dear. You stop playing the fool. I'll deal with our red-headed baronet, but I want you to tell me about your syringe. And no fairy tales, I want the truth!' He growled so fiercely that she shrank back in alarm.

At supper she sat there staring down into her plate. She always ate with such an excellent appetite, but today she had hardly even touched her sautéed eels. Her eyes were red and swollen and every now and then her lips gave a slight tremor.

But Watchdog was in a genial, even magnanimous mood. He looked at Renate frequently with some severity, but his glance was fatherly rather than hostile. Commissioner Gauche was not as formidable as he would like to appear.

'A very impressive piece,' he said with an envious glance at the Big Ben clock standing in the corner of the saloon. 'Some people have all the luck.'

The monumental prize was too big to fit in Fandorin's cabin and so it had been installed temporarily in Windsor. The oak tower continually ticked, jangled and wheezed deafeningly, and on the hour it boomed out a chime that caught everyone by surprise and made them gasp. At breakfast, when Big Ben informed everyone (with a ten minute delay) that it was nine o'clock, the doctor's wife had almost swallowed a teaspoon. And in addition to all of this, the base of the tower was obviously a bit too narrow and every strong wave set it swaying menacingly. Now, for instance, when the wind had freshened and the white curtains at the windows had begun fluttering in surrender, Big Ben's squeaking had become positively alarming.

The Russian seemed to take the commissioner's genuine admiration for irony and began making apologetic excuses.

'I t-told them to give the clock to fallen women too, but M. Driet was adamant. I swear by Christ, Allah and Buddha that when we g-get to Calcutta I shall leave this monster on the steamer. I won't allow anyone to foist this nightmare on me!'

He squinted anxiously at Lieutenant Renier, who remained diplomatically silent. Then the diplomat turned to Renate for sympathy, but all she gave him in reply was a stern, sullen glance. In the first place, she was in a terribly bad mood, and in the second, Fandorin had been out of favour with her for some time.

There was a story to that.

It all started when Renate noticed that the sickly Mrs Truffo positively blossomed whenever she was near the darling little diplomat. And Mr Fandorin himself seemed to belong to that common variety of handsome males who manage to discover something fascinating in every dull woman they meet and never neglect a single one. In principle, Renate regarded this subspecies of men with respect and actually found them quite attractive. It would be terribly interesting to know what precious ore the blue-eyed, brown-haired Russian had managed to unearth in the dismal doctor's wife. There certainly could be no doubt that he felt a distinct interest in her.

A few days earlier Renate had witnessed an amusing little scene played out by those two actors: Mrs Truffo (in the role of female vamp) and Mr Fandorin (in the role of perfidious seducer). The audience had consisted of one young lady (quite

exceptionally attractive, despite being in a certain delicate condition) concealed behind the tall back of a deckchair and following the action in her make-up mirror. The scene of the action
was set at the stern of the ship. The time was a romantic sunset.
The play was performed in English.

The doctor's wife had executed her lumbering approach to
the diplomat with all the elephantine grace of a typical British
seduction (both dramatis personae were standing at the rail, in
profile towards the aforesaid deckchair). Mrs Truffo began, as
was proper, with the weather:

'The sun is so very bright in these southern latitudes!' she
bleated with passionate feeling.

'Oh yes,' replied Fandorin. 'In Russia at this time of the year
the snow has still not melted, and here the temperature is
already thirty-five degrees Celsius, and that is in the shade. In
the sunlight it is even hotter.'

Now that the preliminaries had been successfully concluded,
Mrs Goatface felt that she could legitimately broach a more
intimate subject.

'I simply don't know what to do!' she began in a modest tone
appropriate to her theme. 'I have such white skin! This intolerable sun will spoil my complexion or even, God forbid, give me
freckles.'

'The problem of f-freckles is one that worries me as well,' the
Russian replied in all seriousness. 'But I was prudent and
brought along a lotion made with extract of Turkish camomile.
Look, my suntan is even and there are no freckles at all.'

The cunning serpent temptingly presented his cute little face
to the respectable married woman.

Mrs Truffo's voice trembled in treacherous betrayal.

'Indeed, not a single freckle . . . And your eyebrows and eyelashes are barely bleached. You have a wonderful epithelium,
Mr Fandorin, quite wonderful!'

Now he'll kiss her, Renate predicted, seeing that the distance
separating the diplomat's epithelium from the flushed features
of the doctor's wife was a mere five centimetres.

But her prediction was mistaken.

Fandorin stepped back and said:

'Epithelium? Are you familiar with the science of physiology?'

'A little,' Mrs Truffo replied modestly. 'Even before I was married I had some involvement with medicine.'

'Indeed? How interesting! You really must t-tell me about it!'

Unfortunately Renate had not been able to follow the performance all the way to its conclusion – a woman she knew had sat down beside her and she had been obliged to abandon her surveillance.

However, this clumsy assault by the doctor's foolish wife had piqued Renate's own vanity. Why should she not try her own charms on this tasty-looking Russian bear cub? Purely out of sporting interest, naturally, and in order to maintain the skills without which no self-respecting woman could get by. Renate had no interest in the thrill of romance. In fact, in her present condition the only feeling that men aroused in her was nausea.

In order to while away the time (Renate's phrase was 'to speed up the voyage') she worked out a simple plan. Small-scale naval manoeuvres, code name Bear Hunt. In fact, of course, men were actually more like the family of canines. Everybody knew that they were primitive creatures who could be divided into three main types: jackals, sheepdogs and gay dogs. There was a different approach for each type.

The jackal fed on carrion – that is, he preferred easy prey. Men of that kind went for availability.

And so the very next time they were alone together, Renate complained to Fandorin about M. Kleber, the tedious banker whose head was full of nothing but figures, the bore who had no time for his young wife. Any halfwit would have realized that here was a woman literally pining away from the tedium of her empty life, ready to swallow any hook, even without bait.

It didn't work, and she had to waste a lot of time parrying inquisitive questions about the bank where her husband worked.

Very well, so next Renate had set her trap for a sheepdog.

This category of men loved weak, helpless women. All they really wanted was to be allowed to rescue and protect you. A fine subspecies, very useful to have around. The main thing here was not to overdo the physical weakness – men were afraid of sick women.

Renate had swooned a couple of times from the heat, slumping gracefully against the ironclad shoulder of her knight and protector. Once she had been unable to open the door of her cabin because the key had got stuck. On the evening of the ball she had asked Fandorin to protect her from a tipsy (and entirely harmless) major of dragoons.

The Russian had lent her his shoulder, opened the door and sent the dragoon packing, but the louse had not betrayed the slightest sign of amorous interest.

Could he really be a gay dog, Renate wondered. You certainly wouldn't think so to look at him. This third type of man was the least complicated, entirely devoid of imagination. Only a coarsely sensual stimulus, such as a chance glimpse of an ankle, had any effect on them. On the other hand, many great men and even cultural luminaries had belonged to precisely this category, so it was certainly worth a try.

With gay dogs the approach was elementary. Renate asked the diplomat to come and see her at precisely midday, so that she could show him her watercolours (which were non-existent). At one minute to 12 the huntress was already standing in front of her mirror, dressed only in her bodice and pantaloons.

When there was a knock at the door she called out:

'Come in, come in. I've been waiting for you!'

Fandorin stepped inside and froze in the doorway. Without turning round, Renate wiggled her bottom at him and displayed her naked back to its best advantage. The wise beauties of the eighteenth century had discovered that it was not a dress open down to the navel that produced the strongest effect on men, but an open neck and a bare back. Obviously the sight of a defenceless spine roused the predatory instinct in the human male.

The diplomat seemed to have been affected. He stood there looking, without turning away. Pleased with the effect, Renate said capriciously:

'What are you doing over there, Jenny? Come here and help me on with my dress. I'm expecting a very important guest any minute.'

How would any normal man have behaved in this situation?

The more audacious kind would have come up behind her without saying a word and kissed the soft curls on the back of her neck.

The average, fair-to-middling kind would have handed her the dress and giggled bashfully.

At that point Renate would have decided the hunt had been successfully completed. She would have pretended to be embarrassed, thrown the insolent lout out and lost all further interest in him. But Fandorin's response was unusual.

'It's not Jenny,' he said in a repulsively calm voice. 'It is I, Erast Fandorin. I shall wait outside while you g-get dressed.'

He was either one of a rare, seduction-proof variety or a secret pervert. If it was the latter, the Englishwomen were simply wasting their time and effort. But Renate's keen eye had not detected any of the characteristic signs of perversion. Apart, that was, from a strange predilection for secluded conversation with Watchdog.

But this was all trivial nonsense. She had more serious reasons for being upset.

At the very moment when Renate finally decided to plunge her fork into the cold sautée, the doors crashed open and the bespectacled professor burst into the dining room. He always looked a little crazy – either his jacket was buttoned crookedly or his shoelaces were undone – but today he looked a real fright: his beard was dishevelled, his tie had slipped over to one side, his eyes were bulging out of his head and there was one of his braces dangling from under the flap of his jacket. Obviously something quite extraordinary must have happened. Renate instantly forgot her own troubles and stared curiously at the learned scarecrow.

Sweetchild spread his arms like a ballet dancer and shouted:

'Eureka, gentlemen! The mystery of the Emerald Rajah is solved!'

'Oh no,' groaned Mrs Truffo. 'Not again!'

'Now I can see how it all fits together,' said the professor, launching abruptly into an incoherent explanation. 'After all, I was in the place, why didn't I think of it before? I kept thinking about it, going round and round in circles, but it just didn't add up. In Aden I received a telegram from an acquaintance of mine in the French Ministry of the Interior and he confirmed my suspicions, but I still couldn't make any sense of the eye, and I couldn't work out who it could be. That is, I more or less know who, but how? How was it done? And now it has suddenly dawned on me!' He ran over to the window. A curtain fluttering in the wind enveloped him like a white shroud, and the professor impatiently pushed it aside. 'I was standing at the window of my cabin knotting my tie and I saw the waves, crest after crest all the way to the horizon. And then suddenly it hit me! Everything fell into place – about the shawl, and about the son! It's a piece of simple clerical work. Dig around in the registers at the École Maritime and you'll find him!'

'I don't understand a word,' growled Watchdog. 'You're raving. What's this about some school or other?'

'Oh no, this is very, very interesting,' exclaimed Renate. 'I simply adore trying to solve mysteries. But my dear professor, this will never do. Sit down at the table, have some wine, catch your breath and tell us everything from the beginning, calmly and clearly. After all, you have such a wonderful way with a story. But first someone must bring me my shawl, so that I don't catch a chill from this draught.'

'Let me close the windows on the windward side, and the draught will stop immediately,' Sweetchild suggested. 'You are right, madam, I should tell you the whole thing starting from the beginning.'

'No, don't close the windows, it will be too stuffy. Well, gentlemen?' Renate inquired capriciously. 'Who will fetch my shawl from my cabin? Here is the key! Monsieur baronet?'

Of course, the Ginger Lunatic did not stir, but Renier jumped to his feet.

'Professor, I implore you, do not start without me!' he said. 'I shall be back in a moment.'

'And I'll go and get my knitting,' sighed the doctor's wife.

She got back first and began deftly clacking away with her needles. She waved her hand at her husband to tell him there was no need to translate.

Meanwhile Sweetchild was readying himself for his moment of triumph. Having taken Renate's advice to heart, he seemed determined to expound his discoveries as spectacularly as possible.

There was absolute silence at the table, with everyone watching the speaker and following every movement he made.

Sweetchild took a sip of red wine and began walking backwards and forwards across the room. Then he halted, picturesquely posed in profile to his audience, and began:

'I have already told you about that unforgettable day when Rajah Bagdassar invited me into his palace in Brahmapur. It was a quarter of a century ago, but I remember everything quite clearly, down to the smallest detail. The first thing that struck me was the appearance of the palace. Knowing that Bagdassar was one of the richest men in the world, I had been expecting to see oriental luxury on a grand scale. But there was nothing of the kind. The palace buildings were rather modest, without any ornamental refinements. And the thought came to me that the passion for precious stones that was hereditary in this family, handed down from father to son, must have displaced every other vainglorious ambition. Why spend money on walls of marble if you could buy another sapphire or diamond? The Brahmapur palace was squat and plain, essentially the same kind of clay casket as that in which that indescribable distillation of magical luminescence was kept. No marble and alabaster could ever have rivalled the blinding radiance of those stones.'

The professor took another sip of wine and adopted a thoughtful pose.

Renier arrived, puffing and panting, respectfully laid Renate's shawl across her shoulders and remained standing beside her.

'What was that about marble and alabaster?' he asked in a whisper.

'It's about the Brahmapur palace, let me listen,' said Renate with an impatient jerk of her chin.

'The interior decor of the palace was also very simple,' Sweetchild continued. 'Over the centuries the halls and rooms had changed their appearance many times, and the only part of the palace that seemed interesting to me from a historical point of view was the upper level, consisting of four halls, each of which faced one of the points of the compass. At one time the halls had been open galleries, but during the last century they were glassed in. At the same time the walls were decorated with quite fascinating frescos depicting the mountains that surround the valley on all sides. The landscape is reproduced with astonishing realism, so that the mountains seem to be reflected in a mirror. From the philosophical point of view, this mirror imaging must surely represent the duality of existence and . . .'

Somewhere nearby a ship's bell began clanging loudly. They heard people shouting and a woman screaming.

'My God, it's the fire alarm!' shouted the lieutenant, dashing for the door. 'That's all we needed!'

They all dashed after him in a tight bunch.

'What's happening?' the startled Mrs Truffo inquired in English. 'Have we been boarded by pirates?'

Renate sat there for a moment with her mouth open, then let out a blood-curdling squeal. She grabbed the tail of the commissioner's coat and stopped him running out after the others.

'Monsieur Gauche, don't leave me!' she begged him. 'I know what a fire on board ship means, I've read about it! Now everyone will dash to the lifeboats and people will be crushed to death, and I'm a weak pregnant woman, I'll just be swept aside! Promise you will look after me!'

'What's that about lifeboats?' the old grandpa mumbled anxiously. 'What kind of nonsense is that! I've been told the fire-fighting arrangements on the *Leviathan* are exemplary. Why, the ship even has its own fire officer. Stop shaking will you, everything will be all right.' He tried to free himself, but Renate was clutching his coat-tail in a grip of iron. Her teeth were chattering loudly.

'Let go of me, little girl,' Watchdog said in a soothing voice. 'I won't go anywhere. I'll just take a look at the deck through the window.'

But no, Renate's fingers didn't release their grip.

The commissioner was proved right. After two or three minutes there was the sound of leisurely footsteps and loud voices in the corridor and one by one the Windsorites began to return.

They had still not recovered from their shock, so they were laughing a lot and talking more loudly than usual.

The first to come in were Clarissa Stamp, the Truffos and Renier, whose face was flushed.

'It was nothing at all,' the lieutenant announced. 'Someone threw a burning cigar into a litter bin with an old newspaper in it. The fire spread to a door curtain, but the sailors were alert and they put the flames out in a moment . . . But I see that you were all prepared for a shipwreck,' he said with a laugh, glancing significantly at Clarissa.

She was clutching her purse and a bottle of orangeade.

'Well, orangeade, in order not to die of thirst in the middle of the ocean,' Renier guessed. 'But what is the purse for? You wouldn't have much use for it in the lifeboat.'

Renate giggled hysterically and Miss Old Maid, embarrassed, put the bottle back on the table. The Truffos were also well equipped: the doctor had managed to grab his bag of medical instruments and his wife was clutching a blanket against her breast.

'This is the Indian Ocean, madam, you would hardly have frozen to death,' Renier said with a serious expression, and the stupid goat nodded her head imbecilically.

The Japanese appeared holding a pathetic, bright-coloured bundle . . . what could he have in there, a travelling hara-kiri kit?

The Lunatic came in looking dishevelled, clutching a small box, the kind normally used for holding writing instruments.

'Who were you planning to write to, Mr Milford-Stokes? Ah, I understand! When Miss Stamp had drunk her orangeade, we could have stuck a letter in the bottle and sent it floating off across the ocean waves,' suggested the lieutenant, who was obviously acting so jovially out of a sense of relief.

Now everyone was there except the professor and the diplomat.

'M. Sweetchild is no doubt packing his scholarly works, and monsieur le russe is putting on the samovar for a final cup of tea,' said Renate, infected by the lieutenant's jolly mood.

And there was the Russian, speak of the devil. He stood by the door, with his handsome face as dark as a storm cloud.

'Well, M. Fandorin, have you decided to take your prize with you in the boat?' Renate inquired provocatively.

Everyone roared with laughter, but the Russian (even though it was rather witty) failed to appreciate the joke.

'Commissioner Gauche,' he said quietly. 'Would you be so kind as to step out into the corridor. As quickly as you can.'

It was strange, but when he spoke these words the diplomat did not stammer once. Perhaps the nervous shock had cured him? Such things did happen.

Renate was on the point of joking about that too, but she bit her tongue. That would probably have been going too far.

'What's all the hurry?' Watchdog asked gruffly. 'Another teller of tales. Later, young man, later. First I want to hear the rest of what the professor has to say. Where has he got to?'

Fandorin looked at the commissioner expectantly, but when he realized that the old man was feeling obstinate and had no intention of going out into the corridor, he shrugged and said:

'The professor will not be joining us.'

Gauche scowled.

'And why would that be?'

'What do you mean, he won't be joining us?' Renate put in. 'He stopped just when it was getting interesting! That's not fair!'

'Professor Sweetchild has just been murdered,' the diplomat announced coolly.

'What's that?' Watchdog roared. 'Murdered? What do you mean, murdered?'

'I believe it was done with a surgical scalpel,' the Russian replied with remarkable composure. 'His throat was cut very precisely.'

Commissioner Gauche

'Are they ever going to let us go ashore?' Mme Kleber asked plaintively. 'Everyone else is out strolling round Bombay, and we're just sitting here doing nothing . . .'

The curtains were pulled across the windows to keep out the searing rays of the sun that scorched the deck and made the air sticky and suffocating. But although it was hot and stuffy in the Windsor saloon, everyone sat there patiently, waiting for the truth to be revealed.

Gauche took out his watch – a presentation piece with a profile portrait of Napoleon III – and replied vaguely:

'Soon, ladies and gentlemen. I'll let you out soon. But not all of you.'

At least he knew what he was waiting for: Inspector Jackson and his men were conducting a search. The murder weapon itself was probably lying at the bottom of the ocean, but some clues might have been left. They must have been left. Of course, there was plenty of circumstantial evidence anyway, but hard evidence always made a case look more respectable. It was about time Jackson put in an appearance . . .

The *Leviathan* had reached Bombay at dawn. Since the evening of the previous day all the Windsorites had been confined to their cabins under house arrest, and immediately the ship arrived in port Gauche had contacted the authorities, informed them of his own conclusions and requested their assistance. They had sent Jackson and a team of constables. Come on, Jackson, get a move on, thought Gauche, wishing the inspector would stop dragging his feet. After a sleepless night the commissioner's head felt as heavy as lead and his liver had started playing up, but despite everything he was feeling rather pleased with himself. He had finally unravelled the knots in the tangled thread, and now he could see where it led.

At half past eight, after finalizing his arrangements with the local police and spending some time at the telegraph office, Gauche had ordered the detainees to be assembled in the Windsor saloon – it would be more convenient for the search. He hadn't even made an exception for Renate, who had been sitting beside him at the time of the murder and could not possibly have cut the professor's throat. The commissioner had been watching over his prisoners for more than three hours now, occupying a strategic position in the deep armchair opposite his *client*, and there were two armed policemen standing outside the door of the saloon, where they could not be seen from inside.

The detainees were all too sweaty and nervous to make conversation. Renier dropped in from time to time, nodded sympathetically to Renate and went off again about his business. The captain looked in twice, but he didn't say anything, just gave the commissioner a savage glance – as if this whole mess was papa Gauche's fault!

The professor's deserted chair was like the gap left by a missing tooth. The Indologist himself was lying ashore, in the chilly vaults of the Bombay municipal morgue. The thought of the dark shadows and the blocks of ice almost made Gauche envy the dead man. Lying there, with all his troubles behind him, with no sweat-drenched collar cutting into his neck . . .

The commissioner looked at Dr Truffo, who did not seem very comfortable either: the sweat was streaming down his olive-skinned face and his English Fury kept whispering in his ear.

'Why are you looking at me like that, monsieur!' Truffo exploded when he caught the policeman's glance. 'Why do you keep staring at me? It's absolutely outrageous! What right do you have? I've been a respectable medical practitioner for fifteen years . . .' he almost sobbed. 'What difference does it make if a scalpel was used? Anyone could have done it!'

'Was it really done with a scalpel?' Mlle Stamp asked timidly.

It was the first time anyone in the saloon had mentioned what had happened.

'Yes, only a very good quality scalpel produces such a clean incision,' Truffo replied angrily. 'I inspected the body. Someone obviously grabbed Sweetchild from behind, put one hand over his mouth and slit his throat with the other. The wall of the corridor is splattered with blood, just above the height of a man. That's because his head was pulled back . . .'

'No great strength would have been required, then?' asked the Russian. 'The element of surprise would have b-been enough?'

The doctor gave a despondent shrug.

'I don't know, monsieur. I've never tried it.'

Aha, at last! The door half-opened and the inspector's bony features appeared in the gap. The inspector beckoned to the commissioner, who grunted with the effort of hoisting himself out of the armchair.

There was a pleasant surprise waiting for the commissioner in the corridor. Everything had worked out quite splendidly! A thorough job, efficient and elegant. Solid enough to bring the jury in straight away, no lawyer would ever demolish evidence like that. Good old papa Gauche, he could still give any young whippersnapper a hundred points' start. And well done Jackson for his hard work!

The four of them went back into the saloon together: the captain, Renier and Jackson, with Gauche bringing up the rear. At this stage he was feeling so pleased with himself that he even started humming a little tune. And his liver had stopped bothering him.

'Well, ladies and gentlemen, this is it,' Gauche announced cheerfully, walking out into the very centre of the saloon. He put his hands behind his back and swayed on his heels. It was a pleasant feeling to know you were a figure of some importance, even, in your own way, a ruler of destinies. The road had been long and hard, but he had reached the end at last. Now for the most enjoyable part.

'Papa Gauche has certainly had to rack his old brains, but an old hunting dog will always sniff out the fox's den, no matter how confused the trail might be. By murdering Professor Sweetchild our criminal has finally given himself away. It was an act of despair. I believe that under questioning the murderer will tell me all about the Indian shawl and many other things as well. Incidentally, I should like to thank our Russian diplomat who, without even knowing it, helped to set me on the right track with several of his comments and questions.'

In his moment of triumph Gauche could afford to be magnanimous. He nodded condescendingly to Fandorin, who bowed his head without speaking. What a pain these aristocrats were, with all their airs and graces, always so arrogant, you could never get a civil word out of them.

'I shall not be travelling with you any further. Thanks for the company, as they say, but all things in moderation. The murderer will also be going ashore: I shall hand him over to Inspector Jackson in a moment, here on board the ship.'

Everyone in the saloon looked warily at the morose, skinny Englishman standing there with his hands in his pockets.

'I am very glad this nightmare is over,' said Captain Cliff. 'I realize you have had to put up with a lot of unpleasantness, but it has all been sorted out now. The head steward will find you places in different saloons if you wish. I hope that the remainder of your cruise on board the *Leviathan* will help you to forget this sad business.'

'Hardly,' said Mme Kleber, answering for all of them. 'This whole experience has been far too upsetting for all of us! But please don't keep us in suspense, monsieur Commissioner, tell us quickly who the murderer is.'

The captain was about to add something to what he had said, but Gauche raised his hand to stop him. This time he had earned the right to a solo performance.

'I must confess that at first my list of suspects included every single one of you. The process of elimination was long and difficult, but now I can reveal the most crucial point: beside

Lord Littleby's body we discovered one of the *Leviathan*'s gold emblems – this one here.' He tapped the badge on his own lapel. 'This little trinket belongs to the murderer. As you know, a gold badge could only have been worn by a senior officer of the ship or a first-class passenger. The officers were immediately eliminated from the list of suspects, because they all had their badges in place and no one had requested the shipping line to issue a new emblem to replace one that had been lost. But among the passengers there were four individuals who were not wearing a badge. Mlle Stamp, Mme Kleber, M. Milford-Stokes and M. Aono. I have kept this quartet under particularly close observation. Dr Truffo found himself here because he is a doctor, Mrs Truffo because husband and wife must not be set asunder, and our Russian diplomat because of his snobbish disinclination to appear like a caretaker.'

The commissioner lit his pipe and started pacing around the salon.

'I have erred, I confess. At the very beginning I suspected monsieur le baronet, but I received timely information concerning his . . . circumstances, and selected a different target. You, madam!' Gauche swung round to face Miss Stamp.

'As I observed,' she replied coldly. 'But I really cannot see what made me appear so suspicious.'

'Oh, come now!' said Gauche, surprised. 'In the first place, everything about you indicates that you suddenly became rich only very recently. That in itself is already highly suspicious. In the second place, you lied about never having been in Paris, even though the words Hôtel Ambassadeur are written on your fan in letters of gold. Of course, you stopped carrying the fan, but old Gauche has sharp eyes. I spotted that trinket of yours straight away. It is the sort of thing that expensive hotels give to their guests as mementoes of their stay. The Ambassador happens to stand on the rue de Grenelle, only five minutes' walk from the scene of the crime. It is a luxurious hotel, very large, and all sorts of people stay in it, so why is the mademoiselle being so secretive, I asked myself. There is something not right here. And I found I couldn't get the idea of Marie Sanfon out of my head . . .' The commissioner smiled disarmingly at Clarissa Stamp. 'Well, I was casting around in the dark for a while, but eventually I hit upon the right trail, so I offer my apologies, mademoiselle.'

Gauche suddenly noticed that the red-headed baronet had turned as white as a sheet: his jaw was trembling and his green eyes were glaring at the commissioner balefully.

'What precisely do you mean by . . . my "circumstances"?' he said slowly, choking on the words in his fury. 'What are you implying, mister detective?'

'Come, come,' said Gauche, raising a conciliatory hand. 'Above all else, you must remain calm. You must not become agitated. Your circumstances are your circumstances and they are no one else's business. I only mentioned them to indicate that you no longer figure among my potential suspects. Where is your emblem, by the way?'

'I threw it away,' the baronet replied gruffly, his eyes still looking daggers at Gauche. 'It's repulsive! It looks like a golden leech! And . . .'

'And it was not fitting for the baronet Milford-Stokes to wear the same kind of nameplate as a rag-tag bunch of nouveaux riches, was it?' the commissioner remarked shrewdly. 'Yet another snob.'

Mlle Stamp also seemed to have taken offence.

'Commissioner, your description of exactly what it is that makes me such a suspicious character was most illuminating. Thank you,' she said acidly, with a jerk of her pointed chin. 'You have indeed tempered justice with mercy.'

'When we were still in Aden I sent a number of questions to the préfecture by telegram. I could not wait for the replies because the inquiries that had to be made took some time, but there were several messages waiting for me in Bombay. One of them concerned you, mademoiselle. Now I know that from the age of fourteen, when your parents died, you lived in the country with a female cousin of your mother. She was rich, but miserly. She treated you, her companion, like a slave and kept you on little more than bread and water.'

The Englishwoman blushed and seemed to regret ever having made her comment. Now, my sweet little bird, thought Gauche, let us see how deeply you blush at what comes next!

'A couple of months ago the old woman died and you discovered she had left her entire estate to you. It is hardly surprising that after so many years under lock and key you should want to get out and travel a bit, to see the world. I expect you had never seen anything of life except in books?'

'But why did she conceal the fact that she visited Paris?' Mme Kleber interrupted rudely. 'Because her hotel was on the street where all those people were killed? She was afraid you would suspect her, was that it?'

'No,' laughed Gauche. 'That was not it. Having suddenly become rich, Mlle Stamp acted as any other woman would have done in her place – the first thing she did was to visit Paris, the capital of the world. To admire the beautiful sights of Paris, to dress in the latest Paris fashion and also, well . . . for romantic adventures.'

The Englishwoman had clenched her fingers together nervously, she was gazing at Gauche imploringly, but nothing was going to stop him now – this fine lady should have known better than to look down her nose at a commissioner of the Paris police.

'Miss Stamp found romance in plenty. In the Ambassador Hotel she made the acquaintance of an exceptionally suave and handsome gentleman, who is listed in the police files under the name of the Vampire. A shady character who specializes in rich, ageing foreign women. The flames of passion were ignited instantly and – as always happens with the Vampire – they were extinguished without warning. One morning, on the thirteenth of March to be exact, madam, you woke alone and forlorn in a hotel room that you could barely recognize because it was so empty. Your friend had made off with everything except the furniture. They sent me a list of the items that were stolen from you.' Gauche glanced into his file. 'Number thirty-eight on the list is "a golden brooch in the form of a whale". When I read that, I began to understand why Miss Stamp does not like to remember Paris.'

The foolish woman was a pitiful sight now – she had covered her face with her hands and her shoulders were heaving.

'I have never really suspected Mme Kleber,' said Gauche, moving on to the next point on his agenda, 'even though she was unable to give a clear explanation of why she had no emblem.'

'But why did you ignore what I told you?' the Japanese butted in. 'I told you something very important.'

'I didn't ignore it!' The commissioner swung round to face the speaker. 'Far from it. I had a word with Mme Kleber and she gave me an explanation that accounted for everything. She suffered so badly during the first stage of pregnancy that her doctor prescribed . . . certain sedative substances. Afterwards the painful symptoms passed, but the poor woman had already become habituated to the medication, which she took for her nerves and insomnia. She was taking larger and larger doses and the habit was threatening to get out of hand. I had a fatherly word with Mme Kleber and afterwards, under my watchful eye, she threw the vile narcotic into the sea.' Gauche cast a glance of feigned severity at Renate, who had stuck out her lower lip like a sulky child. 'Remember, my dear, you promised papa Gauche on your word of honour.'

Renate lowered her eyes and nodded.

Clarissa erupted. 'Ah, what touching concern for Mme Kleber! Why could you not spare my blushes, monsieur detective? You have humiliated me in front of the entire company.'

But the commissioner had no time for her now – he was still gazing at the Japanese, and his gaze was grave and unrelenting. The quick-witted Jackson understood, without having to be told, that it was time. There was a funereal gleam of burnished steel as he took his hand out of his pocket. He held the revolver with the barrel pointing straight at the Oriental's forehead.

'I believe that you Japanese think of us as ginger-haired monkeys?' Gauche said in a hostile voice. 'I've heard that's what you call Europeans. We are hairy barbarians and you are cunning, subtle and so highly cultured. White people are not even fit to lick your boots.' The commissioner puffed out his cheeks sarcastically and blew a thick cloud of smoke out to one side. 'Killing ten monkeys means nothing to you, you don't even think of it as wrong.'

Aono sat there tense and still. His face was like stone.

'You accuse me of killing Lord Littleby and his vassals . . . that is, servants?' the Oriental asked in a flat, lifeless voice. 'Why do you accuse me?'

'For every possible reason criminal science has to offer, my dear chap,' the commissioner declared. Then he turned away from the Japanese, because the speech he was about to make was not intended for this yellow dog, it was intended for History. The time would come when they would print it in the textbooks on criminology!

'First, gentlemen, allow me to present the circumstantial evidence indicating that this person *could have* committed the crimes of which I accuse him.' (Ah, but he shouldn't be giving this speech to an audience of ten people, he should be addressing a packed hall in the Palais de Justice!) 'And then I shall present to you the evidence which demonstrates beyond all possible doubt that M. Aono not only could have, but actually *did* murder eleven people – ten on the fifteenth of March on the rue de Grenelle and one yesterday, the fourteenth of April, on board the steamer *Leviathan*.'

As he spoke, an empty space formed around Aono. The Russian was the only one left sitting beside the prisoner, and the inspector was standing just behind him with his revolver at the ready.

'I hope nobody here has any doubt that the death of Professor Sweetchild is directly connected with the crime on the rue de Grenelle. As our investigation has demonstrated, the goal of that murder most foul was to steal, not the golden Shiva, but the silk shawl . . .' Gauche scowled sternly, as if to say: *Yes, indeed, the investigation has established the facts, so you can stop making that wry face, monsieur diplomat. '. . .* which is the key to the hidden treasure of the rajah of Brahmapur, Bagdassar. We do not yet know how the accused came to learn the secret of the shawl, and we are all aware that the Orient holds many impenetrable mysteries for our European minds. However, the deceased professor, a genuine connoisseur of oriental culture, had succeeded in solving this mystery. He was on the point of sharing his discovery with us when the fire alarm was sounded. Fate itself had sent the criminal a golden opportunity to stop Sweetchild's mouth for ever. Afterwards all would be silence again, just like at the rue de Grenelle. But the killer failed to take into account one very important circumstance: this time Commissioner Gauche was on hand, and he is not one to be trifled with. It was a risky move, but it might have worked. The criminal knew that the scholar would dash straight to his cabin to save his papers, that is, his manuscripts. It was there, concealed by the bend in the corridor, that the murderer committed his foul deed. And there we have the first piece of circumstantial evidence . . .' the commissioner raised a finger to emphasize his point '. . . M. Aono ran out of the salon and therefore he could have committed this murder.'

'Not only I,' said the Japanese. 'Six other people ran out of the salon: M. Renier, M. and Mme Truffo, M. Fandorin, M. Milford-Stokes and Mlle Stamp.'

'Correct,' Gauche agreed. 'But I merely wished to demonstrate to the jury, by which I mean the present company, the connection between these two crimes, and also that you *could have* committed yesterday's murder. Now let us return to the "Crime of the Century". M. Aono was in Paris at the time, a fact of which there can be no doubt, and which is confirmed by a telegram that I recently received.'

'One and a half million other people were also in Paris,' the Japanese interjected.

'Perhaps, but nonetheless we now have our second piece of circumstantial evidence,' said Gauche.

'Too circumstantial by far,' put in the Russian.

'I won't dispute that.' Gauche tipped some tobacco into his pipe before he made his next move. 'However, the fatal injections were administered to Lord Littleby's servants by a medic of some sort, and there are certainly not one and a half million medics in Paris, are there?'

No one contested that, but Captain Cliff asked:

'True, what of it?'

'Ah, monsieur capitaine,' said Gauche, his eyes flashing brightly, 'the point is that our friend Aono here is not a military man, as he introduced himself to all of us, but a qualified surgeon, a recent graduate from the medical faculty at the Sorbonne! I learned that from the same telegram.'

A pause for effect. A muffled hum of voices in the hall of the Palais de Justice, the rustling of the newspaper artists' pencils on their sketchpads: 'Commissioner Gauche Plays His Trump Card.' Ah, but you must wait for the ace, my friends, the ace is yet to come.

'And now, ladies and gentlemen, we move from circumstantial evidence to hard facts. Let M. Aono explain why he, a doctor, a member of a respected and prestigious profession, found it necessary to pose as an army officer. Why such deception?'

A drop of sweat slithered down the waxen face of the Japanese. Aono said nothing. He certainly hadn't taken long to run out of steam!

'There is only one answer: he did it to divert suspicion from himself. The murderer was a doctor!' the commissioner summed up complacently. 'And that brings us to our second piece of hard evidence. Gentlemen, have you ever heard of Japanese boxing?'

'I've not only heard of it, I've seen it,' said the captain. 'One time in Macao I saw a Japanese navigator beat three American sailors senseless. He was a puny little tyke, you'd have thought you could blow him over, but you should have seen the way he skipped about and flung his arms and legs around. He laid three hulking whalers out flat. He hit one of them on the arm with the edge of his hand and twisted the elbow the other way. Broke the bone, can you imagine? That was some blow!'

Gauche nodded smugly.

'I have also heard that the Japanese possess the secret of killing with their bare hands in combat. They can easily kill a man with a simple jab of the finger. We have all seen M. Aono practising his gymnastics. Fragments of a shattered gourd – a remarkably hard gourd – were discovered under the bed in his cabin. And there were several whole ones in a sack. The accused obviously used them for perfecting the precision and strength of his blow. I cannot even imagine how strong a man must be to smash a hard gourd with his bare hand, and into several pieces . . .'

The commissioner surveyed his assembled audience before introducing his second piece of evidence.

'Let me remind you, ladies and gentlemen, that the skull of the unfortunate Lord Littleby was shattered into several fragments by an exceptionally strong blow with a blunt object. Now would you please observe the calluses on the hands of the accused.'

The Japanese snatched his small, sinewy hands off the table.

'Don't take your eyes off him, Jackson. He is very dangerous,' warned Gauche. 'If he tries anything, shoot him in the leg or the shoulder. Now let me ask M. Aono what he did with his gold emblem. Well, have you nothing to say? Then let me answer the question myself: the emblem was torn from your chest by Lord Littleby at the very moment when you struck him a fatal blow to the head with the edge of your hand!'

Aono half-opened his mouth, as though he was about to say something, but he only bit his lip with his strong, slightly crooked teeth and closed his eyes. His face took on a strange, detached expression.

'And so, the picture that emerges of the crime on the rue de Grenelle is as follows,' said Gauche, starting his summing-up. 'On the evening of the fifteenth of March, Gintaro Aono went to

Lord Littleby's mansion with the premeditated intention of killing everyone in the house and taking possession of the triangular shawl from the owner's collection. At that time he already had a ticket for the *Leviathan*, which was due to sail for India from Southampton four days later. The defendant was obviously intending to search for the Brahmapur treasure in India. We do not know how he managed to persuade the unfortunate servants to submit to an "inoculation against cholera". It is very probable that the accused showed them some kind of forged document from the mayor's office. That would have been entirely convincing because, as I have been informed by telegram, medical students from the final year at the Sorbonne are quite often employed in prophylactic public health programmes. There are quite a lot of Orientals among the students and interns at the university, so the evening caller's yellow skin was unlikely to alarm the servants. The most monstrous aspect of the crime is the infernal callousness with which two innocent children were murdered. I have considerable personal experience of dealing with the scum of society, ladies and gentlemen. In a fit of rage a criminal thug may toss a baby into a fire, but to kill with such cold calculation, with hands that do not even tremble . . . You must agree, gentlemen, that is not the French way, indeed it is not the European way.'

'That's right!' exclaimed Renier, incensed, and Dr Truffo supported him wholeheartedly.

'After that everything was very simple,' Gauche continued. 'Once he was sure that the poisonous injections had plunged the servants into a sleep from which they would never wake, the murderer walked calmly up the stairs to the second floor and into the hall where the collection was kept, and there he began helping himself to what he wanted. After all, he was certain that the master of the house was away. But an attack of gout had prevented Lord Littleby from travelling to Spa and he was still at home. The sound of breaking glass brought him out into the hall, where he was murdered in a most barbarous manner. It was this unplanned murder that shattered the killer's diabolical composure. He had almost certainly planned to take several items from the collection in order not to draw attention to the celebrated shawl, but now he had to hurry. We do not know, but perhaps his Lordship called out before he died and the killer was afraid his cries had been heard in the street. For whatever reason, he took only a golden Shiva that he did not need and beat a hasty retreat, without even noticing that his *Leviathan* badge had been left behind in the hand of his victim. In order to throw the police off the scent, Aono left the house through the window of the conservatory . . . No, that was not the reason!' Gauche slapped himself on the forehead. 'Why did I not think of it before? He could not go back the way he had come if his victim had cried out! For all he knew, passers-by were already gathering at the door of the mansion! That was why Aono smashed the window in the conservatory, jumped down into the garden and then made his escape over the fence. But he need not have been so careful – at that late hour the rue de Grenelle was empty. If there were any cries, no one heard them . . .'

The impressionable Mme Kleber sobbed. Mrs Truffo listened to her husband's translation and blew her nose with feeling.

Clear, convincing and unassailable, thought Gauche. The evidence and the investigative hypotheses reinforce each other perfectly. And old papa Gauche still hasn't finished with you yet.

'This is the appropriate moment to consider the death of Professor Sweetchild. As the accused has quite rightly observed, in theory the murder could have been committed by six other people apart from himself. Please, do not be alarmed, ladies and gentlemen!' The commissioner raised a reassuring hand. 'I shall now prove that you did not kill the professor and that he was in fact killed by our Japanese friend here.'

The blasted Japanese had completely turned to stone. Was he asleep? Or was he praying to his Japanese god? Pray as much as you like, my lad, that old slut Mme Guillotine will still have your head!

Suddenly the commissioner was struck by an extremely unpleasant thought. What if the English nabbed the Japanese

for the murder of Sweetchild? The professor was a British subject after all. Then the criminal would be tried in an English
court and he would end up on a British gallows instead of a
French guillotine! Anything but that! The 'Crime of the Century' could not be tried abroad! The trial must be held in the
Palais de Justice and nowhere else! Sweetchild may have been
killed on board an English ship, but there were ten bodies in
Paris and only one here. And in any case the ship wasn't entirely
British property, there were two partners in the consortium!

Gauche was so upset that he lost track of his argument. Not
on your life, he thought to himself, you will not have my client.
I'll put an end to this farce and then go straight to the French
consul. I'll take the murderer to France myself. And immediately he could see it: the crowded quayside, the police
cordons, the journalists . . .

But first the case had to be brought to a conclusion.

'Now Inspector Jackson will tell us what was found when the
defendant's cabin was searched.'

Gauche gestured to Jackson to say his piece.

Jackson launched into a monotonous rigmarole in English,
but the commissioner soon put a stop to that:

'This investigation is being conducted by the French police,'
he said sternly, 'and the official language of this inquiry is also
French. Apart from which, monsieur, not everyone here understands your language. And most importantly of all, I am not sure
that the accused knows English. And you must admit that he has
a right to know the results of your search.'

The protest was made as a matter of principle, in order to put
the English in their place from the very beginning. They had to
realize that they were the junior partners in this business.

Renier volunteered to act as interpreter. He stood beside the
inspector and translated phrase by phrase, enlivening the Englishman's flat, truncated sentences with his own dramatic
intonation and expressive gestures.

'Acting on instructions received, a search was carried out. In
cabin number twenty-four. The passenger's name is Gintaro

Aono. We acted in accordance with the Regulations for the Conduct of a Search in a Confined Space. A rectangular room with a floor area of two hundred square feet. Was divided into twenty squares horizontally and forty-four squares vertically.' The lieutenant asked what that meant and then explained to the others. 'Apparently the walls also have to be divided into squares – they tap on them in order to identify secret hiding places. Although I can't see how there could be any secret hiding places in a steamship cabin . . . The search was conducted in strict sequence: first vertically, then horizontally. No hiding places were discovered in the walls . . .' At this point Renier gave an exaggerated shrug, as if to say: who would ever have thought it? 'During the examination of the horizontal plane. The following items relevant to the case were discovered. Item one: notes in a hieroglyphic script. They will be translated and studied. Item two: a long dagger of oriental appearance with an extremely sharp blade. Item three: a sack containing eleven Egyptian gourds. And finally, item four: a bag for carrying surgical instruments. The compartment for holding a large scalpel is empty.'

The audience gasped. The Japanese opened his eyes and glanced briefly at the commissioner, but still did not speak.

He's going to crack any moment, thought Gauche, but he was wrong. Without getting up off his chair, the Oriental swung round to face the inspector standing behind him and struck the hand holding the revolver a sharp blow from below. While the gun was still describing a picturesque arc through the air, the athletic Japanese had already reached the door, but when he jerked it open the two policemen standing outside jammed the barrels of their Colts into his chest. A split second later the inspector's weapon completed its trajectory, crashed onto the centre of the table and detonated with a deafening roar. There was a jangling sound and the air was filled with smoke. Someone screamed.

Gauche quickly summed up the situation: the prisoner was backing towards the table; Mrs Truffo was in a dead faint; there seemed to be no other casualties; there was a hole in Big Ben just below the dial and its hands weren't moving. The clock was jangling. The ladies were screaming. But in general the situation was under control.

The Japanese was returned to his seat and shackled with handcuffs; the doctor's wife was revived and everyone went back to their places. The commissioner smiled and began talking again, demonstrating his superior presence of mind.

'Gentlemen of the jury, you have just witnessed a scene that amounts to a confession of guilt, even though it was played out in a somewhat unusual manner.'

He'd made that slip about the jury again, but he didn't bother to correct himself. After all, this was his dress rehearsal.

'As the final piece of evidence, it could not possibly have been more conclusive,' Gauche summed up smugly. 'And you, Jackson, may consider yourself reprimanded. I told you that he was dangerous.'

The inspector was as scarlet as a boiled crayfish. That would teach him.

All in all, everything had turned out quite excellently.

The Japanese sat there with three guns pointing at him, pressing his shackled hands to his chest. He had closed his eyes again.

'That is all, Inspector. You can take him away. He can be kept in your lock-up for the time being. When all the formalities have been completed, I shall take him to France. Goodbye, ladies and gentlemen, old papa Gauche is disembarking, I wish you all a pleasant journey.'

'I am afraid, Commissioner, that you will have to travel with us a little further,' the Russian said in that monotonous voice of his.

For a moment Gauche thought he had misheard.

'Eh?'

'Mr Aono is not guilty of anything, so the investigation will have to be continued.'

The expression on Gauche's face must have looked extremely stupid – wildly staring eyes and bright scarlet cheeks . . .

Before the outburst of fury came, the Russian continued with quite astonishing self-assurance:

'Captain, on b-board ship you are the supreme authority. The commissioner has just acted out a mock trial in which he took the part of prosecutor and played it with great conviction. However, in a civilized court, after the prosecution has made its case the defence is offered the floor. With your permission, I should like to take on that assignment.'

'Why waste any more time?' the captain asked in surprise. 'It all seems cut and dried to me. The commissioner of police explained everything very clearly.'

'Putting a passenger ashore is a serious m-matter, and the responsibility is ultimately the captain's. Think what damage will be done to the reputation of your shipping line if it turns out that you have made a mistake. And I assure you,' said Fandorin, raising his voice slightly, 'that the commissioner is mistaken.'

'Nonsense!' exclaimed Gauche. 'But I have no objections. It might even be interesting. Carry on, monsieur, I'm sure I shall enjoy it.'

After all, a dress rehearsal had to be taken seriously. This boy was no fool, he might possibly expose some gaps in the prosecution's logic that needed patching up. Then if the prosecutor made a mess of things during the trial, Commissioner Gauche would be able to give him a hand.

Fandorin crossed one leg over the other and clasped his hands around his knee.

'You gave a brilliant and convincing speech. At first sight your arguments appear conclusive. Your logic seems almost beyond reproach, although, of course, the so-called "circumstantial evidence" is worthless. Yes, Mr Aono was in Paris on the fifteenth of March. Yes, Mr Aono was not in the saloon when the p-professor was killed. In themselves these two facts mean nothing, so let us not even take them into consideration.'

'Very well,' Gauche agreed sarcastically. 'Let us move straight on to the hard facts.'

'Gladly. I counted five more or less significant elements. Mr Aono is a doctor, but for some reason he concealed that from us. That is one. Mr Aono is capable of shattering a hard object such as a gourd – and perhaps also a head – with a single blow. That is two. Mr Aono does not have a *Leviathan* emblem. That is three. A scalpel, which might be the one that killed Professor Sweet-child, is missing from the defendant's medical bag. That is four. And finally, five: we have just witnessed an attempted escape by the accused, which sets his guilt beyond all reasonable doubt. I don't think I have forgotten anything, have I?'

'There is a number six,' put in the commissioner. 'He is unable to offer an explanation for any of these points.'

'Very well, let us make it six,' the Russian agreed readily.

Gauche chuckled.

'I'd say that's more than enough for any jury to send our little pigeon to the guillotine.'

Inspector Jackson jerked his head up and growled in English: 'To the gallows.'

'No, to the gallows,' Renier translated.

Ah, the black-hearted English! He had warmed a viper in his bosom!

'I beg your pardon,' fumed Gauche. 'The investigation has been conducted by the French side. So our villain will go to the guillotine!'

'And the decisive piece of evidence, the missing scalpel, was discovered by the British side. He'll be sent to the gallows,' the lieutenant translated.

'The main crime was committed in Paris. To the guillotine!'

'But Lord Littleby was a British subject. And so was Professor Sweetchild. It's the gallows for him.'

The Japanese appeared not to hear this discussion that threatened to escalate into an international conflict. His eyes were still closed and his face was completely devoid of all expression. These yellow devils really are different from us, thought Gauche. And just think of all the trouble they would have to take with him: a prosecutor, a barrister, a jury, judges in robes.

Of course, that was the way it ought to be, democracy is democracy after all, but this had to be a case of casting pearls before swine.

When there was a pause Fandorin asked:

'Have you concluded your debate? May I p-proceed?'

'Carry on,' Gauche said gloomily, thinking about the battles with the British that lay ahead.

'And let us not d-discuss the shattered gourds either. They also prove nothing.'

This whole comedy was beginning to get on the commissioner's nerves.

'All right. We needn't waste any time on trifles.'

'Excellent. Then that leaves five points: he concealed the fact that he is a doctor; he has no emblem; the scalpel is missing; he tried to escape; he offers no explanations.'

'And every point enough to have the villain sent . . . for execution.'

'The problem is, Commissioner, that you think like a European, but M-Mr Aono has a different, Japanese, logic, which you have not made any effort to fathom. I, however, have had the honour of conversing with this gentleman, and I have a better idea of how his mind works than you do. Mr Aono is not simply Japanese, he is a samurai, and he comes from an old and influential family. This is an important point for this particular case. For five hundred years every man in the clan of Aono was a warrior. All other professions were regarded as unworthy of such a distinguished family. The accused is the third son in the family. When Japan decided to move a step closer to Europe, many noble families began sending their sons abroad to study, and Mr Aono's father did the same. He sent his eldest son to England to study for a career as a naval officer, because the principality of Satsuma, where the Aono clan resides, provides officers for the Japanese navy. In Satsuma the navy is regarded as the senior service. Aono senior sent his second son to a military academy in Germany. Following the Franco-German War of 1870 the Japanese decided to restructure their army on the German model, and all of their military advisers are Germans. All this information about the clan of Aono was volunteered to me by the accused himself.'

'And what the devil do we want with all these aristocratic details?' Gauche asked irritably.

'I observed that the accused spoke with pride about his older brothers but preferred not to talk about himself. I also noticed a long time ago that for an alumnus of St Cyr, Mr Aono is remarkably ignorant of military matters. And why would he have been sent to a French military academy when he himself had told me that the Japanese army was being organized along German lines? I have formed the following impression. In keeping with the spirit of the times, Aono senior decided to set his third son up in a peaceful, non-military profession and make him a doctor. From what I have read in books, in Japan the decision of the head of the family is not subject to discussion, and so the defendant travelled to France to take up his studies in the faculty of medicine, even though he felt unhappy about it. In fact, as a scion of the martial clan of Aono, he felt disgraced by having to fiddle with bandages and tinker with clysters! That is why he said he was a soldier. He was simply ashamed to admit his true profession, which he regards as shameful. From a European point of view this might seem absurd, but try to see things through his eyes. How would your countryman D'Artagnan have felt if he had ended up as a physician after dreaming for so long of winning a musketeer's cloak?'

Gauche noticed a sudden change in the Japanese. He had opened his eyes and was staring at Fandorin in a state of obvious agitation, and crimson spots had appeared on his cheeks. Could he possibly be blushing? No, that was preposterous.

'Ah, how very touching,' Gauche snorted. 'But I'll let it go. Tell me instead, monsieur counsel for the defence, about the emblem. What did your bashful client do with it? Was he ashamed to wear it?'

'That is absolutely right,' the self-appointed barrister said with a nod. 'That is the reason. He was ashamed. Look at what it says on the badge.'

Gauche glanced down at his lapel.

'It doesn't say anything. There are just the initials of the Jasper–Artaud Partnership.'

'Precisely.' Fandorin traced out the three letters in the air with his finger. 'J – A – P. The letters spell "jap", the term of abuse that foreigners use for the Japanese. Tell me, Commissioner, how would you like to wear a badge that said "frog"?'

Captain Cliff threw his head back and burst into loud laughter. Even the sour-faced Jackson and stand-offish Miss Stamp smiled. The crimson spots spread even further across the face of the Japanese.

A terrible premonition gnawed at Gauche's heart. His voice was suddenly hoarse.

'And why can he not explain all this for himself?'

'That is quite impossible. You see – again as far as I can understand from the books that I have read – the main difference between the Europeans and the Japanese lies in the moral basis of their social behaviour.'

'That's a bit high-flown,' said the captain.

The diplomat turned to face him.

'Not at all. Christian culture is based on a sense of guilt. It is bad to sin, because afterwards you will be tormented by remorse. The normal European tries to behave morally in order to avoid a sense of guilt. The Japanese also strive to observe certain moral norms, but their motivation is different. In their society the moral restraints derive from a sense of shame. The worst thing that can happen to a Japanese is to find himself in a situation where he feels ashamed and is condemned or, even worse, ridiculed by society. That is why the Japanese are so afraid of committing any faux pas that offends the sense of decency. I can assure you that shame is a far more effective civilizing influence than guilt. From Mr Aono's point of view it would be quite unthinkable to speak openly of "shameful" matters, especially with foreigners. To be a doctor and not a soldier is shameful. To confess that he has lied is even more shameful. And to admit that he, a samurai, could attach any importance to offensive nicknames – why, that is entirely out of the question.'

'Thank you for the lecture,' said Gauche, with an ironic bow. 'And was it shame that made your client attempt to escape from custody too?'

'That's the point,' agreed Jackson, suddenly transformed from enemy to ally. 'The yellow bastard almost broke my wrist.'

'Once again you have guessed correctly, Commissioner. It is impossible to escape from a steamship, there is nowhere to go. Believing his position to be hopeless and anticipating nothing but further humiliation, my client (as you insist on calling him) undoubtedly intended to lock himself in his cabin and commit suicide according to samurai ritual. Is that not right, Mr Aono?' Fandorin asked, addressing the Japanese directly for the first time.

'You would have been disappointed,' the diplomat continued gently. 'You must have heard that your ritual dagger was taken by the police during their search.'

'Ah, you're talking about that – what's it called? – hira-kira, hari-kari.' Gauche smirked into his moustache. 'Rubbish. I don't believe that a man could rip his own belly open. If you've really had enough of this world, it's far better to brain yourself against the wall. But I won't take you up on that either. There is one piece of evidence you can't shrug off – the scalpel that is missing from his medical instruments. How do you explain that? Do you claim that the real culprit stole your client's scalpel in advance because he was planning the murder and wanted to shift the blame onto Aono? That just won't wash! How could the murderer know the professor would decide to tell us about his discovery immediately after dinner? And Sweetchild himself had only just guessed the secret of the shawl. Remember the state he was in when he came running into the saloon!'

'Nothing could be easier for me than to explain the missing scalpel. It is not even a matter of supposition, but of hard fact.

Do you remember how things began disappearing from people's cabins after Port Said? The mysterious spate of thefts ended as suddenly as it had begun. And do you remember when? It was after our black stowaway was killed. I have given a lot of thought to the question of why he was on board the *Leviathan*, and this is my explanation. The negro was probably brought here from darkest Africa by Arab slave traders, and naturally he arrived in Port Said by sea. Why do I think that? Because when he escaped from his masters, the negro didn't simply run away, he boarded a ship. He evidently believed that since a ship had taken him away from his home, another ship could take him back.'

'What has all this got to do with our case?' Gauche interrupted impatiently. 'This negro of yours died on the fifth of April, and Sweetchild was killed yesterday! To hell with you and your fairy tales! Jackson, take the prisoner away!'

The commissioner set off decisively towards the door, but the diplomat grabbed his elbow in a vice-like grip and said in a repulsively obsequious voice:

'Dear M. Gauche, I would like to follow my arguments through to their conclusion. Please be patient for just a little while longer.'

Gauche tried to break free, but this young whippersnapper had fingers of steel. After his second attempt failed, the commissioner decided not to make himself look even more foolish. He turned to face Fandorin.

'Very well, five more minutes,' he hissed, glaring into the insolent youth's serene blue eyes.

'Thank you. Five minutes will be more than enough to shatter your final piece of hard evidence . . . I knew that the runaway slave must have a lair somewhere on the ship, so I looked for it. But while you were searching the holds and the coal-holes, Captain, I started with the upper deck. The black man had only been seen by first-class passengers, so it was reasonable to assume that he was hiding somewhere close by. I found what I was looking for in the third lifeboat from the bow on the starboard side: the remains of his food and a bundle of his belongings. There were several pieces of coloured cloth, a string of beads and all sorts of shiny objects, including a small mirror, a sextant, a pince-nez and also a large scalpel.'

'Why should I believe you?' roared Gauche. His case was crumbling to dust before his very eyes.

'Because I am a disinterested party who is prepared to confirm his testimony under oath. May I continue?' The Russian smiled his sickening little smile. 'Thank you. Our poor negro was evidently a thrifty individual who did not intend to return home empty-handed.'

'Stop, stop!' cried Renier, with a frown. 'M. Fandorin, why did you not report your discovery to the captain and me? What right did you have to conceal it?'

'I didn't conceal it. I left the bundle where it was. But when I came back to the lifeboat a few hours later, after the search, the bundle was gone. I was sure it must have been found by your sailors. But now it seems that the professor's murderer got there before you and claimed all the negro's trophies, including Mr Aono's scalpel. The c-criminal could have foreseen that he might need to take . . . extreme measures and carried the scalpel around with him as a precaution. It might help to put the police off the scent. Tell me, Mr Aono, was the scalpel stolen from you?'

The Japanese hesitated for a moment before nodding reluctantly.

'And you did not mention it, because an officer of the imperial army could not possibly possess a scalpel, am I right?'

'The sextant was mine!' declared the red-headed baronet. 'I thought . . . but that doesn't matter. So it turns out that savage stole it. Gentlemen, if someone's head is smashed in with my sextant, please bear in mind that it is nothing to do with me.'

Bewildered by this final and absolute disaster, Gauche squinted inquiringly at Jackson.

'I'm very sorry, Commissioner, but it seems you will have to continue your voyage,' the inspector said in French, twisting his thin lips into a smile of sympathy. 'My apologies, Mr Aono. If you would just hold out your hands . . . Thank you.'

The handcuffs jangled plaintively as they were removed.

The silence that ensued was broken by Renate Kleber's frightened voice:

'I beg your pardon, gentlemen, but then who is the murderer?'

PART THREE
Bombay to the Palk Strait

Gintaro Aono

The 18th day of the fourth month
In view of the southern tip of the Indian peninsula

It is now three days since we left Bombay, and I have not opened my diary even once since then. This is the first time such a thing has happened to me since I made it a firm rule to write every day. But I made the break deliberately. I had to come to terms with an overwhelming torrent of thoughts and feelings.

The essential significance of what has happened to me is best conveyed by a haiku that was born spontaneously at the very moment when the inspector of police removed the iron shackles from my wrists.

Lonely is the flight
Of the nocturnal butterfly,
But stars throng the sky.

I realized immediately that it was a very good poem, the best that I have ever written, but its meaning is not obvious and requires elucidation. I have meditated for three days on the changes within my being, until I think I have finally discovered the truth.

I have been visited by the great miracle of which every man dreams – I have experienced satori, or catharsis, as the ancient Greeks called it. How many times has my mentor told me that if satori comes, it comes when it will and on its own terms, it cannot be induced or impeded! A man may be righteous and wise, he may sit in the zazen pose for many hours each day and read mountains of sacred texts, but still die unenlightened. And yet the radiant majesty of satori may be revealed to some ne'er-do-well who wanders aimlessly and foolishly through life, transforming his worthless existence in an instant! I am that ne'er-do-well. I have been lucky. At the age of 27 I have been born again.

Illumination and purification did not come to me in a moment of spiritual and physical concentration, but when I was wretched, crushed and empty, when I was reduced to no more than the wrinkled skin of a burst balloon. But the dull clanking of those irons signalled my transformation. Suddenly I knew with a clarity beyond words that I am not I, but . . . No, that is not it. That I am *not only I*, but also an infinite multitude of other lives. That I am not some Gintaro Aono, third son of the senior counsellor to His Serene Highness Prince Simazu: I am a small and yet precious particle of the One. I am in all that exists, and all that exists is in me. How many times I have heard those words, but I only understood them . . . no, I only experienced their truth, on the 15th day of the fourth month of the 11th year of Meiji, in the city of Bombay, on board an immense European steamship. The will of the Supreme is truly capricious.

What is the meaning of this tercet that was born of my inner intuition? Man is a solitary firefly in the gloom of boundless night. His light is so weak that it illuminates only a minute segment of space; beyond that lie cold, darkness and fear. But if you turn your frightened gaze away from the dark earth below and look upwards (you need only turn your head!), you see that the sky is covered with stars, shining with a calm, bright, eternal light. You are not alone in the darkness. The stars are your friends, they will help you. They will not abandon you in your distress. And a little while later one understands something else, something equally important: a firefly is also a star like all the others. Those in the sky above see your light and it helps them to endure the cold darkness of the universe.

My life will probably not change. I shall be the same as I was before – trivial and absurd, at the mercy of my passions. But this certain knowledge will always dwell in the depths of my soul, my salvation and comfort in times of difficulty. I am no longer a shallow puddle that any strong gust of wind can spill across the ground. I am the ocean, and the storm that drives the all-destroying tsunami across my surface can never touch my inmost depths.

When my spirit was flooded with joy at this realization, I recalled that the greatest of virtues is gratitude. The first star I glimpsed glowing in the blackness around me was Fandorin-san. Thanks to him I know that the world is not indifferent to me, Gintaro Aono, that the Great Beyond will never abandon me in misfortune.

But how can I explain to a man from a different culture that he is my *onjin* for all time? The European languages do not have such a word. Today I plucked up my courage and tried to speak with him about this, but I fear that the conversation came to nothing.

I waited for Fandorin-san on the boat deck, knowing that he would come there with his weights at precisely eight.

When he appeared, wearing his striped tricot (I must inform him that loose clothes, not close-fitting ones, are best suited for physical exercise), I approached him and bowed low in obeisance. 'Why, Mr Aono, what's wrong?' he asked in surprise. 'Why do you stay bent over and not straighten up?' Since it was impossible to make conversation in such a posture, I drew myself erect, although in such a situation I knew that I ought to maintain my bow for longer. 'I am expressing my eternal gratitude to you,' I said, greatly agitated. 'Oh, forget it,' he said, with a careless wave of his hand. This gesture pleased me greatly – Fandorin-san wished to belittle the significance of the boon he had bestowed on me and spare his debtor excessive feelings of gratitude. In his place any nobly raised Japanese would have done the same. But the effect was the reverse – my spirit was inspired with even greater gratitude. I told him that henceforth I was irredeemably in his debt. 'Nothing irredeemable about it,' he said with a shrug. 'I simply wished to take that smug turkey down a peg or two.' (A turkey is an ugly American bird whose pompous, strutting gait seems to express a risible sense of self-importance: figuratively speaking, a conceited and foolish person.) Once again I was struck by Fandorin-san's sensitivity and tact, but I had to make him understand how much I owed to him. 'I thank you for saving my worthless life,' I said and bowed again. 'I thank you three times over for saving my honour. And I thank you an infinite number of times for opening my third eye, with which I see what I could not see before.' Fandorin-san glanced (it seemed to me, with some trepidation) at my forehead, as if he were expecting another eye to open up and wink at him.

I told him that he is my *onjin*, that henceforth my life belongs to him, and that seemed to frighten him even more. 'O how I dream that you might find yourself in mortal danger so that I can save your life, as you have saved me!' I exclaimed. He crossed himself and said: 'I think I'd rather avoid that. If it is not too much trouble, please dream of something else.'

The conversation was turning out badly. In despair I cried out: 'Know that I will do anything for you!' And then I qualified my oath to avoid any subsequent misunderstanding: 'If it is not injurious to the emperor, my country or the honour of my family.'

My words provoked a strange reaction from Fan-

dorin-san. He laughed! I am certain that I shall never understand the redheads. 'All right then,' he said, shaking me by the hand. 'If you insist, then by all means. I expect we shall be travelling together from Calcutta to Japan. You can repay your debt by giving me Japanese lessons.'

Alas, this man does not take me seriously. I wished to be his friend, but Fandorin-san is far more interested in Senior Navigator Fox, a limited man lacking in wisdom, than in me. My benefactor spends much time in the company of this windbag, listening attentively to his bragging of nautical adventures and amorous escapades. He even goes on watch with Fox! I must confess that I feel hurt by this. Today I heard Fox's lurid description of his love affair with an 'aristocratic Japanese lady' from Nagasaki. He talked about her small breasts and her scarlet mouth and all the other charms of this 'dainty little doll'. It must have been some cheap slut from the sailors' quarter. A girl from a decent family would not even have exchanged words with this foreign barbarian! The most hurtful thing of all was that Fandorin-san was clearly interested in these ravings. I was about to intervene, but just at that moment Captain Renier approached them and sent Fox off on some errand.

Oh yes! I have not mentioned a most important event that has taken place in the life of the ship! A firefly's feeble glow blinds his own eyes, so that he cannot see his surroundings in their true proportions.

On the eve of our departure from Bombay a genuine tragedy occurred, a calamity beside which my own sufferings pale into insignificance.

At half past eight in the morning, when the steamer had already weighed anchor and was preparing to cast off, a telegram was delivered from ashore to Captain Cliff. I was standing on the deck looking at Bombay, the scene of such a crucial event in my life. I wanted that view to remain engraved on my heart for ever. That was how I came to witness what happened.

The captain read the telegram and his face underwent a startling transformation. I have never seen anything like it! It was as if an actor of the Noh theatre had suddenly cast off the mask of the Fearsome Warrior and donned the mask of Insane Grief. The old sea dog's rough, weather-beaten face began to tremble. Then the captain uttered a groan that was also a sob and began pacing frantically around the deck. 'Oh God,' he cried out in a hoarse voice. 'My poor girl!' He dashed down the steps from the bridge, on his way to his cabin – as we discovered later.

The preparations for sailing were interrupted. Breakfast began as usual, but Lieutenant Renier was late. Everyone spoke of nothing but the captain's strange behaviour and tried to guess what could have been in the telegram. Renier-san called into the saloon as the meal was coming to an end. The first mate appeared distraught. He informed us that Cliff-san's only daughter (I have mentioned earlier that the captain doted on her) had been badly burned in a fire at her boarding school. The doctors feared for her life. The lieutenant said that Mr Cliff was beside himself. He had decided to leave the *Leviathan* and return to England on the first available packet boat. He kept saying that he must be with his little daughter. The lieutenant repeated over and over again: 'What is going to happen now? What an unlucky voyage!' We tried our best to comfort him.

I must admit that I strongly disapproved of the captain's decision. I could understand his grief, but a man who has been entrusted with a task has no right to allow personal feelings to govern his actions. Especially if he is a captain in charge of a ship. What would become of society if the emperor or the president or the prime minister were to set personal concerns above their duty? There would be chaos. The very meaning and purpose of authority is to fight against chaos and maintain harmony.

I went back out on deck to see Mr Cliff leave the ship that had been entrusted to him. And the Most High taught me a new lesson, the lesson of compassion.

Stooping low, the captain half-walked and half-ran across the gangway. He was carrying a travelling bag in one hand and there was a sailor following him with a single suitcase. When the captain halted on the quayside and turned to face the *Leviathan*, I saw that his broad face was wet with tears. The next moment he began to sway and collapsed forward onto his face.

I rushed across to him. From his fitful breathing and the convulsive twitching of his limbs, I deduced that he had suffered a severe haemorrhagic stroke. When Dr Truffo arrived he confirmed my diagnosis.

It often happens that the strident discord between the voice of the heart and the call of duty is too much for a man's brain to bear. I had wronged Captain Cliff.

After the sick man was taken away to hospital the *Leviathan* was detained at its mooring for a long time. Renier-san, ashen-faced with shock, drove to the telegraph office to conduct negotiations with the shipping company in London. It was dusk before he returned. He brought the news that Cliff-san had not recovered consciousness; Renier-san was to assume temporary command of the ship and a new captain would come aboard in Calcutta.

We sailed from Bombay after a delay of ten hours.

For days now I do not walk, I fly. I am delighted by the sunshine and the landscapes of the Indian coastline and the leisurely regularity of life on this great ship. Even the Windsor saloon, which I used to enter with such a heavy heart, has now become almost like home to me. My companions at table behave quite differently with me now – the antagonism and suspicion have disappeared. Everyone is very kind and considerate now, and I also feel differently about them. Even Kleber-san, whom I was prepared to throttle with my bare hands (the poor woman!) no longer seems repulsive. She is just a young woman preparing to become a mother for the first time and entirely absorbed in the naïve egotism of her new condition. Having learned that I am a doctor, she plagues me with medical questions about all manner of minor complaints. Formerly her only victim was Dr Truffo, but now we share the strain. And almost unbelievably, I do not find it oppressive. On the contrary, I now possess a higher status than when I was taken for a military officer. It is astounding!

I hold a privileged position in the Windsor saloon. Not only am I a doctor and an 'innocent martyr', as Mrs Truffo puts it, of police brutality. I am – more importantly – *definitely not the murderer*. It has been proved and officially confirmed. In this way I have been elevated to Windsor's highest caste – together with the commissioner of police and our new captain (whom we almost never see – he is very busy and a steward takes his food up to the bridge on a tray). We three are above suspicion and no one casts stealthy, frightened glances in our direction.

I feel sorry for the Windsor group, I really do. With my recently acquired spiritual vision I can see clearly what none of them can see, even the sagacious Fandorin-san.

There is no murderer among my companions. None of them is suited for the role of a scoundrel. When I examine these people closely, I see that they have faults and weaknesses, but there is no black-hearted villain who could have killed II innocent victims, including two children, in cold blood. I would have detected the vile odour of their breath. I do not know whose hand felled Sweetchild-sensei, but I am sure it must have been someone else. The commissioner's assumptions are not entirely correct: the criminal is on board the steamship, but not in the Windsor saloon. Perhaps he was listening at the door when the professor began telling us about his discovery.

If Gauche-san were not so stubborn and took a more impartial view of the Windsor group, he would realize that he is wasting his time.

Let me run through all the members of our company.

Fandorin-san. It is obvious that he is innocent. Otherwise why would he have diverted suspicion from me when no one doubted that I was guilty?

Mr and Mrs Truffo. The doctor is rather comical, but he is a very kind man. He would not harm a grasshopper. His wife is the very embodiment of English propriety. She could not have killed anyone, because it would simply be indecent.

M.-S.-san. He is a strange man, always muttering to himself, and his manner can be sharp, but there is profound and genuine suffering in his eyes. People with eyes like that do not commit cold-blooded murders.

Kleber-san. Nothing could be clearer. Firstly, it would be inhuman for a woman preparing to bring a new life into the world to extinguish other lives so casually. Pregnancy is a mystery that teaches us to cherish human life. Secondly, at the time of the murder Kleber-san was with the police commissioner.

And finally, Stamp-san. She has no alibi, but it is impossible to imagine her creeping up behind someone she knows, covering his mouth with one slim, weak hand and raising my scalpel in the other . . . The idea is utter nonsense. Quite impossible.

Open your eyes, Commissioner-san. This path is a dead end.

Suddenly I find it hard to catch my breath. Could there be a storm approaching?

Commissioner Gauche

His blasted insomnia was really running wild now. Five nights of sheer misery, and it was getting worse all the time. And Lord protect him if he did drop off just before dawn, his dreams were so appalling that he woke up a broken man, his mind so numbed by his nocturnal visions that it concocted all sorts of nonsense. Maybe it really was time to retire and just forget about everything? But he couldn't. Nothing on earth was worse than a squalid old age spent in poverty. Someone here was all set to nab a treasure worth one and a half billion francs, and this old *flic* would have to live out the pitiful remainder of his days on a miserly 125 francs a month!

All night long the sheet lightning had flashed across the sky, the wind had howled in the masts and *Leviathan* had pitched ponderously to and fro on the heaving black rollers. Gauche lay in his bed, staring up at the ceiling which was alternately dark and stark white – when it was lit up by lightning. The lashing rain drummed on the deck, and the glass that held his forgotten liver medicine skidded backwards and forwards across the table, with the spoon tinkling inside it.

It was Gauche's first storm at sea, but he wasn't afraid. A sea monster like this couldn't possibly sink! It might get rattled and shaken about a bit, but certainly nothing more. His only problem was that he couldn't get to sleep with the thunder booming away like that. The moment he started nodding off, there it went again – crash, boom!

But he must have fallen asleep somehow, because he suddenly jerked upright in bed, wondering what was happening. The cabin was echoing with the heavy, laboured beating of his heart.

No, it wasn't his heart. It was someone pounding on the door.

'Commissioner! (Bang-bang-bang) Commissioner! (Bang-bang-bang-bang) Open up! Quick!'

Whose voice was that? It couldn't be Fandorin!

'Who's there? What do you want?' cried Gauche, pressing his hand to the left side of his chest. 'Have you lost your mind?'

'Open up, damn you!'

Oho! What kind of a way was that for a diplomat to talk? Something really serious must have happened.

'Just a moment!'

Gauche pulled off his nightcap with the tassel (his old Blanche had knitted it for him), stuck his arms into the sleeves of his dressing gown and slipped on his bedroom slippers.

When he peeped through the crack of the half-open door he saw it really was Fandorin. In a frock coat and tie, holding a walking cane with an ivory knob. His eyes were blazing.

'What is it?' Gauche asked suspiciously, certain his nocturnal visitor could only have brought bad news.

The diplomat began speaking in an untypical jerky manner, but without stammering.

'Get dressed. Bring a gun. We have to arrest Captain Renier. Urgently. He's steering the ship onto the rocks.'

Gauche shook his head – maybe it was just another of those awful dreams he'd been having.

'Monsieur le russe, have you been smoking hashish?'

'I am not here alone,' replied Fandorin.

The commissioner stuck his head out into the corridor and saw two other men standing beside the Russian. One was the half-crazy baronet. But who was the other? The senior navigator, that's right. What was his name now? . . . Fox.

'Pull yourself together!' said the diplomat, launching a new staccato assault. 'There's not much time. I was reading in my cabin. There was a knock. Sir Reginald. He measured our position at one in the morning. With his sextant. The course was wrong. We should go left of the Isle of Mannar. We're going to the right. I woke the navigator. Fox. Tell him.'

The navigator stepped forward. He looked badly shaken. 'There are shoals there, monsieur,' he said in broken French. 'And rocks. Sixteen thousand tonnes, monsieur. If it runs aground it will break in half like a French loaf. A baguette, you understand? Another half-hour on this course and it will be too late to turn back!'

Wonderful news! Now old Gustave had to be a master mariner and lift the curse of the Isle of Mannar!

'Why don't you just tell the captain that . . . that he's following the wrong course?'

The navigator glanced at the Russian.

'Mr Fandorin says we shouldn't.'

'Renier must have decided to go for broke.' The Russian began jabbering away again. 'He's capable of anything. He could have the navigator arrested. For disobeying orders. He could even use a gun. He's the captain. His word is law on board the ship. Only the three of us know what is happening. We need a representative of authority. You, Commissioner. Let's get up there!'

'Wait, wait!' Gauche pressed his hands to his forehead. 'You're making my head spin. Has Renier gone insane, then?'

'No. But he's determined to destroy the ship. And everyone on board.'

'What for? What's the point?'

No, no, this couldn't really be happening. It was all a nightmare.

Realizing that the commissioner wasn't going to be lured out of his lair that easily, Fandorin began speaking more slowly and clearly.

'I have only a hunch to go on. An appalling suspicion. Renier wants to destroy the ship and everyone on it to conceal his crime and cover his tracks. Hide all the evidence at the bottom of the ocean. If you find it hard to believe that anyone could snuff out thousands of lives so callously, then think of the rue de Grenelle and remember Sweetchild. In the hunt for the Brahmapur treasure human life is cheap.'

Gauche gulped.

'In the hunt for the treasure?'

'Yes,' said Fandorin, controlling himself with an effort. 'Renier is Rajah Bagdassar's son. I'd guessed, but I wasn't sure. Now there can be no doubt.'

'What do you mean, his son? Rubbish! The rajah was Indian, and Renier is a pure-blooded Frenchman.'

'Have you noticed that he doesn't eat beef or pork? Do you realize why? It's a habit from his childhood. In India the cow is regarded as a sacred animal, and Moslems do not eat pork. The rajah was an Indian, but he was a Moslem by religion.'

'That proves nothing!' Gauche said with a shrug. 'Renier said he was on a diet.'

'What about his dark complexion?'

'A suntan from sailing the southern seas.'

'Renier has spent the last two years sailing the London–New York and London–Stockholm routes. Renier is half-Indian, Gauche. Think! Rajah Bagdassar's wife was French and at the time of the Sepoy Mutiny their son was being educated in Europe. Most probably in France, his mother's homeland. Have you ever been in Renier's cabin?'

'Yes, he invited me in. He invited everybody.'

'Did you see the photograph on the table? "Seven feet under the keel. Françoise B."?'

'Yes, I saw it. It's his mother.'

'If it's his mother, then why B instead of R? A son and his mother should have the same surname.'

'Perhaps she married a second time.'

'Possibly. I haven't had time to check that. But what if Françoise B. means Françoise Bagdassar? In the European manner, since Indian rajahs don't have surnames.'

'Then where did the name Renier come from?'

'I don't know. Let's suppose he took his mother's maiden name when he was naturalized.'

'Conjecture,' Gauche retorted. 'Not a single hard fact. Nothing but "what if?" and "let's suppose".'

'I agree. But surely Renier's behaviour at the time of Sweetchild's murder was suspicious? Remember how the lieutenant offered to fetch Mme Kleber's shawl? And he asked the professor not to start without him. I think the few minutes Renier was away were long enough for him to set fire to the litter bin and pick up the scalpel from his cabin.'

'And why do you think it was he who had the scalpel?'

'I told you the negro's bundle disappeared from the boat after the search. And who was in charge of the search? Renier!'

Gauche shook his head sceptically. The steamer swung over hard and he struck his shoulder painfully against the doorpost, which didn't help to improve his mood.

'Do you remember how Sweetchild began?' Fandorin continued. He took a watch out of his pocket, glanced at it and began speaking faster. ' "Suddenly it hit me! Everything fell into place – about the shawl, and about the son! It's a simple piece of clerical work. Dig around in the registers at the École Maritime and you'll find him!" Not only had he guessed the secret of the shawl, he had discovered something about the rajah's son as well. For instance, that he studied at the École Maritime in Marseille. A training school for sailors. Which our Renier also happens to have attended. Sweetchild mentioned a telegram he sent to an acquaintance of his in the French Ministry of the Interior. Perhaps he was trying to find out what became of the child. And he obviously did find out something, but he didn't guess that Renier is the rajah's son, otherwise he would have been more careful.'

'And what did he dig up about the shawl?' Gauche asked eagerly.

'I think I can answer that question as well. But not now, later. We're running out of time!'

'So you think Renier himself set the fire and took advantage of the panic to shut the professor's mouth?' Gauche mused.

'Yes, damn it! Use your brains! I know there's not much hard evidence, but we have only twenty minutes left before *Leviathan* enters the strait!'

But the commissioner still wasn't convinced.

'The arrest of a ship's captain on the high seas is mutiny. Why did you believe what this gentleman told you?' He jerked his chin in the direction of the crazy baronet. 'He's always talking all sorts of nonsense.'

The red-headed Englishman laughed disdainfully and looked at Gauche as if he were some kind of woodlouse or flea. He didn't dignify his comment with a reply.

'Because I have suspected Renier for a long time,' the Russian said rapidly. 'And because I thought what happened to Captain Cliff was strange. Why did the lieutenant need to negotiate for so long with the shipping company over the telegraph? It means they did not know that Cliff's daughter had been involved in a fire. Then who sent the telegram to Bombay? The governors of the boarding school? How would they know the *Leviathan*'s route in such detail? Perhaps it was Renier himself who sent the message? My guidebook says that Bombay has at least a dozen telegraph offices. Sending a telegram from one office to another would be very simple.'

'And why in damnation's name would he want to send such a telegram?'

'To gain control of the ship. He knew that if Cliff received news like that he would not be able to continue the voyage. The real question is, why did Renier take such a risk? Not out of idle vanity – so that he could command the ship for a week and then let everything go hang. There is only one possible explanation: he did it so he could send the *Leviathan* to the bottom, with all the passengers and crew on board. The investigation was getting too close for comfort and he could feel the noose tightening around his neck. He must know the police will carry on hounding all the suspects. But if there's a shipwreck with all hands lost, the case is closed. And then there's nothing to stop him picking up the casket at his leisure.'

'But he'll be killed along with the rest of us!'

'No, he won't. We've just checked the captain's launch and it is ready to put to sea. It's a small craft, but sturdy. It can easily weather a storm. It has a supply of water and a basket of provisions and something else that is rather touching – a travelling bag all packed and ready to go. Renier must be planning to abandon ship as soon as the *Leviathan* has entered the narrow channel and can no longer turn back. The ship will be unable to swing around, and even if the engines are stopped the current will still carry it onto the rocks. A few people might be saved, since we are not far from the shore, but everyone who disappears will be listed as missing at sea.'

'Don't be such a stupid ass, monsieur policeman!' the navigator butted in. 'We've wasted far too much time already. Mr Fandorin woke me up and said the ship was on the wrong course. I wanted to sleep and I told Mr Fandorin to go to hell. He offered me a bet, a hundred pounds to one that the captain was off course. I thought, the Russian's gone crazy, everyone knows how eccentric the Russians are, this will be easy money. I went up to the bridge. Everything was in order. The captain was on watch, the pilot was at the helm. But for the sake of a hundred pounds I checked the course anyway, and then I started sweating, I can tell you! But I didn't say a word to the captain. Mr Fandorin had warned me not to say anything. And that,' the navigator looked at his watch, 'was twenty-five minutes ago.'

Then he added something in English that was obviously uncomplimentary about the French in general and French policemen in particular. The only word Gauche could understand was 'frog'.

The sleuth hesitated for one final moment and then made up his mind. Immediately he was transformed, and began getting dressed with swift, precise movements. Papa Gauche might be slow to break into a gallop, but once he started moving he needed no more urging.

As he pulled on his jacket and trousers he told the navigator:

'Fox, bring two sailors up onto the top deck, with carbines. The captain's mate should come too. No, better not, there's no time to explain everything all over again.'

He put his trusty Lefaucheux in his pocket and offered the diplomat a four-cylinder Marietta.

'Do you know how to use this?'

'I have my own, a Herstal-Agent,' replied Fandorin, showing him a handsome, compact revolver unlike any Gauche had ever seen before. 'And this as well.'

With a single rapid movement he drew a slim, pliable sword blade out of his cane.

'Then let's go.'

Gauche decided not to give the baronet a gun – who could tell what the lunatic might do with it?

The three of them strode rapidly down the long corridor. The door of one of the cabins opened slightly and Renate Kleber glanced out, with a shawl over her brown dress.

'Gentlemen, why are you stamping about like a herd of elephants?' she exclaimed angrily. 'I can't get any sleep as it is with this awful storm.'

'Close the door and don't go anywhere,' Gauche told her sternly, shoving her back into the cabin without even slowing his stride. This was no time to stand on ceremony.

The commissioner thought he saw the door of cabin No. 24, which belonged to Mlle Stamp, tremble and open a crack, but he had no time now to worry about minor details.

On deck the wind drove the rain into their faces. They had to shout to make themselves heard.

There were the steps leading to the wheelhouse and the bridge. Fox was already waiting at the bottom with two sailors from the watch.

'I told you to bring carbines!' shouted Gauche.

'They're in the armoury!' the navigator yelled in his ear. 'And the captain has the key!'

'Never mind, let's go up,' Fandorin communicated with a gesture. There were raindrops glistening on his face.

Gauche looked around and shuddered: in the flickering lightning the rain glittered like steel threads in the night sky, and the waves frothed and foamed white in the darkness. It was an awesome sight.

Their heels clattered as they climbed the iron steps, their eyes half-closed against the lashing rain. Gauche went first. At this moment he was the most important person on the whole *Leviathan*, this immense 200-metre monster sliding on unsuspectingly towards disaster. The detective's foot slipped on the top step and he only just grabbed hold of the banister in time. He straightened up and caught his breath.

They were up. There was nothing above them now except the funnels spitting out occasional sparks and the masts, almost invisible in the darkness.

There was the metal door with its steel rivets. Gauche raised his finger in warning: quiet! The precaution was not really necessary – the sea was so loud that no one in the wheelhouse could have heard a thing.

'This is the door to the captain's bridge and the wheelhouse,' shouted Fox. 'No one enters without the captain's permission.'

Gauche took his revolver out of his pocket and cocked it. Fandorin did the same.

'You keep quiet!' the detective warned the over-enterprising diplomat. 'I'll do the talking. Oh, I should never have listened to you.' He gave the door a determined shove.

But of course the damned door didn't budge.

'He's locked himself in,' said Fandorin. 'You say something, Fox.'

The navigator knocked loudly and shouted in English:

'Captain, it's me, Jeremy Fox! Please open up! We have an emergency!'

They heard Renier's muffled voice from behind the door:

'What's happened, Jeremy?'

The door remained closed.

The navigator glanced at Fandorin in consternation. Fandorin pointed at the commissioner, then put a finger to his own temple and mimed pressing the trigger. Gauche didn't understand what the pantomime meant, but Fox nodded and roared at the top of his voice:

'The French cop's shot himself!'

The door immediately swung open and Gauche presented his

wet but living face to Renier. He trained the barrel of his Lefaucheux on the captain.

Renier screamed and leapt backwards as if he had been struck. Now that was real hard evidence for you: a man with a clear conscience wouldn't shy away from a policeman like that. Gauche grabbed hold of the sailor's tarpaulin collar.

'I'm glad you were so distressed by the news of my death, my dear Rajah,' the commissioner purred, then he barked out the words known and feared by every criminal in Paris. 'Get your hands in the air! You're under arrest.'

The most notorious cut-throats in the city had been known to faint at the sound of those words.

The helmsman froze at his wheel, with his face half-turned towards them.

'Keep hold of the wheel, you idiot!' Gauche shouted at him. 'Hey you!', he prodded one of the sailors from the watch with his finger, 'bring the captain's mate here immediately so he can take command. In the meantime you give the orders, Fox. And look lively about it! Give the command "halt all engines" or "full astern" or whatever, don't just stand there like a dummy.'

'Let me take a look,' said the navigator, leaning over a map. Maybe it's not too late just to swing hard to port.'

Renier's guilt was obvious. The fellow didn't even pretend to be outraged, he just stood there hanging his head, with his hands raised in the air and his fingers trembling.

'Right then, let's go for a little talk, shall we?' Gauche said to him. 'Ah, what a lovely little talk we'll have.'

Renate Kleber

Renate arrived for breakfast later than everyone else, so she was the last to hear about the events of the previous night. Everyone threw themselves on her, desperate to tell her the incredible, nightmarish news.

Apparently, Captain Renier was no longer captain.

Apparently, Renier was not even Renier.

Apparently, he was the son of that rajah.

Apparently, he was the one who had killed everybody.

Apparently, the ship had almost sunk in the night.

'We were all sound asleep in our cabins,' whispered Clarissa Stamp, her eyes wide with terror, 'and meanwhile *that man* was sailing the ship straight onto the rocks. Can you imagine what would have happened? The sickening scraping sound, the impact, the crunching as the metal plating is ripped away. The shock throws you out of bed onto the floor and for a moment you can't understand what's happening. Then the shouting, the running feet. The floor tilting over further and further. And the terrible realization that the ship isn't moving, it has stopped. Everyone runs out on deck, undressed . . .'

'Not me!' the doctor's wife declared resolutely.

'. . . The sailors try to lower the lifeboats,' Clarissa continued in the same hushed, mystical voice, ignoring Mrs Truffo's comment, 'but the crowds of passengers milling around on the deck get in their way. Every new wave throws the ship further over onto its side. Now we are struggling to stay on our feet, we have to hold on to something. The night is pitch-black, the sea is roaring, the thunder rumbles in the sky . . . One lifeboat is finally lowered, but so many people crazed by fear have packed into it that it overturns. The little children . . .'

'P-please, no more,' Fandorin interrupted the word-artist gently but firmly.

'You should write novels about the sea, madam,' the doctor remarked with a frown.

But Renate had frozen motionless with one hand over her heart. She had already been pale from lack of sleep and now she had turned quite green at all the news.

'Oh!' she said, and then repeated it: 'Oh!'

Then she turned on Clarissa with a stern face.

'Why are you saying these awful things? Surely you know I mustn't listen to such things in my condition?'

Watchdog was not at the table. It was not like him to miss breakfast.

'But where is M. Gauche?' Renate asked.

'Still interrogating his prisoner,' the Japanese told her. In the last few days he had stopped being so surly and given up glaring at Renate like a wild beast.

'Has M. Renier really confessed to all these appalling crimes?' she gasped. 'He is slandering himself. He must be confused in his mind. You know, I noticed some time ago that he was not quite himself. Did he himself say that he is the rajah's son? Well, I suppose it's better than Napoleon's son. It's obvious the poor man has simply gone mad.'

'Yes, that too, madam, that too,' Commissioner Gauche's weary voice said behind her.

Renate had not heard him come in. But that was only natural – the storm was over, but the sea was still running high, the steamship was rolling on the choppy waves and every moment there was something squeaking, clanging or cracking. Big Ben's pendulum was no longer swinging since the clock had been hit by a bullet, but the clock itself was swaying to and fro – sooner or later the oak monstrosity was bound to keel over, Renate thought in passing, before concentrating her attention on Watchdog.

'What's going on, tell me!' she demanded.

The policeman walked unhurriedly across to his chair and sat down. He gestured to the steward to pour him some coffee.

'Oof, I am absolutely exhausted,' the commissioner complained. 'What about the passengers? Do they know?'

'The whole ship is buzzing with the news, but so far not many people know the details,' the doctor replied. 'Mr Fox told me everything, and I considered it my duty to inform everyone here.'

Watchdog looked at Fandorin and the Ginger Lunatic and shook his head in surprise.

'I see that you gentlemen, however, are not inclined to gossip.'

Renate did not understand the meaning of his remark, but it was irrelevant to the matter in hand.

'What about Renier?' she asked. 'Has he really confessed to all these atrocities?'

Watchdog took a sip from his cup, relishing it. There was something different about him today. He no longer looked like an old dog that yaps but doesn't bite. This dog looked as though it would snap at you. And if you weren't careful it would even take a bite out of you. Renate decided to rechristen the commissioner Bulldog.

'A nice drop of coffee,' Bulldog said appreciatively. 'Yes, he confessed, of course he did. What else could he do? It took a bit of coaxing, but old Gauche has plenty of experience. Your friend Renier is sitting writing out his confession as we speak. He's got into the flow, there's just no stopping him. I left him there to get on with it.'

'Why is he "mine"?' Renate asked in alarm. 'Don't be ridiculous. He's just a polite man who gave a pregnant woman a helping hand. And I don't believe that he is such a monster.'

'When he's finished his confession, I'll let you read it,' Bulldog promised. 'For old times' sake. All those hours we've spent sitting at the same table. And now it's all over, the investigation's finished. I trust you won't be acting for my client this time, M. Fandorin? There's no way this one can avoid the guillotine.'

'The insane asylum more likely,' said Renate.

The Russian was also on the point of saying something, but he held back. Renate looked at him curiously. He looked as fresh and fragrant as if he had spent the whole night dreaming sweetly in his own bed. And as always, he was dressed impeccably: a white jacket and a silk waistcoat with a pattern of small stars. He was a very strange character; Renate had never met anyone like him before.

The door burst open so violently that it almost came off its hinges and a sailor with wildly staring eyes appeared on the threshold. When he spotted Gauche he ran over and whispered something to him, waving his arms about despairingly.

Renate listened, but she could only make out the English words 'bastard' and 'by my mother's grave'.

'Now what's happened?'

'Doctor, please come out into the corridor.' Bulldog pushed away the plate with his omelette in a gesture of annoyance. 'I'd like you to translate what this lad is muttering about for me.'

The three of them went out.

'What!' the commissioner's voice roared in the corridor. 'Where were you looking, you numskull?'

There was the sound of hasty footsteps retreating into the distance, then silence.

'I'm not going to set foot outside this room until M. Gauche comes back,' Renate declared firmly.

The others all seemed to feel much the same.

The silence that descended in the Windsor saloon was tense and uncomfortable.

The commissioner and Truffo came back half an hour later. Both of them looked grim.

'What we ought to have expected has happened,' the diminutive doctor announced, without waiting for questions. 'This tragic story has been concluded. And the final word was written by the criminal himself.'

'Is he dead?' exclaimed Renate, jumping abruptly to her feet.

'He has killed himself?' asked Fandorin. 'But how? Surely you took precautions?'

'In a case like this, of course I took precautions,' Gauche said in a dispirited voice. 'The only furniture in the cell where I interrogated him is a table, two chairs and a bed. All the legs are bolted to the floor. But if a man has really made up his mind that he wants to die, there's nothing you can do to stop him. Renier smashed his forehead in against the corner of the wall. There's a place in the cell where it juts out . . . And he was so cunning about it that the sentry didn't hear a thing. They opened the door to take in his breakfast, and he was lying there in a pool of blood. I ordered him not to be touched. Let him stay there for a while.'

'May I take a look?' asked Fandorin.

'Go ahead. Gawp at him as long as you like, I'm going to finish my breakfast.' And Bulldog calmly pulled across his cold omelette.

Four of them went to look at the suicide: Fandorin, Renate, the Japanese and, strangely enough, the doctor's wife. Who'd have thought the prim old nanny goat would be so inquisitive?

Renate's teeth chattered as she glanced into the cell over Fandorin's shoulder. She saw the familiar body with its broad shoulders stretched out diagonally on the floor of the cell, its dark head towards the projecting corner of the wall. Renier was lying face down, with his right arm twisted into an unnatural position.

Renate did not go into the cell, she could see well enough without that. The others went in and squatted down beside the corpse.

The Japanese raised the dead man's head and touched the bloodied forehead with his finger. Oh yes, he was a doctor, wasn't he?

'O Lord, have mercy on this sinful creature,' Mrs Truffo intoned piously in English.

'Amen,' said Renate, and turned her eyes away from this distressing sight.

They walked back to the saloon without speaking.

They got back just in time to see Bulldog finish eating, wipe his greasy lips with a napkin and pull over his black file.

'I promised to show you the testimony of our former dining companion,' he said impassively, setting out three pieces of paper on the table: two full sheets and a half-sheet, all covered with writing. 'It's turned out to be his farewell letter as well as his confession. But that doesn't really make any difference. Would you like to hear it?'

There was no need to repeat the invitation – they all gathered round the commissioner and waited with bated breath. Bulldog picked up the first sheet, held it away from his eyes and began reading.

To Commissioner Gustave Gauche,
Representative of the French police

19 April 1878, 6.15 a.m.
On board the Leviathan

I, Charles Renier, do hereby make the following confession of my own free will and without duress, solely and exclusively out of a desire to unburden my conscience and clarify the motives that have led me to commit heinous criminal acts.

Fate has always treated me cruelly . . .

'Well that's a song I've heard a thousand times over,' remarked the commissioner. 'No murderer, robber or corrupter of juveniles has ever told the court that fate had showered its gifts on him but he squandered them all, the son of a bitch. All right then, let us continue.'

Fate has always treated me cruelly, and if it pampered me at the dawn of my life, it was only in order to torment me all the more painfully later on. I was the only son and heir of a fabulously rich rajah, a very good man who was steeped in the wisdom of the East and the West. Until the age of nine I did not know the meaning of anger, fear, resentment or frustrated desire. My mother, who felt homesick for her own country, spent all her time with me, telling me about la belle France and gay Paris, where she grew up. My father fell head over heels in love the first time he saw her at the Bagatelle Club, where she was the lead dancer. Françoise Renier (that was my mother's surname, which I took for my own when I became a French citizen) could not resist the temptation of everything that marriage to an oriental sovereign seemed to promise, and she became his wife. But the marriage did not bring her happiness, although she genuinely respected my father and has remained faithful to him to this day.

When India was engulfed by a wave of bloody rebellion, my father sensed danger and sent his wife and son to France. The rajah had known for a long time that the English coveted his cherished casket of jewels and would not hesitate to resort to some underhand trick in order to obtain the treasure of Brahmapur.

At first my mother and I were rich – we lived in our own mansion in Paris, surrounded by servants. I studied at a privileged lycée, together with the children of crowned monarchs and millionaires. But then everything changed and I came to know the very depths of poverty and humiliation.

I shall never forget the black day when my mother wept as she told me that I no longer had a father, or a title, or a homeland. A year later the only inheritance my father had left me was finally delivered via the British embassy in Paris. It was a small Koran. By that time my mother had already had me christened and I attended mass, but I swore to myself that I would learn Arabic so that I could read the notes made in the margins of the Holy Book by my father's hand. Many years later I fulfilled my intention, but I shall write about that below.

'Patience, patience,' said Gauche with a cunning smile. 'We'll get to that later. This part is just the lyrical preamble.'

We moved out of the mansion as soon as we received the terrible news. At first to an expensive hotel. Then to a cheaper hotel, then to furnished apartments. The number of servants grew less and less until finally the two of us were left alone. My mother had never been a practical person, either during the wild days of her youth or later. The jewels she had brought with her to Europe were enough for us to live on for two or three years, and then we fell into genuine poverty. I attended an ordinary school, where I was beaten and called 'darky'. That life taught me to be secretive and vengeful. I kept a secret diary, in which I noted the names of everyone who offended me, in order to take my revenge on every one of them. And sooner or later the opportunity always came. I met one of the enemies of my unhappy adolescence many years later. He did not recognize me; by that time I had changed my name and I no longer resembled the skinny, persecuted 'hindoo' – the name they used to taunt me with in school. One evening I lay in wait for my old acquaintance as he was on his way home from a tavern. I introduced myself by my former name and then cut short his cry of amazement with a blow of my penknife to his right eye, a trick I learned in the drinking dens of Alexandria. I confess to this murder because it can hardly make my position any more desperate.

'Well, he's quite right there,' Bulldog agreed. 'One corpse more or less doesn't make much difference now.'

When I was 13 years old we moved from Paris to Marseille because it was cheaper to live there and my mother had relatives in the city. At 16, after an escapade which I do not wish to recall, I ran away from home and enlisted as a cabin boy on a schooner. For two years I sailed the Mediterranean.

It was a hard life, but it was useful experience. I became strong, supple and ruthless, and later this helped me to become the best cadet at the École Maritime in Marseille. I graduated from the college with distinction and ever since then I have sailed on the finest ships of the French merchant fleet. When applications were invited for the post of first lieutenant on the super-steamship *Leviathan* at the end of last year, my service record and excellent references guaranteed me success. But by that time I had already acquired a Goal.

As he picked up the second sheet of paper, Gauche warned his listeners:

'This is the point where it starts to get interesting.'

I had been taught Arabic as a child, but my tutors were too indulgent with the heir apparent and I did not learn much. Later, when my mother and I were in France, the lessons stopped altogether and I rapidly forgot the little that I knew. For many years the Koran with my father's notes in it seemed to me like an enchanted book written in a magical script that no mere mortal could ever decipher. How glad I was later that I never asked anyone who knew Arabic to read the jottings in the margins! I had decided that I must fathom this mystery for myself, no matter what it cost me. I took up Arabic again while I was sailing to Maghrib and the Levant, and gradually the Koran began speaking to me in my father's voice. But many years went by before the handwritten notes – ornate aphorisms by Eastern sages, extracts from poems and worldly advice from a loving father to his son – began hinting to me that they made up a kind of code. If the notes were read in a certain order, they acquired the sense of precise and detailed instructions, but that could only be understood by someone who had committed the notes to memory and engraved them on his heart. I struggled longest of all with a line from a poem that I did not know:

Death's emissary shall deliver unto you
The shawl dyed crimson with your father's blood.

One year ago, as I was reading the memoirs of a certain English general who boasted of his 'feats of courage' during the Great Mutiny (the reason for my interest in the subject should be clear), I read about the gift the rajah of Brahmapur had sent to his son before he died. The Koran had been wrapped in a shawl. The scales seemed to fall away from my eyes. Several months later Lord Littleby exhibited his collection in the Louvre. I was the most assiduous of all the visitors to that exhibition. When I finally saw my father's shawl the meaning of the following lines was revealed to me:

Its tapering and pointed form
Is like a drawing or a mountain.

And:

The blind eye of the bird of paradise
Sees straight into the secret heart of mystery.

What else could I dream of during all those years of exile if not the clay casket that held all the wealth in the world? How many times in my dreams I saw that coarse earthen lid swing open to reveal once again, as in my distant childhood, the unearthly glow that filled the entire universe.

The treasure was mine by right – I was the legitimate heir. The English had robbed me, but they had gained nothing by their treachery. That repulsive vulture Littleby, who prided himself on his plundered 'rarities', was really no better than a vulgar dealer in stolen goods. I felt not the slightest doubt that I was in the right and the only thing I feared was that I might fail in the task I had set myself.

But I made several terrible, unforgivable blunders. The first was the death of the servants, and especially of the poor children. Of course, I did not wish to kill these people, who were entirely innocent. As you have guessed, I pretended to be a doctor and injected them with tincture of morphine. I only wished to put them to sleep, but due to my inexperience and fear that the soporific would not work, I miscalculated the dose.

A shock awaited me upstairs. When I broke the glass of the display case and pressed my father's shawl to my face with fingers trembling in reverential awe, one of the doors into the room suddenly opened and the master of the house came limping in. According to my information his Lordship was supposed to be away from home, but suddenly there he was in front of me with a pistol in his hand. I had no choice. I grabbed a statuette of Shiva and struck the English lord on the head with all my might. Instead of falling backwards, he slumped forwards, grabbing me in his arms and splashing blood onto my clothes. Under my white doctor's coat I was wearing my dress uniform – the dark-blue sailor's trousers with red piping are very similar to the trousers worn by the municipal medical service. I was very proud of my cunning, but in the end it was to prove my undoing. In his death throes my victim tore the *Leviathan* emblem off the breast of my jacket under the open white coat. I noticed that it was gone when I returned to the steamship. I managed to obtain a replacement, but I had left a fatal clue behind.

I do not remember how I left the house. I know I did not dare to go out through the door and I recall climbing the garden fence. When I recovered my wits I was standing beside the Seine. In one bloody hand, I was holding the statuette, and in the other the pistol – I have no idea why I took it. Shuddering in revulsion, I threw both of them into the water. The shawl lay in the pocket of my uniform jacket, where it warmed my heart.

The following day I learned from the newspapers that I had murdered nine other people as well as Lord Littleby. I will not describe here how I suffered because of that.

'I should think not,' the commissioner said with a nod. 'This stuff is a bit too sentimental already. Anybody would think he was addressing the jury: I ask you, gentlemen, how could I have acted in any other way? In my place you would have done the same. Phooee.' He carried on reading.

The shawl drove me insane. The magical bird with a hole instead of an eye acquired a strange power over me. It was as if I were not in control of my actions, as if I were obeying a quiet voice that would henceforth guide me in all I did.

'There he goes building towards a plea of insanity,' Bulldog laughed. 'That's an old trick, we've heard that one before.'

The shawl disappeared from my writing desk when we were sailing through the Suez Canal. I felt as if it had abandoned me to the whim of fate. It never even occurred to me that the shawl had been stolen. By that time I was already so deeply in thrall to its mystical influence that I thought of the shawl as a living being with a soul of its own. I was absolutely disconsolate. The only thing that prevented me from taking my own life was the hope that the shawl would take pity on me and come back. The effort required to conceal my despair from you and my colleagues was almost more than I could manage.

And then, on the eve of our arrival in Aden, a miracle happened! When I heard Mme Kleber's frightened cry and ran into her cabin, I saw a negro, who had appeared out of nowhere, wearing my lost shawl round his neck. Now I realize that the negro must have taken the bright-coloured piece of cloth from my cabin a few days earlier, but at the time I experienced a genuine holy terror, as if the Angel of Darkness in person had appeared from the netherworld to return my treasure to me.

In the tussle that followed I killed the black man, and while Mme Kleber was still in a faint I surreptitiously removed the shawl from the body. Since then I have always worn it on my chest, never parting with it for a moment.

I murdered Professor Sweetchild in cold blood, with a calculated deliberation that exhilarated me. I attribute my super-
natural foresight and rapid reaction entirely to the magical
influence of the shawl. I realized from Sweetchild's first enig-
matic words that he had solved the mystery of the shawl and
picked up the trail of the rajah's son – my trail. I had to stop the
professor from talking and I did. The silk shawl was pleased
with me – I could tell from the way its warmth soothed my
poor tormented heart.

But by eliminating Sweetchild I had done no more than
postpone the inevitable. You had me hemmed in on all sides,
Commissioner. Before we reached Calcutta you, and especially
your astute assistant Fandorin . . .

Gauche chuckled grimly and squinted at the Russian.

'My congratulations, monsieur, on earning a compliment
from a murderer. I suppose I must be grateful that he has at
least made you my assistant, and not the other way round.'

Bulldog would obviously have been only too happy to cross
out that line so that his superiors in Paris would not see it. But a
song isn't a song without the words. Renate glanced at the
Russian. He tugged on the pointed end of his moustache and
gestured to the policeman to continue.

. . . assistant Fandorin, would undoubtedly have eliminated
all the suspects one by one until I was the only one left. A
telegram to the naturalization department of the Ministry
of the Interior would have been enough to discover the
name now used by the son of Rajah Bagdassar. And the
student records of the École Maritime would have shown
that I joined the college under one name and graduated
under another.

I realized that the road through the blank eye of the bird of
paradise did not lead to earthly bliss, but to the eternal abyss. I
decided that I would not depart this world as an abject failure,
but as a great rajah. My noble ancestors had never died alone.

They were followed onto the funeral pyre by their servants, wives and concubines. I had not lived as a ruler, but I would die as a true sovereign should – as I had decided. And I would take with me on my final journey not slaves and hand-maidens, but the flower of European society. My funeral carriage would be a gigantic ship, a miracle of European technical progress. I was enthralled by the scale and grandeur of this plan. It is a prospect even more vertiginous than limit-less wealth.

'He's lying here,' Gauche interjected sharply. 'He was going to drown us, but he had the boat all ready for himself.'

The commissioner picked up the final sheet, or rather half-sheet.

I confess that the trick I played on Captain Cliff was vile. I can only offer the partial excuse that I did not anticipate such a tragic outcome. I regard Cliff with genuine admiration. Although I wished to seize control of the *Leviathan*, I also wished to save the grand old man's life. I knew that concern for his daughter would make him suffer, but I thought he would soon discover that she was all right. Alas, malicious fate dogs my steps relentlessly. How could I have foreseen that the captain would suffer a stroke? That cursed shawl is to blame for everything!

I burned the bright-coloured triangle of silk on the day the *Leviathan* sailed from Bombay. I have burned my bridges.

'He burned it!' gasped Clarissa Stamp. 'Then the shawl has been destroyed?'

Renate stared hard at Bulldog, who shrugged indifferently and said:

'And thank God it's gone. To hell with the treasure, that's what I say, ladies and gentlemen. We'll all be far better off without it.'

The new Seneca had pronounced judgement. Renate rubbed her chin and thought hard.

Do you find that hard to believe? Well then, to prove my sincerity I shall tell you the secret of the shawl. There is no point in hiding it now.

The commissioner broke off and cast a cunning glance at the Russian.

'As I recall, monsieur, last night you boasted of having guessed that secret. Why don't you share your guess with us, and we shall see if you are as astute as our dead man thought.'

Fandorin was not taken aback in the least.

'It is not very c-complicated,' he said casually.

He's bluffing, thought Renate, but he does it very well. Can he really have guessed?

'Very well, what do we know about the shawl? It is triangular, with one straight edge and two that are rather sinuous. That is one. The picture on the shawl shows a mythical bird with a hole in place of its eye. That is two. I am sure you remember the description of the Brahmapur palace, in particular its upper level: a mountain range on the horizon, reflected in a mirror image on the wall. That is th-three.'

'We remember, but what of it?' asked the Lunatic.

'Oh, come now, Sir Reginald,' the Russian exclaimed in mock surprise. 'You and I both saw Sweetchild's little sketch. It contained all the clues required to guess the truth: the triangular shawl, the zigzag line, the word "palace".'

He took a handkerchief out of his pocket and folded it along a diagonal to make a triangle.

'The shawl is the key that indicates where the treasure is hidden. The shape of the shawl corresponds to the outline of one of the mountains depicted in the frescos. All that is required is to position the upper corner of the shawl on the peak of that mountain, thus.' He put the triangle on the table and ran his finger round its edge. 'And then the eye of the bird Kalavinka will indicate the spot where one must search. Not on the painted mountain, of course, but on the real one. There must be a cave or something of the kind there. Have I got it right, Commissioner, or am I mistaken?'

Everyone turned towards Gauche, who thrust out his chubby lips and knitted his bushy eyebrows so that he looked exactly like a gruff old bulldog.

'I don't know how you pull these things off,' he grumbled. 'I read the letter back there in the cell and I haven't let it out of my hands for a second . . . All right then, listen to this.'

In my father's palace there are four halls which were used for official ceremonies: winter ceremonies were held in the North Hall, summer ceremonies in the South Hall, spring ceremonies in the East Hall and autumn ceremonies in the West Hall. You may remember the deceased Professor Sweetchild speaking about this. The murals in these halls do indeed portray the mountainous landscape that can be seen through the tall windows stretching from the floor to the ceiling. Even after all these years, if I close my eyes I can still see that landscape before me. I have travelled so far and seen so many things, but nowhere in the world is there any sight more beautiful! My father buried the casket under a large brown rock on one of the mountains. To discover which mountain peak it is, you must set the shawl against each of the mountains depicted on the walls in turn. The treasure is on the mountain with the outline that perfectly matches the form of the cloth. The place where the rock should be sought is indicated by the empty eye of the bird of paradise. Of course, even if someone knew in which general area to look, it would take him many hours, or even days, to find the stone – the search would have to cover many square metres of ground. But there can be no possibility of confusion. There are many brown boulders on the mountains, but there is only one in that particular area of the mountain side. 'A mote lies in the single eye / A lone brown rock among the grey,' says the note in the Koran. How many times I have pictured myself pitching my tent on that mountain side and searching for that 'mote'. But it is not to be.

The emeralds, sapphires, rubies and diamonds are fated to lie there until an earthquake sends the boulder tumbling down the mountain. It may not happen for a hundred thousand years, but the precious stones can wait – they are eternal.

But my time is ended. That cursed shawl has drained all my strength and addled my wits. I am crushed, I have lost my reason.

'Well, he's quite right about that,' the commissioner concluded, laying the half-sheet of paper on the table. 'That's all, the letter breaks off at that point.'

'I must say that Renier-san has acted correctly,' said the Japanese. 'He lived an unworthy life, but he died a worthy death. Much can be forgiven him for that, and in his next birth he will be given a new chance to make amends for his sins.'

'I don't know about his next birth,' said Bulldog, carefully gathering the sheets of paper together and putting them into his black file,' but this time around my investigation is concluded, thank God. I shall take a little rest in Calcutta and then go back to Paris. The case is closed.'

But then the Russian diplomat presented Renate with a surprise.

'The case is certainly not closed,' he said loudly. 'You are being too hasty again, Commissioner.' He turned to face Renate and trained the twin barrels of his cold blue eyes on her. 'Surely Mme Kleber has something to say to us?'

Clarissa Stamp

This question caught everyone by surprise. But no, not everyone – Clarissa was astonished to realize that the mother-to-be
was not disconcerted in the least. She turned a little paler and bit
her plump lower lip for a moment, but she replied in a loud,
confident voice with barely any hesitation:

'You are right, monsieur, I do have something to tell. But not
to you, only to a representative of the law.'

She glanced helplessly at the commissioner and implored
him:

'In God's name, sir, I should like to make my confession in
private.'

Gauche did not seem to have anticipated this turn of events.
The sleuth blinked and cast a suspicious glance at Fandorin.
Then he thrust out his double chin pompously and growled:

'Very well, if it's so important to you, we can go to my cabin.'

Clarissa had the impression that the policeman had no idea
what Mme Kleber intended to confess to him.

But then, the commissioner could hardly be blamed for that –
Clarissa herself had been struggling to keep up with the rapid
pace of events.

The moment the door closed behind Gauche and his companion, Clarissa glanced inquiringly at Fandorin, who seemed to
be the only one who really knew what was going on. It was a
whole day since she had dared to look at him so directly, instead
of stealing furtive glances or peering from under lowered eyelashes.

She had never before seen Erast (oh yes, she could call him
that to herself) looking so dismayed. There were wrinkles on his
forehead and alarm in his eyes, his fingers were drumming

nervously on the table. Could it be that even this confident man, with his lightning-fast reactions, was no longer in control of the situation? Clarissa had seen him disconcerted the previous night, but only for the briefest of moments, and then he had rapidly recovered his self-control.

It was after the Bombay catastrophe.

She had not shown herself in public for three whole days. She told the maid she was not well, took meals in her cabin and only went out walking under cover of darkness, like a thief in the night.

There was nothing wrong with her health, but how could she show herself to these people who had witnessed her shame, and especially to *him*? That scoundrel Gauche had made her a general laughing stock, humiliated her, destroyed her reputation. And the worst thing was that she could not even accuse him of lying – it was all true, every last word of it. Yes, as soon as she came into possession of her inheritance, she had gone dashing to Paris, the city she had heard and read so much about. Like a moth to the flame. And she had singed her wings. Surely it was enough that the shameful affair had deprived her of her final shred of self-respect. Why did everyone else have to know that Miss Stamp was a loose woman and a gullible fool, the contemptible victim of a professional gigolo?

Mrs Truffo had visited her twice to enquire about her health. Of course, she wanted to gloat over Clarissa's humiliation; she gasped affectedly and complained about the heat, but there was a gleam of triumph in her beady, colourless eyes: well my darling, which of us is the lady now?

The Japanese called in and said it was their custom 'to pay a visit of condolence' when someone was unwell. He offered his services as a doctor and looked at her with sympathy.

Finally, Fandorin had come knocking. Clarissa had spoken to him sharply and not opened the door – she told him she had a migraine.

Never mind, she said to herself as she sat there all alone, picking listlessly at her beefsteak. Only nine days to hold out until Calcutta. Nine days was no great time to spend behind closed doors. It was child's play if you had been imprisoned for almost a quarter of a century. It was still better here than in her aunt's house. Alone in her comfortable cabin with good books for company. And once she reached Calcutta she would quietly slip ashore and turn over a brand new leaf.

But in the evening of the third day she began having very different thoughts. Oh, how right the Bard had been when he penned those immortal lines:

Such sweet release new freedom does beget,
When cherished bonds are shed without regret!

Now she really did have nothing to lose. Late that night (it was already after 12) Clarissa had resolutely arranged her hair, powdered her face lightly, put on the ivory-coloured Parisian dress that suited her so well and stepped out into the corridor. The ship's motions tossed her from one wall to the other.

Clarissa halted outside the door of cabin No. 18, trying not to think about anything. When she raised her hand it faltered – but only for a moment, just a single brief moment. She knocked on the door.

Erast opened it almost immediately. He was wearing a blue Hungarian robe with cord fastenings and his white shirt showed through the wide gap at the front.

'G-good evening, Miss Stamp,' he said, speaking quickly. 'Has something happened?'

Then without waiting for a reply he added:

'Please wait for a moment and I'll get changed.'

When he let her in he was already dressed in a frock coat with an impeccably knotted tie. He gestured for her to take a seat.

Clarissa sat down, looked him in the eyes and began:

'Please do not interrupt me. If I lose the thread then it will be even worse . . . I know I am a lot older than you. How old are you? Twenty-five? Less? It doesn't matter. I am not asking you to marry me. But I like you. I am in love with you. My entire upbringing was designed to ensure that I would never under any circumstances say those words to any man, but at this moment I do not care. I do not want to lose any more time. I have already wasted the best years of my life. I am fading away without ever having blossomed. If you like me even a little, tell me so. If not, then tell me that also. Nothing could be more bitter than the shame that I have already endured. And you should know that my . . . adventure in Paris was a nightmare, but I do not regret it. Better a nightmare than the stupor in which I have spent my whole life. Well then, answer me, don't just sit there saying nothing!'

My God, how could she have said such things aloud? This was something she could really feel proud of.

For an instant Fandorin was taken aback, he even blinked those long lashes in a most unromantic fashion. Then he began to speak, stammering more than usual:

'Miss Stamp . . . C-Clarissa . . . I do like you. I like you very much. I admire you. And I envy you.'

'You envy me? For what?' she asked, amazed.

'For your courage. For the fact that you are not afraid to b-be refused and appear ridiculous. You see, I am b-basically very timid and uncertain of myself.'

'You, timid?' Clarissa asked, even more astounded.

'Yes. There are two things I am really afraid of: appearing foolish or ridiculous and . . . dropping my guard.'

No, she could not understand this at all.

'What guard?'

'You see, I learned very early what it means to lose some-one, and it frightened me very badly – probably for the rest of my life. While I am alone, my defences against fate are strong, and I fear nothing and nobody. For a man like me it is best to be alone.'

'I have already told you, Mr Fandorin, that I am not laying claim to a place in your life, or even a place in your heart. Let alone attempting to penetrate your "defences".'

She said no more, because everything had already been said.

And just at that very moment, of course, someone started hammering on the door. She heard Milford-Stokes's agitated voice in the corridor:

'Mr Fandorin, sir! Are you awake? Open up! Quickly! This is a conspiracy!'

'Stay here,' Erast whispered. 'I shall be back soon.'

He went out into the corridor. Clarissa heard muffled voices, but she could not make out what they were saying. Five minutes later Fandorin came back in. He took some small, heavy object out of a drawer and put it in his pocket, then he picked up his elegant cane and said in an anxious voice:

'Wait here for a while and then go back to your cabin. Things seem to be coming to a head.'

She knew now what he had meant by that . . . Later, when she was back in her cabin, Clarissa had heard footsteps clattering along the corridor and the sound of excited voices, but of course it had never even entered her head that death was hovering above the masts of the proud *Leviathan*.

'What is it that Mme Kleber wants to confess?' Dr Truffo asked nervously. 'M. Fandorin, please tell us what is going on. How can she be involved in all this?'

But Fandorin just put on an even gloomier expression and said nothing.

Rolling in time to the regular impact of the waves, *Leviathan* was sailing northwards full steam ahead, carving through the waters of the Palk Strait, which were still murky after the storm. The coastline of Ceylon was a green stripe on the distant horizon. The morning was overcast and close. From time to time a gust of hot air blew a whiff of decay in through the open windows on the windward side of the salon, but the draught could find no exit and it foundered helplessly, hardly even ruffling the curtains.

'I think I have made a mistake,' Erast muttered, taking a step towards the door. 'I'm always one step or half a step behind . . .'

When the first shot came, Clarissa did not immediately realize what the sound was – it was just a sharp crack, and any number of things could go crack on a ship sailing across a rough sea. But then there was another.

'Those are revolver shots!' exclaimed Sir Reginald. 'But where from?'

'The commissioner's cabin!' Fandorin snapped, dashing for the door.

Everybody rushed after him.

There was a third shot, and then, when they were only about 20 steps away from Gauche's cabin, a fourth.

'Stay here!' Fandorin shouted without turning round, pulling a small revolver out of his back pocket.

The others slowed down, but Clarissa was not afraid, she was determined to stay by Erast's side.

He pushed open the door of the cabin and held the revolver out in front of him. Clarissa stood on tiptoes and peeped over his shoulder.

The first thing she saw was an overturned chair. Then she saw Commissioner Gauche. He was lying on his back on the other side of the polished table that stood in the centre of the room. Clarissa craned her neck to get a better look at him and shuddered: Gauche's face was hideously contorted and there was dark blood bubbling out of the centre of his forehead and dribbling onto the floor in two narrow rivulets.

Renate Kleber was in the opposite corner, huddled against the wall. She was sobbing hysterically and her teeth were chattering. There was a large black revolver with a smoking barrel in her trembling hand.

'Aaa! Ooo!' howled Mme Kleber, pointing to the dead body. 'I . . . I killed him!'

'I had guessed,' Fandorin said coolly.

Keeping his revolver trained on the Swiss woman, he went up to her and deftly snatched the gun out of her hand. She made no attempt to resist.

'Dr Truffo!' Erast called, following Renate's every move closely. 'Come here!'

The diminutive doctor glanced into the gunsmoke-filled cabin with timid curiosity.

'Examine the body, please,' said Fandorin.

Muttering some lamentation to himself in Italian, Truffo knelt beside the dead Gauche.

'A fatal wound to the head,' he reported. 'Death was instantaneous. But that's not all . . . There is a gunshot wound to the right elbow. And one here, to the left wrist. Three wounds in all.'

'Keep looking. There were four shots.'

'There aren't any more. One of the bullets must have missed. No, wait! Here it is, in the right knee!'

'I'll tell you everything,' Renate babbled, shuddering and sobbing. 'Only take me out of this awful room!'

Fandorin put the little revolver in his pocket and the big one on the table.

'Very well, let's go. Doctor, inform the head of the watch what has happened here and have him put a guard on this door. And then rejoin us. There is no one apart from us now to conduct the investigation.'

'What an ill-starred voyage!' Truffo gasped as he walked along the corridor. 'Poor *Leviathan!*'

In the Windsor saloon Mme Kleber sat at the table, facing the door, and everyone else sat facing her. Fandorin was the only one who took a chair beside the murderess.

'Gentlemen, do not look at me like that,' Mme Kleber said in a pitiful voice. 'I killed him, but I am the innocent victim. When I tell you what happened, you will see . . . But for God's sake, give me some water.'

The solicitous Japanese poured her some lemonade – the table had not yet been cleared after breakfast.

'So what did happen?' asked Clarissa.

'Translate everything she says,' Mrs Truffo sternly instructed her husband, who had already returned. 'Everything, word for word.'

The doctor nodded, wiping the perspiration induced by fast walking from his forehead with a handkerchief.

'Don't be afraid, madam. Just tell the truth,' Sir Reginald encouraged Renate. 'This person is no gentleman, he has no idea how to treat a lady, but I guarantee that you will be treated with respect.'

These words were accompanied by a glance in Fandorin's direction – a glance filled with such fierce hatred that Clarissa Stamp was startled. What on earth could have happened between Erast and Milford-Stokes since the previous day to cause this hostility?

'Thank you, dear Reginald,' Renate sobbed.

She drank her lemonade slowly, snuffling and whining under her breath. Then she looked imploringly at her interrogators and began:

'Gauche is no guardian of the law! He is a criminal, a madman! That loathsome shawl has driven everybody insane! Even a police commissioner!'

'You said you had something to confess to him,' Clarissa reminded her in an unfriendly tone of voice. 'What was it?'

'Yes, there was something that I was hiding . . . Something important. I was going to confess to everything, but first I wanted to expose the commissioner!'

'Expose him? As what?' Sir Reginald asked sympathetically.

Mme Kleber stopped crying and solemnly declared:

'A murderer. Renier did not kill himself. Commissioner Gauche killed him!' Seeing how astounded her listeners were by this claim, she continued rapidly. 'It's obvious! You try smashing your skull by running at the wall in a room of only six square metres. It can't be done. If Charles had decided to kill himself, he would have taken off his tie, tied it to the ventilation grille and jumped off a chair. No, Gauche killed him! He struck him on the head with some heavy object and then made it look like suicide by smashing the dead man's head against the wall.'

'But why would the commissioner want to kill Renier?' Clarissa asked with a sceptical shake of her head. Mme Kleber was obviously talking nonsense.

'I told you, greed had driven him completely insane. That

shawl is to blame for everything. Either Gauche was angry with Charles for burning the shawl, or he didn't believe him – I don't know which. But anyway it's quite clear that Gauche killed him. And when I told him so to his face, he didn't try to deny it. He took out his pistol and started waving it about and threatening me. He said that if I didn't keep my mouth shut I'd go the same way as Renier . . .' Renate began sniffling again and then – miracle of miracles – the baronet offered her his handkerchief.

What mysterious transformation was this? He had always shunned Renate like the plague!

'. . . Well, then he put the pistol on the table and started shaking me by the shoulders. I was so afraid, so afraid! I don't know how I managed to push him away and grab the gun from the table. It was terrible! I ran away from him and he started chasing me round the table. I turned and pressed the trigger. I kept pressing it until he fell . . . And then Mr Fandorin came in.'

Renate began sobbing at the top of her voice. Milford-Stokes patted her shoulder tentatively, as if he were touching a rattle-snake.

Clarissa started when the silence was suddenly broken by the sound of loud clapping.

'Bravo!' said Fandorin with a mocking smile, still clapping his hands. 'Bravo, Mme Kleber. You are a great actress.'

'How dare you!' exclaimed Sir Reginald, choking with indignation, but Erast cut him short with a wave of his hand.

'Sit down and listen. I shall tell you what really happened.' Fandorin was absolutely calm and seemed quite certain that he was right. 'Mme Kleber is not only a superb actress, she is quite exceptionally talented in every respect. She possesses true brilliance and breadth of imagination. Unfortunately, her greatest talent lies in the criminal sphere. You are an accomplice to a whole series of murders, madam. Or rather, not an accomplice, but the instigator, the leading lady. It was Renier who was your accomplice.'

'Look,' Renate appealed plaintively to Sir Reginald. 'Now this one's gone crazy too. And he was such a quiet boy.'

'The most amazing thing about you is the superhuman speed with which you react to a situation,' Erast continued as though she hadn't even spoken. 'You never defend yourself – you always strike first, Mlle Sanfon. You don't mind if I call you by your real name, do you?'

'Sanfon! Marie Sanfon? Her?' Dr Truffo exclaimed.

Clarissa realized she was sitting there with her mouth open. Milford-Stokes jerked his hand away from Renate's shoulder. Renate herself looked at Fandorin pityingly.

'Yes, you see before you the legendary, brilliant, ruthless international adventuress Marie Sanfon. Her style is breathtakingly daring and inventive. She leaves no clues or witnesses. And last, but not least, she cares nothing for human life. The testimony of Charles Renier, which we shall come to later, is a mixture of truth and lies. I do not know, my lady, when you met him and under what circumstances, but two things are beyond all doubt. Firstly, Renier genuinely loved you and he tried to divert suspicion from you until his very last moment. And secondly, it was you who persuaded the son of the Emerald Rajah to go in search of his inheritance – otherwise why would he have waited for so many years? You made Lord Littleby's acquaintance, acquired all the information you required and worked out a p-plan. Obviously at first you had counted on obtaining the shawl by cunning and flattery – after all, his Lordship had no idea of the significance of that scrap of cloth. But you soon became convinced that it would never work: Littleby was absolutely crazy about his collection and he would never have agreed to part with any of the exhibits. It was not possible to obtain the shawl by stealth either – there were armed guards constantly on duty beside the display case. So you decided to keep the risk to a minimum and leave no traces behind, the way you always prefer to do things. Tell me, did you know that Lord Littleby had not gone away, that he was at home on that fateful evening? I am sure you did. You needed to bind Renier to you with blood. It was not he who killed the servants – you did.'

'Impossible!' said Dr Truffo, throwing his hand in the air.

'Without medical training and practice, no woman could give nine injections in three minutes! It's quite out of the question.'

'Firstly, she could have prepared nine loaded syringes in advance. And secondly . . .' Erast took an apple from a dish and cut a piece off it with an elegant flourish. 'M. Renier may have had no experience in using a syringe, but Marie Sanfon does have such experience. Do not forget that she was raised in a convent of the Grey Sisters of St Vincent, an order founded to provide medical assistance to the poor, and their novices are trained from an early age to work in hospitals, leper colonies and hospices. All these nuns are highly qualified nurses and, as I recall, young Marie was one of the best.'

'But of course. I forgot. You're right,' the doctor said, lowering his head penitently. 'Please continue. I shall not interrupt you again.'

'Well then, Paris, the rue de Grenelle, the evening of the fifteenth of March. T-two people arrive at the mansion of Lord Littleby: a young doctor with a dark complexion and a nurse with the hood of her grey nun's habit pulled down over her eyes. The doctor presents a piece of p-paper with a seal from the mayor's office and asks for everyone in the house to be gathered together. He probably says it is getting late and they still have a lot of work to do. The inoculations are given by the nun – deftly, quickly, painlessly. Afterwards the pathologist will not discover any sign of bruising at the sites of the injections. Marie Sanfon has not forgotten what she learned in her charitable youth. What happened after that is clear, so I shall omit the details: the servants fall asleep, the criminals climb the stairs to the second floor, Renier has a brief tussle with the master of the house. The murderers fail to notice that his gold *Leviathan* badge has been left behind in Lord Littleby's hand. Which meant that afterwards, my lady, you had to give him your own emblem – it would be easier for you to avoid suspicion than the captain's first mate. And I expect that you had more confidence in yourself than in him.'

Up to this point Clarissa had been gazing spellbound at Erast, but now she glanced briefly at Renate. She was listening carefully with an expression of offended amazement on her face. If she was Marie Sanfon, she had not thrown her hand in yet.

'I began to suspect both of you from the day that poor African supposedly fell on top of you,' Fandorin confided to Renate. He bit off a piece of the apple with his even white teeth. 'That was Renier's fault, of course – he panicked and got carried away. You would have invented something more cunning. Let me try to reconstruct the sequence of events and you can correct me if I get any of the details wrong. All right?'

Renate shook her head mournfully and propped her plump cheek on her hand.

'Renier saw you to your cabin – you certainly had things to discuss, since your accomplice states in his confession that the shawl had mysteriously disappeared only a short while before. You went into your cabin, saw the huge negro rummaging through your things and for a moment you must have been frightened – if you are acquainted at all with the feeling of fear. But a second later your heart leapt when you saw the precious shawl on the negro's neck. That explained everything: when the runaway slave was searching Renier's cabin, the colourful piece of material had caught his eye and he decided to wear it round his massive neck. When you cried out Renier came running in, saw the shawl and, unable to control himself, he pulled out his dirk . . . You had to invent the story about the mythical attack, lie down on the floor and hoist the negro's hot, heavy body onto yourself. I expect that was not very pleasant, was it!'

'I protest, this is all pure invention!' Sir Reginald exclaimed heatedly. 'Of course the negro attacked Mme Kleber, it is obvious! You are fantasizing again, mister Russian diplomat!'

'Not in the least,' Erast said mildly, giving the baronet a look of either sadness or pity. 'I told you that I had seen slaves from the Ndanga people before, when I was a prisoner of the Turks. Do you know why they are valued so highly? Because for all their great strength and stamina, they are exceptionally gentle and have absolutely no aggressive instincts. They are a tribe of farmers, not hunters, and have never fought a war against anyone. The Ndanga could not possibly have attacked Mme Kleber, not even if he was frightened to death. Mr Aono was surprised at the time that the savage's fingers left no bruises on the delicate skin of your neck. Surely that is strange?'

Renate bowed her head thoughtfully, as though she herself were amazed at the oversight.

'Now let us recall the murder of Professor Sweetchild. The moment it became clear that the Indologist was close to solving the mystery you, my lady, asked him not to hurry but to tell the whole story in detail from the beginning, and meanwhile you sent your accomplice out, supposedly to fetch your shawl, but in actual fact to make preparations for the murder. Your partner understood what he had to do without being told.'

'It's not true!' Renate protested. 'Gentlemen, you are my witnesses! Renier volunteered of his own accord! Don't you remember? M. Milford-Stokes, I swear I'm telling the truth. I asked you first, do you remember?'

'That's right,' confirmed Sir Reginald. 'That was what happened.'

'A t-trick for simpletons,' said Fandorin, with a flourish of the fruit knife. 'You knew perfectly well, my lady, that the baronet could not stand you and never indulged your caprices. Your little operation was carried through very deftly, but on this occasion, alas, not quite neatly enough. You failed to shift the blame onto Mr Aono, although you came very close to succeeding.' At this point Erast lowered his eyes modestly to allow his listeners to recall precisely who had demolished the chain of evidence against the Japanese.

He is not entirely without vanity, thought Clarissa, but to her eyes the characteristic appeared quite charming and only seemed to make the young man even more attractive. As usual, it was poetry that provided the resolution of the paradox:

For even the beloved's limitation
Is worthy, in love's eyes, of adoration.

Ah, mister diplomat, how little you know of Englishwomen. I believe you will be making a protracted halt in Calcutta.

Fandorin maintained his pause, as yet quite unaware that his faults were 'worthy of adoration' or that he would arrive at his new post later than planned, and then continued:

'Now your situation has become genuinely perilous. Renier described it quite eloquently in his letter. And so you take a terrible decision that is nonetheless, in its own way, a stroke of genius: to sink the ship together with the punctilious commissioner of police, the witnesses and a thousand others. What do the lives of a thousand people mean to you, if they prevent you from becoming the richest woman in the world? Or, even worse, if they pose a threat to your life and liberty.'

Clarissa looked at Renate with horrified fascination. Could this young woman, who was rather bitchy, but otherwise seemed perfectly ordinary, really be so utterly wicked? It couldn't be true. But not to believe Erast was also impossible. He was so eloquent and so handsome!

A huge tear the size of a bean slithered down Renate's cheek. Her eyes were filled with mute appeal: why are you tormenting me like this? What did I ever do to you? The martyr's hand slipped down to her belly and her face contorted in misery.

'Fainting won't help,' Fandorin advised her calmly. 'The best way to bring someone round is to massage the face by slapping. And don't pretend to be weak and helpless. Dr Truffo and Dr Aono think you are as strong as an ox. Sit down, Sir Reginald!' There was a steely ring to Erast's voice. 'You will have your chance to intervene on behalf of your damsel in distress. Afterwards, when I am finished . . . Meanwhile, ladies and gentlemen, you should know that we have Sir Reginald to thank for saving all our lives. If not for his . . . unusual habit of taking the ship's position every three hours, we would have been breakfasting on the b-bottom of the sea today. Or rather others would have been breakfasting on us.'

'Where's Polonius?' the baronet blurted out with a laugh. 'At supper. Not where he eats but where he is eaten.' Very funny!

Clarissa shuddered. A wave that was larger than the others had struck the side of the ship, clinking the dishes against each other on the table and setting Big Ben swaying ponderously to and fro.

'Other people are no more than extras in your play, my lady, and the extras have never really meant anything to you. Especially in a matter of some fifty million pounds. A sum like that is hard to resist. Poor Gauche went astray, for instance. But how clumsy our master detective was as a murderer! You are right, of course, the unfortunate Renier did not commit suicide. I would have realized that for myself if your assault tactics had not thrown me off balance. What force does a 'letter of f-farewell' carry on its own? From the tone of the letter it was clearly not a final testament – Renier is still playing for time, hoping to plead insanity. Above all, he is relying on you, Mlle Sanfon, he has grown used to trusting you implicitly. Gauche calmly tore off a third of a page at the point which he thought was best suited for an ending. How clumsy! The idea of the treasure of Brahmapur had driven our commissioner completely insane. After all, it was his salary for three hundred thousand years!' Fandorin gave a sad chuckle. 'Do you remember how enviously Gauche told us the story of the gardener who sold his stainless reputation to a banker for such a good price?'

'But why kill M. Renier?' asked the Japanese. 'The shawl had been burned.'

'Renier very much wanted the commissioner to believe that, and to make his story more convincing he even gave away the shawl's secret. But Gauche did not believe him,' said Fandorin. He paused for a moment and said: 'And he was right.'

You could have heard a pin drop in the salon. Clarissa had just breathed in, but she forgot to breathe out. She wondered why her chest felt so tight, then realized and released her breath.

'Then the shawl is unharmed?' the doctor asked tentatively, as though he was afraid of startling a rare bird. 'But where is it?'

'That scrap of fine material has changed hands three times this morning. At first Renier had it. The commissioner did not believe what was in the letter, so he searched his prisoner and f-found the shawl on him. The thought of the riches that were almost in his grasp deranged him and he committed murder. The temptation was too much. Everything fitted together so neatly: it said in the letter that the shawl had been burned, the murderer had confessed to everything and the steamer was heading for Calcutta, which is only a stone's throw from Brah-mapur. So Gauche went for broke. He struck his unsuspecting prisoner on the head with some heavy object, rigged things to look like a suicide and came back here to wait for the sentry to discover the body. But then Mlle Sanfon took a hand and out-played both of us – the commissioner and myself. You are a most remarkable woman, my lady,' said Erast, turning towards Renate. 'I had expected you to start making excuses and blaming your accomplice for everything, now that he is dead. It would have been very simple, after all. But no, that is not your way. You guessed from the way the commissioner was behaving that he had the shawl, and your first thought was not of defence, but attack! You wanted to get back the key to the treasure, and you did.'

'Why must I listen to this nonsense?' Renate exclaimed in a tearful voice. 'You, monsieur, are nobody and nothing. A mere foreigner! I demand that my case be handled by one of the ship's senior officers!'

The little doctor suddenly straightened his shoulders, stroked a strand of hair forward across his olive-skinned bald patch and declared:

'There is a senior ship's officer present, madam. You may regard this interrogation as sanctioned by the ship's command. Continue, M. Fandorin. You say that this woman managed to get the shawl away from the commissioner?'

'I am certain of it. I do not know how she managed to get hold of Gauche's revolver. The poor fool was probably not afraid of her at all. But somehow she managed it and demanded the shawl. When the old man wouldn't give it to her, she shot him, first in one arm, then in the other, then in the knee. She tortured him! Where did you learn to shoot like that, madam? Four shots, and all perfectly placed. I'm afraid it is rather hard to believe that Gauche chased you round the table with a wounded leg and two useless arms. After the third shot he couldn't stand any more pain and gave you the shawl. Then you finished your victim off with a shot to the centre of the forehead.'

'Oh God!' Mrs Truffo exclaimed unnecessarily.

But Clarissa was more concerned about something else.

'Then she has the shawl?'

'Yes,' said Erast with a nod.

'Nonsense! Rubbish! You're all crazy!' Renate (or Marie Sanfon?) laughed hysterically. 'Lord, this is such grotesque nonsense!'

'This is easy to check,' said the Japanese. 'We must search Mme Kleber. If she does not have the shawl, then Mr Fandorin is mistaken. In such cases in Japan we cut our bellies open.'

'No man's hands shall ever search a lady in my presence!' declared Sir Reginald, rising to his feet with a menacing air.

'What about a woman's hands?' asked Clarissa. 'Mrs Truffo and I will search this person.'

'Oh yes, it would take no time at all,' the doctor's wife agreed eagerly.

'Do as you like with me,' said Renate, pressing her hands together like a sacrificial victim. 'But afterwards you will be ashamed . . .'

The men went out and Mrs Truffo searched the prisoner with quite remarkable dexterity. She glanced at Clarissa and shook her head.

Clarissa suddenly felt afraid for poor Erast. Could he really have made a mistake?

'The shawl is very thin,' she said. 'Let me have a look.'

It was strange to feel her hands on the body of another woman, but Clarissa bit her lip and carefully examined every seam, every fold and every gather on the underwear. The shawl was not there.

'You will have to get undressed,' she said resolutely. It was terrible, but it was even more terrible to think that the shawl would not be found. What a blow for Erast. How could he bear it?

Renate raised her arms submissively to make it easier to remove her dress and said timidly:

'In the name of all that is holy, Mlle Stamp, do not harm my child.'

Gritting her teeth, Clarissa set about unfastening Renate's dress. When she reached the third button there was a knock at the door and Erast's cheerful voice called out:

'Ladies, stop the search! May we come in?'

'Yes, yes, come in!' Clarissa shouted, quickly fastening the buttons again.

The men had a mysterious air about them. They took up a position by the table without saying a word. Then, with a magician's flourish, Erast spread out on the tablecloth a triangular piece of fabric that shimmered with all the colours of the rainbow.

'The shawl!' Renate screeched.

'Where did you find it?' asked Clarissa, feeling totally confused.

'While you were searching Mlle Sanfon, we were busy too,' Fandorin explained with a smug expression. 'It occurred to me that this prudent individual could have hidden the incriminating clue in the commissioner's cabin. But she only had a few seconds, so she could not have hidden it too thoroughly. It did not take long to find the crumpled shawl where she had thrust it under the edge of the carpet. So now we can all admire the famous bird of paradise, Kalavinka.'

Clarissa joined the others at the table and they all gazed spellbound at the scrap of cloth for which so many people had died.

The shawl was shaped like an isosceles triangle, with sides no longer than about 20 inches. The colours of the painting were brilliant and savage. A strange creature with pointed breasts, half-woman and half-bird like the sirens of ancient times,

stood with its wings unfurled against a background of brightly
coloured trees and fruit. Her face was turned in profile and instead of an eye the long curving lashes framed a small hole that
had been painstakingly trimmed with stitches of gold thread.
Clarissa thought she had never seen anything more beautiful in
her life.

'Yes, it's the shawl all right,' said Sir Reginald. 'But how does
your find prove Mme Kleber's guilt?'

'What about the travelling bag?' Fandorin asked in a low
voice. 'Do you remember the travelling bag that we found in
the captain's launch yesterday? One of the things I saw in it was
a cloak that we have often seen on the shoulders of Mme
Kleber. The travelling bag is now part of the material evidence.
No doubt other items belonging to our good friend here will
also be found in it.'

'What reply can you make to that, madam?' the doctor asked
Renate.

'The truth,' she replied, and in that instant her face changed
beyond all recognition.

Reginald Milford-Stokes

. . . then suddenly her face was transformed beyond all recognition, as though someone had waved a magic wand and the weak, helpless little lamb crushed by a cruel fate was instantly changed into a ravening she-wolf. She straightened her shoulders and lifted her chin, her eyes suddenly ablaze and her nostrils flaring as if the woman before us had turned into a deadly predator – no, not a she-wolf, one of the big cats, a panther or lioness who has scented fresh blood. I recoiled, I could not help it. My protection was certainly no longer required here!

The transformed Mme Kleber cast Fandorin a glance of searing hatred that pierced even that imperturbable gentleman's defences. He shuddered.

I could sympathize entirely with this strange woman's feelings. My own attitude to the contemptible Russian has also changed completely. He is a terrible man, a dangerous lunatic with a fantastic, monstrously depraved imagination. How could I ever have respected and trusted him? I can hardly even believe it now!

I simply do not know how to tell you this, my sweet Emily. My hand is trembling with indignation as it holds the pen. At first I intended to conceal it from you, but I have decided to tell you after all. Otherwise it will be hard for you to understand the reason for the metamorphosis in my feelings towards Fandorin.

Yesterday night, after all the shocks and upheavals that I have described above, Fandorin and I had an extremely strange conversation that left me feeling both perplexed and furious. The Russian approached me and thanked me for saving the ship, and then, positively oozing sympathy and stammering over every word, he began talking the most unimaginable, monstrous drivel. What he said was literally this – I remember it word for word: 'I know of your grief, Sir Reginald. Commissioner Gauche told me everything a long time ago. Of course, it is none of my business, and I have thought long and hard before deciding to speak to you about it, but when I see how greatly you are suffering, I cannot remain indifferent. The only reason I dare to say all this is that I have suffered a similar grievous loss, and my reason was also undermined by the shock. I have managed to preserve my reason, and even hone its edge to greater sharpness, but the price I had to pay for survival was a large piece of my heart. But believe me, in your situation there is no other way. Do not hide from the truth, no matter how terrible it might be, and do not seek refuge in illusion. Above all, do not blame yourself. It is not your fault that the horses bolted, or that your pregnant wife was thrown out of the carriage and killed. This is a trial, a test ordained for you by fate. I cannot understand what need there could possibly be to subject a man to such cruelty, but one thing I do know: if you do not pass this test, it means the end, the death of your very soul.'

At first I simply could not understand what the scoundrel was getting at. Then I realized. He imagined that you, my precious Emily, were dead! That you were the pregnant lady who was thrown from a carriage and killed. If I had not been so outraged, I should have laughed in the crazy diplomat's face. How dare he say such a thing, when I know that you are waiting there for me beneath the azure skies of the islands of paradise! Every hour brings me closer to you, my darling Emily. And now there is nobody and nothing that can stop me.

Only – it is very strange – I cannot for the life of me remember how you came to be in Tahiti, alone without me. There certainly must have been some important reason for it. No matter. When we meet, my dear friend, you will explain everything to me.

But let me return to my story.

Mme Kleber straightened up, suddenly seeming taller (it is amazing how much the impression of height depends on posture and the set of the head), and began speaking, for the most part addressing Fandorin:

'All these stories you have hatched up here are absolute nonsense. There is not a single piece of proof or hard evidence. Nothing but assumptions and unfounded speculation. Yes, my real name is Marie Sanfon, but no court in the world has ever been able to charge me with any crime. Yes, my enemies have often slandered me and intrigued against me, but I am strong. Marie Sanfon's nerve is not so easily broken. I am guilty of only one thing – that I loved a criminal and a madman to distraction. Charles and I were secretly married, and it is his child that I am carrying under my heart. It was Charles who insisted on keeping our marriage secret. If this misdemeanour is a crime, then I am willing to face a judge and jury, but you may be sure, mister home-grown detective, that an experienced lawyer will scatter your chimerical accusations like smoke. What charges can you actually bring against me? That in my youth I lived in a convent with the Grey Sisters and eased the suffering of the poor? Yes, I used to give myself injections, but what of that? The moral suffering caused by a life of secrecy and a difficult pregnancy led me to become addicted to morphine, but now I have found the strength to break free of that pernicious habit. My secret but entirely legitimate husband insisted that I should embark on this voyage under an assumed name. That was how the mythical Swiss banker Kleber came to be invented. The deception caused me suffering, but how could I refuse the man I loved? I had absolutely no idea about his other life and his fatal passion, or his insane plans!

'Charles told me that it was not appropriate for the captain's first mate to take his wife with him on a cruise, but he was concerned for the health of our dear child and could not bear to be parted from me. He said it would be best if I sailed under a false name. What kind of crime is that, I ask you?

'I could see that Charles was not himself, that he was in the grip of strange passions that I did not understand, but never in my worst nightmare could I have dreamed that he committed that terrible crime on the rue de Grenelle! And I had no idea that he was the son of an Indian rajah. It comes as a shock to me that my child will be one-quarter Indian. The poor little mite, with a madman for a father. I have no doubt at all that Charles has been completely out of his mind for the last few days. How could anyone sane attempt to sink a ship? It is obviously the act of a sick mind. Of course I knew nothing at all about that insane plan.'

At this point Fandorin interrupted her and asked with a hideous *little grin:* 'And what about your cloak that was packed so thoughtfully in the travelling bag?'

Mme Kleber – Miss Sanfon – that is, Mme Renier . . . Or Mme Bagdassar? I do not know what I ought to call her. Very well, let her remain Mme Kleber, since that is what I am used to. Mme Kleber replied to her inquisitor with great dignity: 'My husband evidently packed everything ready for our escape and was intending to wake me at the last minute.'

But Fandorin was unrelenting. 'But you were not asleep,' he said, with a haughty expression on his face. 'We saw you when we were walking along the corridor. You were fully clothed and even had a shawl on your shoulders.'

'I could not sleep because I felt strangely alarmed,' replied Mme Kleber. 'I must have felt in my heart that something was wrong . . . I was shivering and I felt cold, so I put on my shawl. Is that a crime?'

I was glad to see that the amateur prosecutor was stumped. The accused continued with calm self-assurance: 'The idea that I supposedly tortured that other madman, M. Gauche, is absolutely incredible. I told you the truth. The old blockhead went insane with greed and he threatened to kill me. I have no idea how I managed to hit the target with all four bullets. But it is pure coincidence. Providence itself must have guided my hand. No, sir, you cannot make anything of that either!'

Fandorin's smug self-assurance had been shattered. 'I beg your pardon!' he cried excitedly. 'But we found the shawl! You hid it under the carpet!'

'Yet another unfounded assertion!' retorted Mme Kleber. 'Of course the shawl was hidden by Gauche, who had taken it from my poor husband. And despite all your vile insinuations, I am grateful to you, sir, for returning my property.'

And so saying, she calmly stood up, walked over to the table and took the shawl.

'I am the legitimate wife of the legitimate heir of the Emerald Rajah,' declared this astonishing woman. 'I have a marriage certificate. I am carrying Bagdassar's grandson in my womb. It is true that *my deceased husband committed a number of serious crimes, but what has that to do with me and our inheritance?'*

Miss Stamp jumped to her feet and tried to grab the shawl from Mme Kleber.

'The lands and property of the rajah of Brahmapur were confiscated by the British government,' my fellow countrywoman declared resolutely. 'That means the treasure belongs to Her Majesty Queen Victoria!' – and there was no denying that she was right.

'Just a moment!' our good Dr Truffo put in. 'Although I am Italian by birth I am a citizen of France and I represent her interests here. The rajah's treasure was the personal property of his family and did not belong to the principality of Brahmapur, which means its confiscation was illegal! Charles Renier became a French citizen of his own free will. He committed a most heinous crime on the territory of his adopted country. Under the laws of the French Republic the punishment for such crimes, especially when committed out of purely venal motives, includes the expropriation of the criminal's property by the state. Give back the shawl, madam! It belongs to France.' And he also took a defiant grip on the edge of the shawl.

The situation was a stalemate, and the crafty Fandorin took advantage of it. With the Byzantine cunning typical of his nation, he said loudly: 'This is a serious dispute that requires arbitration. Permit me, as the representative of a neutral power, to take temporary possession of the shawl, so that you do not tear it to pieces. I shall place it over here, a little distance away from the contending parties.'

And so saying, he took the shawl and carried it across to the side table on the leeward side of the salon, where the windows were closed. You will see later, my beloved Emily, why I mention these details.

Thus the bone of contention, the shawl, was lying there on the side table, a bright triangle of shimmering colour sparkling with gold. Fandorin was standing with his back to the shawl in the pose of a guard of honour. The rest of us were bunched together at the dining table. Add to this the rustling of the curtains on the windward side of the room, the dim light of an overcast afternoon and the irregular swaying of the floor beneath our feet, and the stage was set for the final scene.

'No one will dare to take from the rajah's grandson what is his by

right!' Mme Kleber declared, with her hands set on her hips. 'I am a Belgian subject and the court hearing will take place in Brussels. All I need to do for the jury to decide in my favour is to promise that a quarter of the inheritance will be donated to charitable work in Belgium . . . A quarter of the inheritance is eleven billion Belgian francs, five times the annual income of the entire kingdom of Belgium!'

Miss Stamp laughed in her face: 'You underestimate Britannia, my dear. Do you really think that your pitiful Belgium will be allowed to decide the fate of fifty million pounds? With that money we shall build hundreds of mighty battleships and triple the size of our fleet, which is already the greatest in the world. We shall bring order to the entire planet!'

Miss Stamp is an intelligent woman. Indeed, civilization could only benefit if our treasury were enriched by such a fantastic sum. Britain is the most progressive and free country in the world. All the peoples of the earth would benefit if their lives were arranged after the British example.

But Dr Truffo was of a different opinion entirely. 'This sum of one and a half billion French francs will not only finance France's recovery from the tragic consequences of the war with Germany, it will allow her to create the most modern and well-equipped army in the whole of Europe. You English have never been Europeans. You are islanders! You do not share in the interests of Europe. M. de Perier, who until recently was the captain's second mate and is now in temporary command of the Leviathan, will not allow the shawl to go to the English. I shall bring M. de Perier here immediately, and he will place the shawl in the captain's safe!'

Then everyone began talking at once, all trying to shout each other down. The doctor became so belligerent that he even dared to push me in the chest, and Mme Kleber kicked Miss Stamp on the ankle.

Then Fandorin took a plate from the table and smashed it on the floor with a loud crash. As everyone gazed at him in amazement, the cunning Byzantine said: 'We shall not solve our problem in this way. You are getting too heated, ladies and gentlemen. Why don't we let a bit of fresh air into the salon – it has become rather stuffy in here.'

He went over to the windows on the leeward side and began opening *them one by one. When Fandorin opened the window above the side table on which the shawl was lying, something startling happened: the draught immediately snatched at the featherlight material, which trembled and fluttered and suddenly flew up into the air. Everyone gasped in horror as the silk triangle went flying away across the deck, swayed twice above the handrails – as if it were waving goodbye to us – and sailed off into the distance, gradually sinking lower and lower. We all stood there dumbfounded, following its leisurely flight until it ended somewhere among the lazy white-capped waves.*

'How very clumsy I am,' said Fandorin, breaking the deadly silence. 'All that money lost at sea! Now neither Britain nor France will be able to impose its will on the world. What a terrible misfortune for civilization. And it was half a billion roubles. Enough for Russia to repay its entire foreign debt.'

That was when things really started hotting up.

With a war cry halfway between a whistle and a hiss that made my skin crawl, Mme Kleber grabbed a fruit knife from the table and made a mad dash at the Russian. The sudden attack caught him by surprise. The blunt silver blade swung through the air and stabbed Fandorin just below his collarbone, but I do not think it went very deep. The diplomat's white shirt was stained red with blood. My first thought was: God does exist, and he punishes scoundrels. As he staggered backwards, the villainous Byzantine dodged to one side, but the enraged Fury was not satisfied with the damage she had inflicted, and taking a firmer grip on the handle, she raised her hand to strike again.

And then our Japanese colleague, who had so far taken no part in the discussion and remained almost unnoticed, astonished us all. With a piercing cry like the call of an eagle, he leapt up almost as high as the ceiling and struck Mme Kleber on the wrist with the toe of his shoe. Not even in the Italian circus have I ever seen a trick to match that!

The fruit knife went flying into the air, the Japanese landed in a squatting position and Mme Kleber staggered backwards with her face contorted, clutching her injured wrist.

But still she would not abandon her bloodthirsty intent! When she felt her back strike the grandfather clock (I have already written to you about that monster), she suddenly bent down and lifted up the hem of her dress. I was already dazed by the speed of events, but this was too much. I caught a glimpse (forgive me, my sweet Emily, for mentioning this) of a slim ankle clad in a silk stocking and the frills of a pair of pink pantaloons, and a second later when Mme Kleber straightened up a pistol had appeared out of nowhere in her left hand. It was very small and double-barrelled, finished with mother-of-pearl.

I do not dare repeat to you word for word exactly what this creature said to Fandorin – in any case you probably do not know the meaning of such expressions. The general sense of her speech, which was most forceful and expressive, was that the 'rotten pervert' (I employ euphemisms, for Mme Kleber expressed herself rather more crudely) would pay for his lousy trick with his life. 'But first I shall neutralize this venomous yellow snake!' cried the mother-to-be: she took a step forward and fired at Mr Aono, who fell on his back with a dull groan.

Mme Kleber took another step and pointed her pistol straight at Fandorin's face. 'I really do never miss,' she hissed. 'And I'm going to put a bullet right between those pretty blue eyes of yours.'

The Russian stood there, pressing his hand to the red patch spreading across his shirt. He was not exactly quaking with fear, but he was pale all right.

The ship heeled over harder than usual – a large wave had struck it amidships – and I saw that ugly monstrosity, Big Ben, lean further and further over, and then . . . it collapsed right onto Mme Kleber! There was a dull thud as the hard wood struck the back of her head and the irrepressible woman collapsed flat on her face, pinned down by the heavy oak tower.

Everyone dashed across to Mr Aono, who was still lying on the floor with a bullet in his chest. The wounded man was conscious and kept trying to get up, but Dr Truffo squatted down beside him and pressed on his shoulders to make him lie back. The doctor cut open his clothes to examine the entry wound and frowned.

'It is nothing,' the Japanese said in a low voice through clenched teeth. 'The lung is barely grazed.'

'And the bullet,' Truffo asked in alarm. 'Can you feel it, my dear colleague? Where is it?'

'I think the bullet is stuck in the right shoulder blade,' replied Mr

Aono, adding with astonishing composure, 'The lower left quadrant. You will have to section the bone from the back. That is very difficult. Please forgive me for causing you such inconvenience.'

Then Fandorin said something very mysterious. He leaned over the wounded man and said in a quiet voice: 'Well now, Aono-san, your dream has come true – now you are my onjin. I am afraid the free Japanese lessons will have to be cancelled.'

Mr Aono, however, seemed to understand this gibberish perfectly well and he even managed a feeble smile.

When the Japanese gentleman had been bandaged up and carried away on a stretcher by sailors, the doctor turned his attention to Mme Kleber.

We were jolly surprised to discover that the solid oak had not smashed her skull, but only given her a substantial bump on the head. We pulled the stunned criminal out from under London's finest sight and moved her to an armchair.

'I'm afraid the baby will not survive the shock,' sighed Mrs Truffo. 'The poor little thing is not to blame for his mother's sins.'

'The baby will be all right,' her husband assured her. 'This . . . lady possesses such tremendous vitality that she will certainly have a healthy child, with an easy birth at full term.'

Fandorin added, with a cynicism that I found offensive: 'There is reason to hope that the birth will take place in a prison hospital.'

'It is terrible to think what will be born from that womb,' Miss Stamp said, with a shudder.

'In any case, the pregnancy will save her from the guillotine,' remarked the doctor.

'Or from the gallows,' laughed Miss Stamp, reminding us of the bitter wrangling between Commissioner Gauche and Inspector Jackson.

'The most serious threat she faces is a short prison sentence for the attempted murder of Mr Aono,' Fandorin remarked with a sour face. 'And extenuating circumstances will be found for that: temporary insanity, shock, the pregnancy. As she herself demonstrated quite brilliantly, it will be quite impossible to prove anything else. I assure you, Marie Sanfon will be at liberty again very soon.'

It is strange, but none of us mentioned the shawl, as if it had never even existed, as if the scrap of silk that had carried off into oblivion a hundred British battleships and the French revanche had also taken with it the feverish stupor that had shrouded our minds and souls.

Fandorin stopped beside his fallen Big Ben, which was now fit for nothing but the rubbish tip: the glass was broken, the mechanism was smashed and the oak panel was cracked from top to bottom.

'A magnificent clock,' said the Russian, confirming yet again the well-known fact that the Slavs have no artistic taste whatever. 'I shall certainly have it repaired and take it with me.'

The Leviathan gave a mighty hoot on its whistle, no doubt in greeting to some passing vessel, and I began thinking that very soon, in just two or three weeks, I shall arrive in Tahiti and we shall meet again, my adored little wife. Everything else is mere mist and vapour, an insubstantial fantasy.

We shall be together and we shall be happy in our island paradise, where the sun always shines.

In anticipation of that joyful day,
I remain your tenderly loving

Reginald Milford-Stokes.